WITCH'S SPIRIT

THE HEMLOCK CHRONICLES: BOOK THREE

EMMA L. ADAMS

I'd always been a terrible liar.

Kind of unfortunate when my task of the day was to lie through my teeth to a roomful of people who could kill me in the blink of an eye. Confronting hordes of zombies was nothing compared to the combined forces of Edinburgh's supernatural community leaders, the local mage council, *and* the Council of Twelve, all looking directly at me as though they could see straight through the web of lies that I'd been forced to construct. I clenched my hands at my sides, making myself shrink back in my seat as though too terrified for words. *Nothing to see here. Just Jas the lowly necromancer, who definitely isn't hosting a power-hungry spirit who'd like to be sitting in your place on a throne made of the skulls of her enemies.*

While Edinburgh's mages ran the show, there were so many supernatural authority figures here that one table hadn't been enough, so someone had placed three regular sized tables end to end, filling the hall-sized meeting room. Even then, I couldn't see everyone's faces. In the spirit realm, they'd appear as a blur of overlapping figures. That included the two members who were actual ghosts. Being living wasn't a requirement of being a member of the Council of Twelve, the UK's only cross-supernatural council. Nor was being present, because my recently deceased mentor Lady Harper had never bothered to show up for meetings.

"Tell us your view of the events a month ago when the Soul Collector attacked the guild," commanded Lord Sutherland, leader of Edinburgh's mage council. His hair was far too glossy and black for someone in his sixties or older, and his face was unnaturally smooth. Spells lined his wrinkled wrists—custom-made witch spells for youth and attractiveness. Despite his obvious vanity, he'd apparently survived over fifty assassination attempts. And while they said mages' magic sometimes faded with age, he'd held onto his position with a steel claw since before the faerie invasion twenty-two years ago.

On my left, my friend and sort-of-mentor Isabel gave me a nudge of encouragement, while on my right, Lady Montgomery, the leader of Edinburgh's necromancer guild and my boss, sat up straighter. Having allies present didn't make me feel less like I'd unwittingly walked to the gallows. I wished Lloyd was here, but he wasn't considered important enough. Neither was I, really, but when you killed an evil god in sort-of-human flesh, people got suspicious.

No pressure, Jas.

"I..." I swallowed, hoping they'd put my reluctance to meet their eyes down to nerves about public speaking. Eye contact made it harder to mask the truth. "The Soul Collector's goal was to collect human souls. When I tried to stop him, he retaliated by capturing a friend of mine as bait to lure my friends and me into his trap. Thanks to Lady Harper, I managed to defeat him."

I should have known that Lady Harper's sacrificing her life to save a lowly necromancer like me would draw suspicion. The death of a Mage Lord, even a former one, had kicked off an inquiry that'd gone on for the better part of a month now. Never mind that they'd all heard the bloody story at least four times before.

"But why would he see *you* as a worthy target?" Lord Sutherland asked. "Aren't you only a novice necromancer?"

"I'm also Lady Montgomery's assistant," I corrected, annoyance flaring at his dismissive tone. Sure, I wanted him to see me as insignificant, but I'd also almost died to save the people of the city he was supposed to be in charge of. "The Soul Collector targeted me because I was part of a team of necromancers who nearly caught him when we thought we were dealing with a regular human murderer."

"How did Lady Harper die, precisely?" he asked. "There were no witnesses, which makes this a difficult case to resolve."

You don't say.

"Lady Harper died the same as the others," I said. "He wanted powerful souls, so he targeted her first. But when he used his weapon to tear the spirit line open, it back-fired on him and he fell through."

Thank the gods I could say that aloud, even if it was a lie. A geas stopped me from speaking of my coven, and no witnesses had seen me confront the Soul Collector with the help of my second soul, Evelyn Hemlock.

Nobody had seen that I was the one who'd thrown the Soul Collector into the void, and used my magic to lock him there. Permanently, I hoped.

"And this weapon of his disappeared, you said," said a blond female mage wearing similar beautifying spells to Lord Sutherland. "And the spirit line… closed? Of its own accord?"

"The spirit lines can't permanently stay open," I said. "Like in the faerie invasion, they closed without the need for magical intervention. Once he and the weapon were gone, that was it."

"Lady Harper's body was found on Waverley Bridge," Lord Sutherland said. "You were nowhere in sight, and you didn't return to the guild until much later. Where were you?"

"I was looking for my friend Keir. The Soul Collector tied him up in the old train station. Nobody dares go in there."

Lord Sutherland glanced at the blond female mage on his right. Both wore the same expression of polite incredulity, as though they didn't think someone like me could survive wandering through a nest of zombies. Admittedly, I didn't exactly look intimidating even to ghosts. I was shorter than average, slight, and had deliberately combed my dyed jet-black hair so it hung in curtains on either side of my face and made me look shy and vulnerable. I'd also removed my lip piercing and gone without make-up in the hope that they'd think I was too sweet and naive to have ever been capable of producing the torrent of power required to yank closed a gaping hole in reality.

In fairness, I was only half responsible. The other half

came from the ghost who'd helpfully left me in charge of explaining both our actions as though everything we'd done was totally in line with magical laws and regulations.

Lord Sutherland shuffled the papers in front of him—the written version of my report. "That's the second time in the last few months that you've been involved in an incident in that train station, correct?"

"That would be because it's on the spirit line that intersects with the necromancer guild," put in Lady Montgomery from my right-hand side. I sent her a silent thank you, and on her other side, Ilsa Lynn gave me a nod of encouragement. She was one of the few people who looked as uncomfortable as I did, wedged between her boyfriend River—the boss's son—and her mother and sister, who worked for the faerie courts. As Gatekeeper of Death, Ilsa had dealt with a fair bit of crap from the Mage Lords herself. She also knew as well as I did that the real reason that particular spirit line had come under attack was due to the Hemlocks' forest being on the other side.

"I'm sure you understand why we need to check the details," said the Mage Lord.

Yes, because you care about paperwork being accurate more than you care about the lives the Soul Collector took. Even Lady Harper's.

I was lucky Lady Harper had called my boss and gave her a bogus cover-up story in the event that she didn't make it, and I'd never be able to thank her for lying for me. Then again, she'd probably grumble that it wasn't me she'd lied for. If anyone found out the Soul Collector had stolen the weapon he'd used directly from my coven, we'd go extinct for real this time.

Lord Sutherland finally looked away to converse with his fellow mages. While both the local council and the Council of Twelve contained representatives from the shifters, witches, necromancers and half-faeries, it was the mages who led and controlled the discussion, including Lord Vance Colton, founder of the Council of Twelve. I gave him a glare across the table to communicate my annoyance that he hadn't tried to get me out of the questioning, but his attention was on Lord Sutherland. Instead, Drake caught my eye and winked at me. Like Vance, he was younger than most of the mages on the council, maybe early thirties. His coppery hair was barely combed, and he had a long, thin scar on one side of his face which he'd acquired in the years since I'd left home. In addition to the Council of Twelve, he and Vance also led the West Midlands mage council. Having childhood friends in high places came in handy, but wouldn't change my fate if the cracks in my story broke open. Thank god the only psychics I knew were also on my side.

On my left, next to Isabel, Ivy Lane stuck out like a sore thumb in her leather and denim getup with her sword propped against the back of her chair. A human with some kind of faerie magic, she'd founded the Council of Twelve alongside Vance. If Ivy could get away with refusing to tell anyone about her magic, you'd think I'd be allowed to do the same, but I was fairly sure Ivy didn't have an extra soul sharing her body.

Since Lady Harper's funeral, Evelyn Hemlock and I had remained at a stalemate. She'd given justifiable reasons for why she'd hijacked my body—namely, that she needed my magic to fight against the godlike Ancients. The Soul Collector, she claimed, was only the beginning, and while the mages knew he wasn't human, they didn't know he was far from alone in his desire to wreak havoc on earth.

One of the shifters suddenly barked out, "Registers? What do you mean, registers?"

The smooth-faced Mage Lord looked in his direction. "Why, an official register would be a better way to keep track of wayward supernaturals, don't you agree?"

"Don't be absurd," said Vance. "Even if we noted down the name and details of every supernatural, new ones are born every day, and it's entirely possible for someone to be born into a human family and develop skill at witchcraft or the spirit sight. These things don't show up until the child is at minimum ten or eleven years old, so unless you're advocating for frequent testing—"

"I don't see why not," said Lord Sutherland. "We do so for mages who take on training as apprentices."

"There are fewer of us," said Vance. "It's not practical to track every supernatural in existence—to say nothing of the chaos this would create with the half-faeries."

"The Sidhe sure as hell wouldn't approve of a register," Ivy said. "Pretty sure they'd turn you into a flowering plant for asking."

Lord Sutherland shifted in his seat, twisting the spell on his wrist. "This city, like others, has an underworld which is woefully under-policed. There could be anyone hiding among us with any dangerous skill, unknown."

"Welcome to real life," Ivy said. "You're wasting your time. I wasn't born with magic and I ended up with it anyway. Necromancers can carry on working for the guild when they're dead. Are you going to require people to sign up to a register from the afterlife?"

Drake snickered. "You tell them."

I didn't laugh. I'd never heard the idea seriously suggested before. Registers for supernaturals? Not only was it impractical, it was downright dangerous for people whose safety depended on staying under the radar. Like, uh, me. And Keir.

"I'm sure your city has a supernatural underworld," Vance said. "As do most cities where supernaturals lived in hiding prior to the invasion. Registers are *not* the answer, and they've been shot down every time anyone has suggested the notion for the last twenty years."

As they should be. If I had to sign a register… being a guild necromancer was a solid cover for my Hemlock witch status, but not everyone was that lucky. What about the vampires? The Soul Collector had tried to exterminate them and most had been forced to temporarily leave the city. Keeping a written list of their names would be sentencing them to death.

"We'll revisit the subject later," said Lord Sutherland. "This meeting has gone on long enough… unless anyone has another topic they wish to address?" He spoke to the mages, for all the world like the other supernaturals weren't even present.

"The Will of Lady Alice Harper," Vance said. "Her fortune has already been distributed, but it seems she had some documents she wanted to bequeath to the Council of Twelve. I had them brought to your office. She also left more possessions from her country house to her living relatives—in that case, Wanda—and to Jas Lyons."

All eyes turned on me again.

"Why would she leave so much for Jas?" enquired Lord Sutherland.

So much for him forgetting about me when the interrogation was done. "She adopted me out of a witch orphanage when I was a kid. Maybe she liked me more than I thought."

True to his word, Vance had granted me the dubious honour of going through all Lady Harper's crap over the holidays. Since she'd owned three mansion-sized houses with all manner of secret nooks and crannies, we still hadn't found everything. Wanda had offered the house she'd inherited to the council to use as a backup meeting place and safe house. Her other two English countryside properties were turned into safe houses, too. After facing Lady Harper's extended family falling over themselves to avoid taking any of her fortune, it was jarring to see the unconcealed expressions of interest on the faces of the other mages. Lord Sutherland, I realised with a shudder of revulsion, would have taken every penny for himself and probably spent it on beautifying spells.

My former mentor had also left me some money, enough to live independently for a few years should I want to leave the guild. I'd donated the ghastly second-hand furniture she'd left to me to the local witch orphanage along with every other material thing I'd inherited and I still didn't feel any better. I'd rather have a living mentor who could save me from execution at the hands of the mage council than a pile of cash.

My hands tingled with static as Evelyn's magic snapped to attention. I quickly buried them in my pockets to hide the glow. *What is it?*

A guttural snarl came from my right. I spun in my seat as the meeting room door flew open, and a huge furred body leapt through. Council members rose to their feet with exclamations of alarm, chairs falling over, and a flurry of snarls and hisses broke out as the shifters already present assumed their animal forms. Claws slashed, teeth bit, and bursts of magic exploded on both sides of the table.

"ENOUGH," bellowed Lord Sutherland.

There was a bang, a crackle of lightning, and a huge gust of wind swept through the room. Everyone in the line of fire fell backwards, knocked flat by the force of the blast. One by one, the shifters all turned human, feathers and fur disappearing instantly. Even the intruder, whoever he was. The council members climbed to their feet, their impeccable clothes ruined.

A gap cleared around an inert body at the far side of the table. Blood streaked the grey swirling patterns on the carpet.

"He's dead," said Lord Sutherland. "Lord Forrest is dead."

Silence fell. Everyone stared around, shocked beyond measure at the sudden explosion of violence.

Vance reached the shifters first, and from the way they drew back, he was the one who'd hit them with magic and startled them back into human form.

"Who did this?" he demanded. "Which of you killed him?"

One of the shifters slowly rose to his feet. In human form, he barely resembled the monster he'd been when he'd jumped at the mage, but the traces of blood on his hands gave him away. I looked from him to the mage's body, tasting bile.

As a necromancer, I spent my days surrounded by death and yet it never ceased to startle me how very final it was. One second someone was alive, the next they were dead, and the world went on, leaving the survivors scrambling to pick up the pieces.

The shifter turned on the spot, and mages immediately moved to surround him. As he broke into a run, Vance raised a hand. The air rippled and the shifter was thrown backwards into the path of the oncoming mages. Vance's ability to displace things extended to being able to move individual air particles around to create a shield or even lift a person into the air. The shifter struggled briefly as his feet left the ground, his gaze darting around in panic.

"Who are you?" Vance demanded.

"Kill him!" shouted one of the other mages.

Vance whirled to face the council, still holding the shifter off the ground. "The barriers on this building cannot be breached by an outsider. I believe that's the responsibility of Lord Clarke. How did this man get inside?"

I was very glad not to be Lord Clarke at the moment. If looks could kill, Vance would have skewered half the room. I could only assume Ivy had some degree of immunity, or she was used to it, being his fiancé. She moved to his side, her sword in her hand, and everyone snapped into action. Several mages ran out of the room, presumably to check on the wards, while Vance procured a pair of handcuffs and snapped them onto the shifter.

As for me, I watched, my heart hammering. The mages and the shifters had a long-standing animosity due to the laws which had meant that until recently, the mages had effectively controlled where the shifters were allowed to live. I couldn't call myself an expert, but I did know it'd been hard to convince the shifters to sign up for the

Council of Twelve at all. And now... one of them had committed murder in full view of the council.

"He can't have broken through the wards," said a tremulous voice from among the mages, presumably belonging to Lord Clarke. "Not alone."

Oh, boy. Since nobody was looking at me, I tapped into the spirit realm. Greyness immediately surrounded me, covering the world in a fog-like filter. The pulsing brightness of the council members' spirits filled the room. I extended my consciousness outwards, into the lobby. Only necromancers stood out as particularly bright, and there weren't any outside this room.

Whatever my Hemlock magic had reacted to was in the physical world, and now it was as still and silent as the mage's inert body lying on the meeting room floor.

I let the spirit realm fade out, unable to quell the suspicion that if someone wanted to destabilise the cross-supernatural council, they might just have succeeded.

2

The meeting broke up as the mages dragged the shifter out of the room. The rest of the council left, talking in hushed voices, and I took Lady Montgomery's departure as an invitation to leave, too.

"Did you see something, Jas?" Isabel whispered from my right-hand side. She was a little taller than me at five feet, with warm brown skin and dark curly hair tied back out of the way for the meeting, her hands clean of their usual chalk stains. Like me, she wore spells in the form of wristbands concealed out of sight. Not that being armed had prepared any of us for the sudden attack.

I shook my head. "I thought the wards were up."

"They were," she whispered. "I put them there myself."

"You did?" Not just anyone could undo witch wards, let alone Isabel's. "How can a shifter have removed them?"

"With the help of another witch."

My heart sank. "Maybe they're still in the building, or close by." I looked through the dispersing crowd for my boss. Lady Montgomery's brows rose questioningly as I approached her. While she might not disguise her greying hair or wrinkles using spells like Lord Sutherland did, her scars and obvious experience in battle made her look much more formidable.

"Lady Montgomery," I said. "Can you sense anyone in the building who shouldn't be? Someone broke the wards on the gate."

"The intruder did," she said. "Nobody else is inside this building who shouldn't be. That does not, however, mean the shifter worked alone."

He couldn't have. "Did you see anything in the spirit realm?"

"I did not," she said. "Jas, I'd advise you not to involve yourself in this investigation. You're here for the guild, not the council."

"Might we summon the dead mage's ghost?" I asked. "That's the quickest way to figure out what really went on."

"Yes, it is," she said. "I will see if the mages will allow that."

With long-legged strides, she approached the mages. Some of them had already taken the shifter into another room, probably to interrogate him before they locked him up. I didn't know what the mages' jail looked like, but he wouldn't spend long there. The penalty for killing a mage was death. The rules were pretty damned clear on that one.

Ilsa Lynn approached us, worry creasing her brow. She was a fair bit taller than Isabel and me, with a curvaceous figure and long dark brown hair grown past her shoulders.

"My mum and sister had to leave," she said. "Did you see anything in the spirit realm, Jas?"

"No. Did you? Lady Montgomery's gone to ask the mages if we can summon Lord Forrest's ghost."

"Good idea," said Ilsa. "You'd think the ghosts would have spotted the intruder coming, but Frank said he wasn't paying attention."

"Who's Frank?" I asked.

"Former necromancer head in Ivy's region," she said.

"Oh, him," said Isabel. "I keep forgetting he's on the council, being a ghost. I don't know about the spirit realm, but that shifter broke through wards I spent hours setting up. And the building was already well protected."

"It's not on a spirit line," I said, frowning. That at least meant it was unlikely for a poltergeist to take up residence here, but we should still be able to reach the mage's ghost. Not that I'd been spending as much time in the spirit realm as I used to, with no magic keeping Evelyn contained.

I rubbed my arms, which prickled with goosebumps. Shifters didn't typically lose control of themselves when it wasn't the full moon. When it *was*, they found themselves confined to their animal forms at dusk, stripped of human reason or sense. In waking hours, though, that sort of thing didn't happen.

River Montgomery walked over to us. Ilsa's boyfriend looked nothing like his mother, having inherited his startling looks from his faerie side of the family. Curly blond hair almost covered his pointed ears, and even in his necromancer coat, he moved with an elegant grace that stood out among the crowd of humans. At the moment, he was the council's only half-faerie representative.

"Lady Montgomery has requested that I summon the spirit of Lord Forrest, in full view of the mage council," he said.

"You mean you're supposed to supervise, right?" said Ilsa, giving him a smile. "I guess it doesn't matter who summons him as long as the mages are witnesses."

For all their power, the mages didn't possess the spirit sight. That type of magic, at least, I didn't have to keep hidden behind a geas.

"We can roll a die to see who gets to do the summoning," I said. "The longer we wait, the more likely it is that the guy disappears for good."

River nodded to his mother's approaching figure. "The mages won't make us wait that long, don't worry. They know how serious it is."

Maybe. Though while the mages could turn everything into an hours-long ceremony, one of their own people had been murdered in plain sight, an even rarer occurrence than a shifter flipping out and attacking someone in public. Now they'd be ready for action. And vengeance. Lord Sutherland's beautified face was tight with anger as he intercepted Lady Montgomery. "Am I to understand you're prepared to summon Lord Forrest's spirit?"

"Several of my necromancers are, yes," she said, in tones that implied she intended Ilsa and me to come along despite the mage's obvious reluctance.

He made a low, displeased noise and selected a free room to host the summoning. When our small group of necromancers was inside, he abruptly shut the door on Isabel and the others. "Go on, then."

Someone had already laid out candles in the room's

centre—twelve, evenly spaced out. They didn't have to be, but like the mages, the necromancers were often sticklers for rules and ceremony. Lady Montgomery snapped her fingers and the candles lit up, while someone turned off the ceiling lights to make it easier to see the spirit realm. Grey smoke filled the circle of candles, swirling lightly.

"I summon Lord Forrest," Lady Montgomery said in clear tones.

For a moment, the space inside the circle remained grey and blurred. Then a faint flickering in the smoke announced a spiritual presence. Normally only necromancers could see into the spirit realm, but the candles made the dead visible to mundane eyes. The image of the murdered mage appeared, transparent and staring. His pallid face was even paler in death.

"What am I doing here?" he gasped. "Who are you?"

"What did you do?" demanded Lord Sutherland, turning on the necromancers with an accusing stare.

"Ghosts are often confused and disorientated after crossing the veil," Lady Montgomery said to him. "They may not even remember their former lives."

"I'm dead?" exclaimed the ghost.

"Yes, you are," said Ilsa, moving closer to the circle. "Can you tell us what you remember about when you died?"

"We know how he died," snapped Lord Sutherland. "If *he* doesn't remember, this is a waste of our time. Were you or were you not attacked by a shifter?" Lord Sutherland spoke slowly and carefully.

The dead man looked into the distance. "I... I was attacked. Someone stabbed me with his claws."

"Do you remember anything else?" I asked him. "Anything, uh, magical?" Maybe we should have gone to question the shifter instead, but there was absolutely no way I'd be allowed to sit in on his interrogation after narrowly escaping my own.

"No," he said, his voice fading. "Am… am I never going to come back? I'm dead?"

"Yep," I said. "If it's any consolation, it's painless. Just pass through the gates."

"Enough," said Lord Sutherland. "Turn the circle off. I don't want ghosts in our headquarters."

The spirit popped out of existence as the candles went out at Lady Montgomery's command. "You did ask us to summon him, Lord Sutherland."

"Everyone saw what that shifter scumbag did," the Mage Lord snapped. "Is that ghost going to stay behind?"

"Only if he has unfinished business," I answered. "Most dead people don't turn into ghosts for that reason." *Frankly, I don't think he'll be going within a mile of you again, if he has any sense.*

"Fascinating," he snarled, twisting the beautifying spells on his wrists in agitation, making his features distort. "We're done here."

Lord Forrest hadn't seen what'd prompted the shifter to attack. Shifters didn't turn for no reason… but the only way to know for sure was to get the killer's account of the story. Before the mages executed him.

Against my better judgement, I tailed Lord Sutherland out of the room. "Has the shifter been questioned yet?"

"What?" he snapped. "He's unconscious, but when he wakes, we will interrogate him. He'll die once he pleads guilty."

Mages were many things. Lenient was not one of them. "Who does the questioning?"

"The mage council, of course."

He swept away across the lobby. Damn. I had no business interrogating killers, but why had my Hemlock magic reacted when the shifter had broken into the headquarters? It'd never responded to a shifter before. As far as I could recall, the only magic it'd ever reacted to was witch magic.

I found Isabel waiting outside the door. "Any luck?" she asked.

"Inconclusive," I said. "The mage didn't remember anything we didn't already see. But the shifter's going to die the instant he tells the mages he's the murderer, and it's just plain weird that he managed to break the wards. Have the mages found out how he did it?"

"No, nor why he shifted during the day," Isabel said. "It's not common."

"Shifters can lose control at any moment, given an incentive," said a voice from behind me. I whirled on the spot, finding myself face to face with Vance Colton. Ah, crap. How long had he been listening in?

"They can?" I asked, resisting the urge to back up a step or two. Vance's light grey eyes weren't quite as intense as they'd been when he'd confronted the shifters, but he was over a foot taller than me and powerfully built. More than that, though, he had a reputation as one of the most powerful mages in a generation, and of all the people who knew anything of my Hemlock witch family, he was most likely to guess the truth.

"Yes," Vance said. "Anger, frustration... most shifters turn in an instant if they're attacked. It's not so unusual for him to have shifted, if he had a grudge against the mage in question and wanted to cause violence."

"And did he?"

I wondered how in the world Vance knew. It wasn't like mages and shifters traditionally got along well.

"I didn't know him, but I expect it'll come out in the questioning," he said. "You won't be allowed in, however."

That figured. Not that I particularly wanted to go anywhere near the mages' interrogation chambers, but Lord Forrest had died in full view of the entire Council of Twelve with zero doubt that the shifter was guilty. Either the killer didn't care about his own fate, or someone had put him up to it. Shifters generally knew when to pick their battles, and despite their brutal reputation, they didn't go around attacking other supernaturals with more magic than they had. They were big on self-preservation, though in more of a pack-oriented way than vampires were. That's why it was unusual to run into a lone shifter. They didn't survive without allies for long.

Vance left to join the mages, at which point, I turned to Isabel. "Obviously I'm going to do it anyway."

"What a surprise," said Ilsa, walking to my side. "Let me guess… you're going in through the spirit realm?"

"You've got it. You won't tell on me to the boss?"

She shook her head. "Nah. I'm not a snitch. I know this isn't the same as… you know, a few weeks ago. But it's still suspicious that he was able to get past those wards."

"Exactly," said Isabel.

"Worth a try," I said. "I don't suppose you know of an empty room nobody will burst in on?"

"The library, maybe," Ilsa suggested. "But we'll have to seal the door."

The library was across the hall from the meeting room, which was too close to the mages for my liking, but none of them gave us a second glance. They were too occupied by the murder and their prisoner.

"Wasn't this place destroyed a few months ago?" I asked, remembering the attack on the mage guild when a bunch of wraiths had appeared above the city.

"The mages fixed it," Ilsa said. "Got any candles? I'm not sure I have enough for a full circle."

"I have a few." I closed the door behind us. "Is one spell enough, Isabel?"

"It should be," she said, and there was a flash as she activated a sealing spell over the door. "This will only hold for about twenty minutes—any more than that and the mages might get suspicious."

Not to mention my boss might question where we'd disappeared to.

"Is River okay with you being here?" I asked Ilsa, setting down my candles.

"He won't be thrilled at hiding things from Lady Montgomery, but it's for a good cause." She laid down the last candle, forming a circle of twelve.

"I've never done this before," I admitted. "But I know how it works."

It wasn't as easy to question the living through the spirit realm as it was the dead, but we were in the same building as the shifter, and two of us had the ability to travel much further in the spirit realm than was believed possible. Perks of having two souls. And being a shade.

Ilsa and I stepped into the candle circle, and the grey fog of spirit realm filled the space. Stepping out of my body was easy—a sudden rush of weightlessness, between one blink and the next, and sensation became floaty noth-ingness. Nowhere near as disorientating as crossing between realms in my physical body, like when I entered the Hemlocks' forest. Part of me expected to see Evelyn Hemlock beside me, but instead Ilsa floated at my side. Her body glowed brighter than mine, enhanced by her Gatekeeper's magic. Like me, she hadn't been born a necromancer, but had developed her powers as a side effect. In her case, it was because she was Gatekeeper between the mortal and spirit worlds, not bound to an evil spirit, but we shared a similar outsider status. The glowing symbol on her forehead which marked her as Gatekeeper proved that, if nothing else.

"Better hope Lady Montgomery's not watching too closely," I said, floating out of the circle. Ilsa did likewise. I reached out with my senses—not the physical sort, but the sixth sense that enabled me to recognise anyone in the spirit realm within reach. I knew what the shifter looked like, but it wasn't as easy to track a stranger as it was a friend.

Ilsa and I passed through the wall as though it wasn't there, then another. If the interrogation had started, the mages wouldn't see us snooping, so it was worth checking either way. Peering into each room took no time at all, and we tracked the shifter to a guarded cell-like room the size of a cupboard. He sat on the floor with his back to the wall. No furniture in the room, but he wouldn't live long enough to need it.

Ilsa tapped the shifter's shoulder—not his physical form, but his presence in the spirit realm. He jumped upright with a stifled cry of alarm. "Holy shit, you're ghosts."

"Not exactly," I said, with a glance at Ilsa. "They're going to question you soon. The mages. All they want to hear is that you're guilty, but if you have anything else to say, tell us. Why did you attack that mage?"

His brow furrowed. "You look like ghosts."

"Let's say we are," I said. "Tell me, why did you attack that mage?"

"I…" He trailed off. "I don't know why I did it."

"Really?" Ilsa said sceptically. "You broke into a highly secure building and murdered a mage. You're saying you have no memory of doing that?"

"No…" He paused. "I do, but I don't know why."

"Was someone telling you what to do?" I asked him, unease skittering down my spine. "Did someone else come with you?"

He shook his head violently. "No, I came here alone. I felt… felt I had to do it."

"You… felt you had to?" I cast my mind around all my magical knowledge and drew a blank. *Felt* implied either a coercion spell or some other kind of influence, but that didn't explain how he'd broken through the wards.

"How did you get into the building?" asked Ilsa, clearly thinking along the same lines.

"I used a spell." He blinked, his gaze going out of focus. "I had to get to the council meeting."

"Why?" I asked. "Was someone telling you what to do? In your mind?"

Ilsa gave a slight head-shake. "We'd know if he was a psychic."

Psychics could only hypnotise other necromancers with psychic sensitivities. His 'feeling' sounded similar, but I'd know if he was a necromancer.

"Where did you get the spell that broke down the wards?" I asked him.

He looked at his feet. "I don't… I don't remember."

Maybe the same spell had forced him to shift, too, though I'd never heard of such a thing before.

"Am I going to die?" he whispered.

"Sorry," I said. "If it's any consolation, it's not so bad over here."

I gestured at the endless grey beyond Ilsa and me, though I hadn't a clue if he could actually see any of it. The murky shape of the endless gates stretched across the horizon, while more fading human figures floated in that direction. Ghosts departing the land of the living. The guy hadn't a hope of getting out of this. Mages did not forgive, especially murder of one of their own.

The door rattled. In an instant, I blinked back into my body. Ilsa reappeared beside me a moment later, and we stepped out of the candle circle.

"Verdict?" Isabel asked.

"A witch spell," I said. "I think."

Ice cracked on my hands, residue from the spirit realm, but the bone-deep chill within me came from somewhere else. Speaking to the almost-dead was freakier than speaking to the recently deceased. The mages were ruthless, but surely they'd see that the shifter hadn't been in control of his own mind.

Oh, who was I kidding? A fair proportion of them believed that they'd come by their gifts through superiority alone and that all other supernaturals were inferior by nature. Mages prided themselves on being fully in control of their own abilities, unlike shifters, though having grown up with them, I'd seen them cause easily as many magical accidents as any other supernaturals. More, if anything.

A witch spell had broken the wards. Not a Hemlock one, unless that's what my magic had responded to. Of course, it was possible that my magic had reacted in response to a potential threat, not against the magic.

But the last time I'd felt a reaction like that was when I was face to face with one of the Ancients.

3

Isabel, Ilsa and I walked back to the necromancer guild accompanied by River. I was sure he'd guessed we'd been snooping around the mages' place behind their backs, but questioning someone via the spirit realm wasn't technically against the law. I hadn't even used my Hemlock magic.

The mage apprentice guarding the guild's iron gates scowled at Isabel as she went to inspect the wards. Shimmering, semi-transparent glyphs formed a barrier in front of the gates and the walls surrounding the mages' headquarters. Their complex patterns looked more technically skilled than I was capable of, but my hands itched to touch them and see if they were as strong as they looked.

"What're you looking at?" said the apprentice, a straw-haired kid who was younger than I was. "We fixed the wards. Nothing else will get in."

"Do you know how they were broken to begin with?" I asked.

The apprentice scowled. "You're not supposed to be here. Get out."

"Technically, we all had an invite," I said, but it wasn't worth starting a fight with a spoiled apprentice who wouldn't know a real witch spell if it set his hair on fire. If I offered to help, he'd laugh in my face, and I was supposed to be keeping my Hemlock magic quiet. I just wished I knew what the shifter had done to break through so easily.

Isabel and I parted ways at the necromancer guild's entrance. It nestled between two equally ancient buildings in Edinburgh's Old Town, with iron built deep into the brick and powerful wards designed to keep out threats from the living and dead alike. These wards were familiar, because I'd made them myself.

"Let me know if you need anything," Isabel said to me. "You know where to find me."

"Sure." I waved goodbye and followed Ilsa and River back into the guild. The visiting members of the Council of Twelve had chosen to stay at a local hotel—specifically, the one I'd accidentally test-driven Evelyn's ward-making skills on—rather than at the mages' headquarters, mostly because they needed somewhere to store all Lady Harper's old junk from her Highland estate until they found a way to dispose of it.

The cold winter air pursued us inside, making our breaths fog and our feet go numb if we stood still for too long. I shivered and buried my hands deep in the pockets of my long, hooded cloak, daydreaming of hot cocoa and a movie night in Lloyd's room with the portable heater his mum had bought him the winter the guild's pipes had frozen over.

"Somehow I don't think the council will be leaving town on schedule," Ilsa said in a low voice.

"They killed the murderer, didn't they?" River said.

"Yes, but..." Ilsa trailed off, looking preoccupied. "I don't know. A murder like that in plain sight in the middle of a meeting looks like someone specifically wanted the Council of Twelve *and* Edinburgh's mage council to witness it. Someone other than the murderer."

"Not to mention the killer got past the wards," I added. "They don't sell unlocking charms powerful enough to undo top-strength witch wards on the market, do they?"

"Are you sure your friend didn't leave a gap in the wards?" River asked, his faerie-bright green eyes as preoccupied as Ilsa's.

"Positive," I said. "Whatever the issue was, it's not ours."

"I'll see what my mother says." River turned on his heel and disappeared upstairs, moving with the light, quick steps of a half-faerie. Like his mother, River could be forthright and domineering, but he seemed to sincerely care for Ilsa, and was one of the guild's top-ranked necromancers.

"The council will sort it, I'm sure." Ilsa took a step towards the stairs. "I should tell Morgan. He'll be pissed that Hazel didn't stop by here, but Mum took off like a bat out of hell after the meeting."

Ilsa's mother and sister were the Summer Gatekeepers who kept the peace between the mortal realm and the Seelie Court of Faerie. Ilsa herself, though she bore the title of Gatekeeper, belonged to a different realm entirely: Death. If *she* hadn't felt anything wrong when the shifter had attacked, surely nothing from the wrong side of the veil was involved. But if I believed the shifter's claim that he'd felt compelled to attack the mage for no discernible reason, a mind-control spell wasn't the sort of the thing you found at the witches' markets. I might have invented a few spells, but I'd never consider making one that could take a person's free will away. I had far too much experience being on the receiving end, thanks to Evelyn Hemlock.

"I guess Lloyd will either be in the archives or the training room," I said, walking upstairs with Ilsa. "Not on patrol."

"Nah, you two are always on the same ones," Ilsa said, with a smile. "Not that I wouldn't do the same, given the chance."

"I'm in charge of the rota for a reason. Besides, the boss owes me for not sticking up for me back then."

"Yeah…" Ilsa's smile faded. "Sorry the mages interrogated you in front of the council again."

I gave a casual shrug. "I'm the one who killed the Soul Collector. They don't like that there were no other witnesses to Lady Harper's death."

"Well, *now* they have a distraction." Her lips pursed. "Honestly, the council seemed edgy before the attack. Almost like they were expecting another… incident."

"What, like from the Soul Collector?" I dropped my voice. "I've seen and heard nothing since." Not from him or the other Ancients—and I knew there must be others, hiding from sight.

Unfortunately for all of us, the people who were most likely to know if there was another imminent attack were no longer speaking to me. The Hemlocks had maintained an icy silence the last few times I'd passed through the forest when I'd been to and from the mages' home over the holidays. Maybe because I'd taken Lady Harper's side over theirs, and now she was dead, so they couldn't challenge her in person.

Ilsa and I checked the weapons room, finding no signs of Lloyd or the others in there.

"I reckon Morgan's with Mackie in the training room," she said. "I did wonder—when the shifter said he *felt* he had to go into the headquarters, it sounded similar to when that vampire controlled Mackie."

"I think we'd know if a psychic shifter was running around the city. Mackie and Morgan would be able to hear the howling every full moon." My light tone failed to conceal my lingering misgivings. Psychic or not, I was positive that someone with access to powerful witchcraft had given the shifter orders. Now the killer was dead, the mages might let the matter drop, but surely they wouldn't overlook the fact that he'd broken through the wards with the help of a spell.

"You said you sensed… witchcraft?" Ilsa asked. "I guess it's possible we didn't catch all the witches working with the enemy."

"Isabel doesn't think we did, if they're as good at hiding as the Soul Collector was." It was hard to catch people who didn't work for one particular coven, and the mages had got one thing right—supernaturals were good at hiding. They'd had to be to survive in the world before the faerie invasion. Hiding not just from humans, but other supernaturals.

Sure enough, we found the others in the training hall that covered a large section of the upper floor. Some areas were designated for sparring or weapons practise, while others were for practising necromancy.

"You're not even trying," Morgan Lynn's voice came from the other side of the wooden doors. He and Mackie Chen, his sort-of-apprentice, stood nose to nose wielding knives. Luckily, they were the blunted, rubber practise knives with no sharp edges. Mackie was tenacious but lacked skill, while Morgan was as likely to accidentally stab himself as anyone else.

Lloyd stood on the side, watching them spar, and grinned at me when I came in. He lounged on a practise mat, reading a comic book rather than making any effort to hit the punching bag over his head. When we fought the dead, I was usually the one who did the actual punching, while he hid his tall lanky frame out of sight. His locs moved as he stood, dropping the comic book. "Hey, Jas."

Mackie dropped the practise knife and swore. "Bloody thing has no grip. I'd do better with the real thing." She and Morgan were the guild's only psychics and she was the stronger of the two, with the ability to disable any enemy without even touching them, let alone using a knife.

"I'm not letting you near me with anything pointy until you apologise for knocking me out," Morgan said to his apprentice.

"It was an accident," she protested. "I didn't know guild necromancers were so freaking delicate."

Morgan threw the rubber knife at her. It bounced off her forehead, and she caught it, throwing it wildly back. Ilsa and I dodged and the knife hit the doors behind us instead.

"Try that in a real battle and you'd be dead," he said to her. "Your footwork's all wrong."

"You can talk," she shot at him. "You walk like a drunken zombie."

"It's a strategy," he retaliated. "If I walk like a drunken zombie, the enemy has no clue what to anticipate."

"Probably because *you* haven't a clue what you're doing," said Ilsa. "Have you been in here the whole time we've been gone?"

Lloyd shrugged. "I expected you back sooner. How'd the meeting go?"

"The mages grilled me for half an hour, made some terrible suggestions, and then one of them got murdered by a shifter intruder," I said. "So, not great."

"What?" Lloyd picked up the practise knife and promptly dropped it again. "Who got killed by a shifter?"

"A mage. Lord Forrest."

"Wait, someone *died?*" said Morgan, as quick on the uptake as usual. "Is that why Lady Montgomery hasn't come to lecture us?"

"You've got it," said Ilsa. "No patrolling today, but we're on the rota for tomorrow, right, Jas? Assuming you don't break anything." She gave Morgan a pointed look.

He pulled a face at his sister. "Yes, mother. Let me guess, you sneaked behind Lady Montgomery's back and interrogated the dead guy's ghost?"

"Uh… he's not wrong." I glanced at Ilsa. "On that topic, did you sense anything in the spirit realm?"

Morgan shook his head. "Nope, nothing here."

"I didn't sense anything." Mackie kicked one of the knives off the ground and caught it in one hand. "But why would I? It's not like a ghost killed him."

No. Not a ghost… and not an Ancient. "I felt something odd. When he broke in."

"You don't need to be all secretive," said Lloyd. "You know that, right, Jas? We're trustworthy—all of us."

Ilsa's head dipped, Morgan grunted in agreement, and even Mackie gave me a rare smile. "Sure we are."

I know. The problem was, the number of people in on my secrets climbed by the week. Lloyd, Ilsa, Morgan and Mackie were sworn to secrecy, but Keir, Ivy and Isabel knew, too, and a fair few of the mages at least knew the Hemlock witches weren't as extinct as they'd pretended. One slip-up in front of the wrong person would cause the life I'd built here at the guild to crumble to ashes.

"Exactly," Ilsa said. "Look, I'm the only official guardian of the gates between life and death. If most of the guild can keep that on the down-low, they can do the same with your secret."

"You've never ripped open the line between realities, have you?" I said. "Or lied to the mage council?"

"I nearly started a riot in Faerie," Ilsa said. "And Morgan's broken every law in both realms."

"Hey!" Morgan said indignantly, darting a look at Lloyd. "I have not."

"We both used blood magic," Ilsa said.

I frowned. "*You* used blood magic?"

"Out of necessity," she said. "Trust me, when you've dealt with the Sidhe, the mages are nothing. When it comes down to it, they want to protect this realm. So do all of us. And we'll do that, right?"

"Damned straight," said Mackie, hitting the punching bag so hard that it swung and smacked Lloyd in the back of the head.

"Ow!" He jumped out the way. "Really, Jas, we've got your back. What's on your mind?"

"Evelyn's magic reacted when the shifter broke in," I admitted. "Isabel set the wards up, and there's no way he should have been able to just stride in. He said he killed the mage because he had a 'feeling' that told him to. He's not psychic, either."

Unease filled the room. We all remembered Mackie's narrow escape when the last Ancient had manipulated her mind and forced her to do his bidding.

Morgan spoke first. "Any supernatural can lose control if they're not paying attention. Like necromancers. One second you're hanging out in Death, the next, everyone in the graveyard next door has come out to party."

"Speaking from experience, are you?" said Lloyd.

He had a point. Necromancers had the highest mortality rate of any supernaturals, because we spent so much time close to the realm of the dead. Shifters weren't far behind either, due to their hair-trigger tempers, but most of those deaths occurred during the full moon. Not in broad daylight in the middle of an important council meeting.

"There's definitely a witch involved, anyway," I said. "But the shifter came alone, or it looked that way."

I'd never forget the horror of watching the Soul Collector hop from one body to another, killing each host as he left them. Since he'd had no physical form, he'd been able to freely move all around England and Scotland and amass a small group of necromancers to persuade count-less humans to do his bidding. And that was just *one* Ancient. Much worse lurked on the other side of the wall between realities.

Lloyd picked up the book he'd been reading. "I declare this training session over. Want to go to the cafe in a bit, Jas?"

"Can't, I'm meeting Keir," I said. "Unless you want to hang out with us at the Redcap's Cave. I think they're doing a karaoke night later."

He shuddered. "Not after the last one. I'll pass. Things are going well with our not-so-fanged friend, then?"

"Sure." I didn't particularly want to discuss my love life in front of a couple of nosy psychics, especially since everyone in this room was aware of the slight issue of Keir needing to feed on my soul to live. "Maybe he knows if the spirit line was involved."

"Or maybe he was trying to sneak into the meeting himself." Lloyd rolled his eyes. "Might a vampire have possessed that shifter?"

"Nope," I said. "Vampires can't possess the living. Not possible. All the evidence suggests it must have been a spell, but one Isabel doesn't know."

"Would the..." He dropped his voice. "Hemlocks?"

"They don't do portable spells." In its purest form, witch magic was made up of energy—wild, raw power. Handmade spells captured that energy, but the Hemlocks were capable of manipulating the raw power on its own without the need to contain it. At least until they'd chained themselves to their forest in order to stop the Ancients breaking free from the realm they were imprisoned in.

That an Ancient had still managed to attack us was proof that their plan hadn't worked as well as they thought. Maybe there *were* other godlike beings walking among us, but I doubted a supernatural register would draw them out of hiding.

I shook my head, feeling rattled. "I need to get outside for a bit. Unless you want to spar? Doesn't look like you've been doing much training."

I was more resilient than most necromancers thanks to the two spirits sharing my body, but that didn't mean I was immune to physical threats. Lady Montgomery had been strongly suggesting that everyone take a hand-to-hand refresher in case of another attack on the guild and I'd restarted my combat training, but nothing would ever hold a candle to my Hemlock magic.

"Look, some people are built for combat, some of us are built to run like hell," Lloyd said.

I snorted. He wasn't wrong. The pair of us spent more time running away from zombies than arm-wrestling them. Still, my Hemlock magic was more than a good enough substitute. I hadn't lied, though, I did need a distraction. I was supposed to be going on a date with Keir in a couple of hours and all I could think about was the dead mage and the doomed shifter. *Think cheery thoughts, Jas.*

"We'll go for a walk, then," I said. "Not near mage territory. I spent entirely too much of today shut in that meeting room."

The two of us left the others and went outside into the cold January air. Typical of this time of year, Edinburgh was bloody freezing but not a snowflake was in sight.

"So, what else came up at the council meeting?" Lloyd's breath puffed out in clouds. "Before the carnage? How'd the report go?"

"Same as the last three, except the mages suggested

putting every supernatural on a register so they can anticipate the next attack."

"A register?" His brow furrowed. "Yeah, that's not gonna work. I didn't know I was a necromancer at all until I raised my sister's dead cat from the grave. Half the guild's the same."

"I'm not sure it was aimed at the guild," I admitted. "The subject was rogues, actually."

"Like Mackie. And Keir."

I dipped my head, perturbed by how easily it'd come to the mages as a solution. Put my name on permanent record? I couldn't even tell anyone my real full name, Jacinda Hemlock. As for Evelyn, she was one of the millions listed as missing, presumed dead, after the faerie invasion. Besides, if I suggested putting my name on a register, she'd probably take over my body and run for the hills. Or just blast the mage council to pieces. I never really knew with Evelyn. While she'd claimed to be on my side, she was incredibly resentful that she was stuck in my body and forced to share her magic with me. Never mind that she was the only one of the pair of us who'd actually volunteered for this arrangement.

"They won't go through with it," he said. "Trust me, it's the mages being way out of touch again. Even the guild doesn't require compulsory registration."

"We almost did." I buried my hands in my pockets in search of warmth. "I don't know, there's got to be a way to look out for bad elements without throwing innocent people under the bus."

The question was, how? The Soul Collector had existed right under the guild's nose for years and still escaped detection. The Ancients were clever, and… well, ancient. Immortal, even. How were us humans even meant to compete?

When Lloyd and I got back to the guild, Keir was already waiting outside. Despite the cold, he wore a thin jacket over a T-shirt and jeans. His longish dark hair had been cut shorter since I'd last seen him face to face, and there was an attractive level of stubble on his defined jawline.

Lloyd cleared his throat. "Okay, I'm going in. Let me know if you wanna watch a movie later, if you don't stay out all night."

"Will do." I waved him off and turned to Keir. "You're early."

"I heard about the mage's death."

"Yeah, it was bad luck," I said. By now, I was half convinced I'd imagined the way Evelyn's magic had responded. She was so unpredictable that even her magic wasn't a reliable indicator. "I'll explain later. I haven't seen you in person for a while."

"Doesn't the spirit realm count?" He smiled and leaned in to hug me. He was surprisingly warm considering his thin clothes, but in the spirit realm, coldness brushed against me, the touch of a vampire eager to feed. Thanks to my shade power, he and I were bound in such a way that he was only capable of feeding on me, nobody else. Luckily for both of us, the sensation of a vampire's touch wasn't unpleasant, more of a full-body massage from head to toe that was as appealing to me as it was to him. By the time we broke apart, his blue-grey eyes were positively glowing.

I reluctantly let go of his hands. "I swear the guild gets colder every year. Why are you so warm?"

"Probably because I was sparring with a friend."

He'd been hitting the gym over the holidays, too, judging by the visible definition in his arms and chest under his thin T-shirt.

"I thought your vampire friends left town."

"Not all my friends are vampires, believe it or not," he said. "Anyway, I've been waiting to give you your present."

Here we go. Our relationship was in its early stages, but he'd told me he'd be getting me a present, so I'd done the same. Lloyd had said I was making too big a deal out of it, but to me, gift-giving signalled a new stage in our relationship I wasn't sure I was ready for. Things had leapt from casual to heated in a heartbeat thanks to the *accidental soul-binding* incident, but it was a little difficult to forget that dating me came with Evelyn Hemlock as the eternal third wheel, while dating him came with the added bonus of a missing brother and a grudge against the mage council. Complicated didn't even begin to cover it.

"Don't look so scared, Jas," he said. "It's not a hand-stitched puppet."

"Lloyd got me monster-patterned socks. We're good." Though after our long walk in the cold, I wished I'd asked for mittens instead. And earmuffs.

Keir handed me a square-shaped package. I took it and dug my free hand into my shoulder bag, handing him his own present. "I wasn't sure what you'd like."

I'd been way more extravagant than normal, thanks to the money Lady Harper had given me, but I knew Keir had more money than I did. Sure enough, I opened the package to find the sort of sketchbook and pencils that would have once cost me my life's savings to buy. "Oh my god, Keir."

"Do you like them?"

"Yes. I do." I tucked them under my arm and gave him a one-armed hug. "Now I feel like you aren't going to like mine."

He smiled, turning over the soft package. "I think I know what this is."

He opened the package, revealing a handmade coat. Market-bought, but well-made and reinforced with a couple of my own embellishments.

"I added some protective spells in case you ran into another knife."

He folded it over one arm and leaned in to kiss me. "Thanks, Jas."

"Least I could do considering the trouble my coven got you into." I put the sketchbook and paints safely in my bag. "Also, you'll catch your death of cold in that thread-bare thing you're wearing."

"Anyone can catch death by touching me. Or you." He winked, then shrugged the new coat on over his jacket.

"You're confident we're not going to run into any monsters tonight?" I adjusted my shoulder bag and fell into step alongside him.

"We'll send them packing if we do." He intertwined his hand with mine. "I missed seeing you in the real world. You'll have to tell me all about what you've been up to."

"You want to hear about the hours I spent ransacking Lady Harper's old houses? We found mice in one of them. No ghosts, though."

We walked along the cobbled street, and I told him

about the shifter's attack on the mage. As predicted, Keir told me not to dismiss Evelyn's instincts.

"Was he carrying any spells on him?" Keir asked.

"If he was, the mages would have confiscated them," I said. "I should have asked Isabel. But if he used the spells, they disintegrate instantly. Mine do, anyway."

"Might be worth looking into." He halted outside the Redcap's Cave, a cosy pub which offered discounts to necromancer guild members as a bonus for the zombie infestation we'd cleared out of the place a few years ago. "All right, we're here. No morbid talk from now on, okay?" He squeezed my hand, an unconscious gesture of reassurance that he had my back.

"I'll do my best, but necromancer habits die hard." I squeezed his hand back, still a little surprised at how easily we'd fallen into familiar ways. Vampires weren't typically touchy-feeling, except in the soul-sucking sense, that is. They didn't have a reputation for being great with long-term relationships, either, but Keir had sworn to make more of an effort with me. And not just because he depended on me to survive.

Keir and I entered the warm pub and ordered food and drinks. We spent a good two hours catching up, listening to the music from the old jukebox—much more pleasant than those awful faerie ballads that somehow showed up on every pub's karaoke list these days—and by my second glass of mead, my head was spinning pleasantly.

"Ah, looks like the karaoke crew is here." Keir leaned over to me as a large group of half-faeries came into the pub. The Redcap's Cave was a popular place to mingle with other supernaturals, but when it came to faerie singalongs, it wasn't uncommon to walk away with no clothes or any memory of the night.

"Wanna go for another drink somewhere else?" I slid off my bar stool, my steps a little unsteady.

"I think you've had enough." He slipped an arm around me to help me walk out the door, sidestepping a group of half-nymphs wearing so little clothing that I was surprised they didn't have icicles hanging from their ears.

I wobbled outside, cursing whoever had come up with the idea of putting all the pubs on cobbled streets which were impossible to walk on in heeled shoes, much less while inebriated. Using Keir for balance, I took a few unsteady steps, and then stopped.

There was a ghost outside. To be precise, the ghost of the shifter who'd killed the mage.

Why wasn't anything in my life ever simple?

4

The ghost floated in the middle of the street, lit with the faint grey light of the spirit realm. It was definitely the same man I'd spoken to in that jail cell. But I'd thought he'd gone beyond the veil after the mages had killed him.

"Hey there," I said, my voice slurred. "What are you doing?"

The shifter turned on the spot. His hands were encased in scaled claws, and the scales stopped somewhere at his elbows. Must be his shifted form, or a partial shift. I hadn't known it was possible for a shifter to change forms as a ghost.

"You!" He pointed with a scaled hand, his eyes widening. "You're not a ghost."

"Uh, you are," I said, some of my fuzzy-headedness disappearing. "What are you doing out here?"

A couple of nearby humans gave me wary looks and quickened their pace. I didn't blame them. In my first year at the guild, I'd given up trying to be discreet when talking to ghosts in public. People expected weirdness from necromancers, after all, drunk or not. But this man definitely shouldn't be here. We were much too far from where he'd died.

"I'm here… because…" His hands twitched, the scales rippling. Shifter forms could be ambiguous, especially on half-shifters, but I'd never seen one with scales before. At least he knew he was dead, which was more than I could say for a fair few of the ghosts I dealt with, but the sight of the gleaming scales chilled me in a way I couldn't explain.

Wait—when he'd attacked the mage, he'd shifted into a wolf. Wolves didn't have scales. *Huh?*

Without warning, he let out a bone-shaking roar. My whole body shook with it, and I cast a wild glance around, half expecting to hear terrified screams—but none of the humans so much as looked in his direction. I grabbed Keir for balance as my feet slipped on the cobblestones and the spirit realm wavered before my eyes. Then the shifter sprinted out of sight, disappearing from view.

I looked at Keir in bewilderment. "Did you see that?"

He'd gone very pale. "Yes, I did. He's gone."

I faced the spot where the ghost had been floating and tapped into the spirit realm. I left my body and felt my drunkenness lift—physical states didn't typically transfer over to the spirit realm. The shifter, however, had gone. *Ran* off. Not beyond the gates of Death, but literally ran, like a pack of werewolf shifters were on his tail.

I returned to my body in a blink. "How'd he do that? He ought to be anchored to the place he died."

Keir held my shoulders tight, peering into my eyes. "You left."

"Yes… Evelyn didn't come back, did she?"

He loosened his hold on me. "No, but I thought you weren't doing that anymore."

"I'm not afraid of her." Maybe I should be, but I was damned if I let her presence stop me from doing my job.

He didn't look convinced. "You know what she did."

"She saved me in the end." My words were sober, my good mood gone. "She won't screw with me as long as I don't bind her again. She wants out of this as much as I do."

Didn't mean I trusted her, but she wanted a body of her own as badly as I wanted to be free. Most shades met an unfortunate end, but most weren't enhanced with Hemlock magic. Together, we might find a solution that didn't result in either of us dying.

"Right." Keir took my hand. "I'll walk you back."

"It's been a nice evening. Ghost notwithstanding."

"Good." He smiled. "You're not patrolling tomorrow?"

"Not until night time. Graveyard shift—literally." I grimaced. "Otherwise, I'm meant to be helping the mages sort out Lady Harper's crap from her country estate in the Highlands. We only found out it existed the other week, since you know, she has three other houses. I think she set them up as safe houses out of paranoia, to be honest, not to actually live in."

"Sometimes it's good to be prepared." His arms enveloped me, and I sighed, relaxing into him. His spirit's touch caressed me head to spine, banishing the night's cold and leaving delicious warmth in its place.

When he released me, he was breathing heavily. "I missed you, Jas."

I knew what he meant. In the spirit realm, it wasn't the

same as touching him, wanting him in a way ghosts couldn't quite have.

Still… those were dangerous words to hear from a vampire. Especially as my own life was just as unstable as his, and with Lady Harper's death, nothing stood between me and punishment if the mages found out about Evelyn.

Yet when I was with Keir, Evelyn stayed away. For now.

———

First thing the next morning, I sent Isabel a text asking if she could find out whether the mages had confiscated any witch spells from the shifter. It seemed a long shot, but after a restless night punctuated by dreams of being pursued by a clawed ghost, I was eager for answers on how the hell the dead shifter had wound up on the wrong side of town.

'Weird' didn't even cover it. Evelyn was quiet, and I still hadn't asked her if she'd felt anything odd when her magic had reacted to the shifter's arrival yesterday. Maybe I should have asked her right away, but I'd been in shock —and besides, there'd been far too many witnesses with the spirit sight in the mages' guild at the time who would have seen her if she'd shown her face.

I have a tracking spell, Isabel replied. *Let's see if the mages missed anything.*

All right. I pulled on my clothes, loaded up on spells, and walked out of the guild's headquarters, texting Lloyd to let him know where I was going.

The air was cool, crisp, the sky as grey as the spirit realm. I shivered, huddling in my cloak for warmth, and quickened my pace until the tall, modern shape of the hotel came into view.

Isabel met me outside the front doors. "Hey, Jas."

"Hey." I ducked into the hotel lobby out of the cold. The interior was bright and cheerful, typical of a witch-owned place, with swirling green and yellow patterns on the wallpaper. "Got the tracking spell?"

"You bet." She held up a band-shaped spell. "I admit it's a long shot. The mages won't let anyone see what they confiscated from the shifter, and they won't let us into their headquarters again either. If we want to get up close, we'll have to use shadow spells."

"Figures." I twisted a shadow spell on my wrist and turned into a human-shaped shadow, and Isabel did like-wise. "I still feel like I should tell the mages I saw the shifter's ghost last night."

"Hmm. Were you drinking?"

"I was, but Keir saw it too. Not that he wants to go near the mages with a ten-foot pole." He held a long-standing grudge against them for refusing to believe that the Ancients had kidnapped his brother eight years ago. While he didn't mention it often, I knew it bothered him that the Soul Collector had perished without revealing whether or not he knew about his missing brother.

The gloomy, overcast day ensured nobody spotted us when we neared the gates of the mages' guild. Isabel picked a spot out of sight of the guards but within view of the gate, and laid down a tracking spell. According to Isabel, tracking spells tended to replay recent important events, and a ward being deactivated would leave a huge magical trace. I took her word for it, because Isabel knew more about that type of thing than me. Maybe Evelyn did, too, but she was still quiet.

Green light engulfed me when I put my hands into the spell-circle. The glare faded, showing a black and white image of the view across the street. As I watched, two cloaked mages approached the gates, their hands glowing as they activated witch spells. The shimmering wards grew brighter.

"It's just replaying the mages resetting the wards this morning." I let the tracking spell die. "I reckon we're too late. We should have ignored that bratty apprentice and used a tracker yesterday instead."

"No, we just need to find a clearer spot." Isabel produced three more spells. She'd probably spent all night making them.

On the fourth attempt, we finally got a glimpse of the shifter. As the spell activated in a flash of green light, a black-and-white image of the shifter walked up to the gates. His head was down, preventing me from reading his expression. He halted outside the gates, which were unguarded. The mages didn't always post actual people outside—usually, the wards were enough.

There was a white flash, so dazzling that I winced, certain that if the scene hadn't been in black and white, I'd have been momentarily blinded. The next second, the man was no longer a man but a giant wolf, shouldering the gates open. He disappeared inside, too quickly for me to see if he had scales on his hands like the spectre Keir and I had seen last night.

"That flash must have been the spell he used," I withdrew my hands from the circle, glancing at Isabel. "Recognise it?"

She shook her head. "I wish there was a way to make trackers that replay events in colour rather than black and white. If I'd seen what colour that flash was, I might have been able to guess the spell type."

"If it was a spell that undoes wards, it'd be..." I paused. "Uh. Help me out here?"

"Depends on the ward type, the aesthetic of the witch in question, and a thousand other factors. Let me have another look." She activated another tracking spell.

I watched her, not participating this time. After a few seconds, Isabel lifted her head, the spell circle collapsing into dust. The chill breeze swept the residue away. Witch magic did leave traces and impressions, but rarely physical ones.

"Anything new?" I asked.

"I was trying to see what the spell looked like before it went off." She shook spell dust from her hands. "It'd have disintegrated the moment he activated it, so the mages will have trampled over all the evidence by now."

"It'd be hard to see either way, from this angle." Isabel's handmade spells looked like stationary, bands or pencils, but the local ones were typically made to look like pieces of jewellery. Small, inconspicuous, and hard to spot, let alone through the lens of a tracking spell. I'd experimented a bit with my own handmade spells, but found the band-shaped ones to be the most practical and easy to conceal.

"A custom job." Isabel rose to her feet. "Specifically put together to undo the mages' security wards—every layer of them. Anti-undead, iron, protection, built-in alarms..."

"Someone got in a few months ago," I reminded her. "I don't know how they bypassed the wards, though."

"Oh, that was a Sidhe," Isabel said. "Not human, so our wards aren't as effective against them. I know the mages like to say they are, but there's only so much you can do against non-humans. Look what happened in the invasion. Half the mages' wards failed then, too."

My stomach sank uneasily. "Our last enemy wasn't human either."

And from what Ilsa had said, the Ancients had proven too powerful for even the Sidhe, the immortal faeries who'd once worshipped them as gods. If the Sidhe could kick the mages' wards down like they were nothing, maybe the Ancients could, too.

It can't be one of them. Not again. I'd know. The shifter had been human, and the mages had easily killed him. Besides, there were definitely still a few rogue witches running around with knowledge of spells I hadn't encountered before.

"We should go." Isabel adjusted the spells on her wrists. "Might nose around the market and ask some questions. What about you?"

"The last time I went to the market, Evelyn wouldn't stop complaining about everything the other witches were doing wrong." I'd never known her so vocal, and it'd been hard to focus on buying spell ingredients when she kept up a constant stream of critiques. "Anyway, I'm supposed to be helping sort Lady Harper's crap from her house in the Highlands before my patrol tonight."

"Sure," said Isabel. "Wanda and Drake will be in. I'll probably only be a couple of hours."

"Sounds good. Let me know if you find anything."

I made my way to the hotel again, firing off a message to Wanda. The two of us had grown up together after the mages adopted me, and Wanda had been the closest to a best friend I'd had as a teenager. She was also Lady Harper's granddaughter, not that you'd know it.

I quickened my pace as I neared the hotel, re-entered the bright lobby, and made my way to the second floor. The mages had rented all the best rooms. While the other guests complained at the noise—and the occasional blast of fire or lightning—the witch owners of the hotel had raked in a fortune from tips.

Wanda greeted me at the door to her room. She was about my age, tall and willowy and dark-haired, having taken after her mother rather than Lady Harper's side of the family.

"Hey, Jas." She waved me into the posh suite, where Drake lounged on the sofa, sipping some kind of fancy alcoholic beverage. The tall, lanky mage hadn't changed much since I was a teenager, especially his penchant for turning everything into a joke. He stood in sharp contrast to his closest friend and fellow Mage Lord, Vance.

"Where's Ivy?" I asked.

"Out," said Drake. "She gets bored being cooped up."

"I would if I had to sit through as many meetings as you guys," I said. "All right, let's see what other crap Lady Harper's left for me to throw out."

Ever since Vance had discovered Lady Harper's secret country estate—up in the Highlands, balanced on a cliff of all places—he and Ivy had been going back and forth between there and here, moving everything pertinent from the house to the hotel so it was easier to search. A mass of boxes covered the floor, and it looked like it'd doubled since the last time I'd come in here.

"The ones we haven't searched yet are here," said

Wanda, wading into the mass of boxes. "Ivy refused to let Vance leave her junk all over their suite, so I volunteered to watch it all. Most of it'll probably have to be tossed out, anyway."

I moved over to the boxes. Cracked ancient wine glasses, crockery... empty picture frames. "Did she not even keep any photos of her family?"

"Oh, she gave them to me," Wanda said, her mouth pinching. "When I was five or so. I don't think she could stand to look at pictures of my dad."

I sat down on the plush carpet, not knowing what to say. Lady Harper's emotions had ranged from irritable to raging mad with little in between, and it'd been easy to forget the years she'd grieved the family she'd lost in the invasion. After all, we'd all lost someone. A lot of some-ones. I tossed the empty picture frames aside, my mind conjuring images of faceless Hemlocks I'd never meet. "Wish she'd been as considerate of the living as the dead. Drake, is there a 'junk' pile?"

"Right here." A flame jumped into his hand. "I'll burn up anything we can't donate."

"Aren't you supposed to be running errands?" Wanda asked.

Drake yawned. "Yeah, Vance told me to talk to Lord Clarke, but he's a dick."

"You'll live," Wanda said. "Go on. We'll handle this, right, Jas?"

Honestly, I'd rather be patrolling in a graveyard right now. "Yeah, sure."

Drake left, while I dove into the box of junk. After a few minutes, the door opened again and Vance walked in.

He wore his knee-length mage coat and rainwater damp-ened his dark hair.

"Hey, Vance," said Wanda. "Come to help?"

"No, I was looking for Drake."

"Don't worry, he went to talk to Lord Clarke," Wanda said. "We could use an extra pair of hands here."

"No, I don't have time. I need the council documents. Lord Sutherland was asking me about them." He moved to open a new box we hadn't touched yet. "Lord Sutherland is insistent that the original Twelve's documents be searched for evidence of any past encounters with…" He glanced at Wanda. "Our enemies."

"The Ancients," I supplied, my heart diving two floors below. Had Lady Harper encountered them before? Given how many other secrets she'd kept from me, it wouldn't be a surprise. "Why does she have the documents? Wouldn't they be kept at the mages' headquarters?"

"Her house used to serve as headquarters," Vance said. "I did wonder, Jas, if she might have told anything to you or Wanda about the Ancients that she didn't mention to me."

"Nope," I said. *Well, aside from the fact that my coven went to war with them. But that's the Hemlocks' secret, not Lady Harper's.* "Not me. Wanda?"

"She didn't," Wanda put in. "Not a word."

"Figures." I rolled my eyes. "I'd have thought she'd tell you, Vance. You're her successor."

Vance lifted the box over to a more central spot on the floor. "I wouldn't put it like that. She never wanted to serve on the mages' council the second time around, and after the invasion, she didn't think anyone would live long enough to succeed her."

"I forget how cheery she was." I moved to the box he'd opened and coughed at all the dust. "Has this not been touched in decades?"

"It was hidden in the attic of the estate she hasn't been to in at least ten years, so quite possibly," Vance said. "These are old council documents from before the invasion."

Dusty stacks of paper filled the box's space. I dug down and pulled out a stack, and a loose sheet of paper fell out. A map, covered in so much dust that its lines were barely visible. I turned it over, trying to figure out which way up it went. A blurred X marked the corner, but the other lines were too faded to make out.

"Good god, her handwriting's worse than yours is," I said, trying to make sense of the scribbles at the page's edges. I'd need a magnifying glass to read it.

Wanda laughed, covering it with a cough as Vance scowled. "I believe her goal was that the documents couldn't be copied."

"Or read." I squinted at the page. "Honestly. For all the hours she spent lecturing *me* about my note-taking skills…"

"That sounds familiar." Vance lifted a stack of documents aside.

"She did that to you, too?" I blinked at him in surprise.

"All the time," he said. "It got worse when she put me in charge of mentoring Drake, because he absolutely refused to do anything I asked."

"Only because you were a brat," Drake said, walking into the room.

Vance looked up. "Aren't you supposed to be talking to Lord Clarke about security?"

"Done. I assume *you're* supposed to be doing something more important than reminiscing with Jas."

"We're looking at Lady Harper's crap," I told him. "Just in case she left any last requests. Know what this map is?"

"A treasure map?" said Drake, leaning over me. "Let's see."

I passed the crumpled page to him. "Might be the map to her wine cellar for all I know."

"Holy crap, it's an actual treasure map," Drake said. "With an X marks the spot and everything."

"Can you picture Lady Harper hiding treasure for fun?" I stood, stretching my legs. "When I was an apprentice, she once tried to kick-start my witch magic by levitating me off the roof. It's probably from a board game or something."

"Are we going roaming around the Highlands in search of hidden treasure?" asked Drake. "Awesome."

"Sorry to burst your bubble, but Lady Harper would rather have cut off her own hand than dug up the ground to bury treasure." I sat down beside the box again. "She used to complain about her countryside house having too much scenery."

"She did at that," said Vance. "Frankly, I could have used a map to find her house. It took nearly three hours of walking around the Highlands before I tracked the place down."

"I thought you could teleport anywhere," I said.

"Only places I've already been."

Drake snickered. "Yeah, otherwise his ability gets confused and we end up in places we're not supposed to be in. He's not kidding, though. Lady Harper hid that estate well. It's covered in so many wards that you could walk right into it and not know."

"The Highlands house wouldn't make a bad safe house," Vance said. "If it wasn't so isolated."

"Oh, come on, Vance, there's not really going to be another war," Drake said, rolling his eyes. "Chill out."

"War?" I echoed, looking between the mages. "What war, exactly?"

Drake shrugged. "Things are getting heated lately, but that's nothing new."

"Heated in what way? I mean, aside from the murder." I thought of the shifter-ghost and my heart gave an uneasy flip. Trouble in the spirit realm… and a mention of the Ancients. Maybe the mages were taking it more seriously than I'd thought.

Vance rose to his feet, brushing dust off the front of his tailored clothes. "Supernatural relations are fragile. Lady Harper's death came at a bad time."

"Yes, because you're paranoid," Drake told Vance.

"It's the reason I'm still alive. I'm going to find Ivy."

"She probably ran off to get away from your overprotective—" Drake said after him, but he was gone in blink.

I raised an eyebrow at Drake. "War? Seriously?"

"It's nothing," said Drake. "He's probably channelling Lady Harper's spirit. Look at how many times she saw enemies following her around."

"Probably because the one time she dismissed the signs, the world got invaded by faeries," Wanda said from the corner.

"What, she told you that?" Wanda and I had both been a year old at the time of the invasion, not old enough to have concrete memories of any of it.

"Erm, not exactly," said Wanda, flushing a little. "I kind of eavesdropped on her on the phone once when I was little. She was on one of her rants."

"She never ranted about the faerie invasion before," I said. "That I know of, anyway." If anything, she avoided the subject. She'd lost her entire family aside from Wanda.

Lady Harper wasn't the only paranoid one. The Hemlock witches seemed convinced there'd be a war, too. I looked down at the stack of documents like if I stared hard enough, the word *Hemlock* would leap out at me. She'd hidden her connection to their coven even from the council, as far as I knew, and the Lady Harper I knew would never have left that information open to discovery after her death. But it was worth a look, if just for an insight into who the bad-tempered mage who'd tried to train me in witchcraft had really been.

I grabbed another box, and dove in.

5

Lloyd and I walked through the graveyard, shivering in the cold night air. I wore three layers under my necromancer coat, but nowhere was as freezing as a cemetery at midnight on top of a spirit line. And quite possibly, nobody was as foolish as a necromancer who willingly walked into it.

The locals had been complaining about creepy howling noises from the cemetery every night. After three attempts to search the place in daylight hours with nothing to show for it, we'd drawn the short straw and been sent here to catch and banish the pesky spirit. Ordinarily, it'd be a rote mission I could have done while sleepwalking… except we'd landed up right in the middle of the spirit line the Soul Collector had tried to break.

"I c-can't feel my toes," Mackie grumbled from behind us.

"You're the one who volunteered," Ilsa said to her.

"I sure as hell didn't," Morgan said, scowling.

"I can light a campfire," said Lloyd. "Don't look at me

like that, Jas. If this ghost appears at midnight on the dot every single day, it won't be put off by a few flames."

"Or we might draw something worse here," I said. "This howling ghost is restricted to midnight, but that doesn't mean everything else is."

"You're so sensible today," he said, pulling a face.

"No, she's right," Ilsa said, resting her hand on the nearest gravestone. "This isn't a key point, but the energy here… I don't know, it feels kinda charged."

I tapped into the spirit realm, unsettled by how blurred it looked. On a spirit line, the blurriness was par for the course, but Ilsa, being Gatekeeper, was more tuned into the line than I was.

"I don't sense anything," I admitted, "but I want this done before we freeze to death. No funny business, and definitely nothing that'll make Lady Montgomery give us extra paperwork. She's being twice as pedantic as usual now the Mage Lords are in town."

"She bloody is," Mackie muttered. "I thought she was gonna handcuff us together to stop me wandering off."

"If you don't want to get devoured by a howling ghost, you'd better not," Morgan said.

"Ghosts don't eat people," she shot at him.

"What makes you think it's a ghost?" He folded his arms. "People are hearing howling noises at night. Sounds more like a werewolf."

"It's not the full moon," I reminded them. "Besides, it's a graveyard. Probably a ghost having a laugh." Creepy howling at midnight was such a poltergeist thing to do, not that there were any signs at the moment. A chill breeze swept through the fog, getting into every gap in my coat and forcing me to use one of my warmth spells early.

"Give me that." Lloyd grabbed me from behind, wrapping his arms around me in a bear hug. "I should have known you were hoarding all the warmth for yourself."

"Hey, back off," I said.

"Lloyd, stop assaulting her," said Ilsa.

"I'm not!" he said, letting go of me when he saw the others watching. "She's hoarding witch spells to keep warm while the rest of us freeze to death."

Morgan raised an eyebrow at him. "All right, then. If anything, we'd be warmer if we moved closer together."

"I'm not touching any of you," said Mackie.

"Quiet," hissed Ilsa.

A quiet whining noise came from somewhere among the gravestones. The small hairs on my arms stood up, and I looked around for the source, one hand gripping the candle in my pocket.

"There it is," muttered Ilsa. "There—*there.*"

She turned on the spot and pointed at a spot between two huge headstones. I squinted, seeing nothing more than a flicker in the spirit realm. I trod closer, and Ilsa caught my arm. Her forehead had ignited with a blue glow, and a similar glow came from her pocket.

"What is it?" I whispered.

"That's no ghost."

Lloyd let out a low curse. The shadows at the edges of the cemetery walls moved. Then several pairs of eyes blinked from within, paws treading towards us. The ground trembled. *Not ghosts.*

"Hellhounds!" yelped Morgan.

With a howl, one of the hellhounds jumped at us. I

dove to the ground, throwing myself behind a headstone. The beast collided with the stone, knocking into it hard enough to crack the surface. I rolled over on the ground, digging in my pocket. Candles wouldn't do much use against hellhounds. They couldn't be tapped in a summoning circle. But I'd bet they weren't immune to witch magic.

"Don't look directly into their eyes," Ilsa warned, a knife in her hand. "And don't get bitten!"

I grabbed my own knife, looking around for Lloyd. He'd pulled Mackie behind a headstone, out of the hellhounds' path—but Morgan, Ilsa and I were right in their way. And there were at least half a dozen of them, solid shadows more the size of wild boars or cows than regular dogs. Fear trickled down my spine as a pair of black eyes scanned us, caught my gaze.

The hellhound roared, leaping at me. Evelyn's magic surged to the surface, and a whipcord of magic appeared in my hands, shimmering silver. I slashed outwards at the beast's neck. Its head came free in a spray of blood, splattering the headstones with blue-red droplets.

"Way to go, Jas," Lloyd said, kicking the hellhound's body and causing its buddy to stumble. He threw a knife between the second hellhound's eyes, but the beast moved its head so the blade sank into its cheek instead. "Ah, crap."

Morgan, having flung himself out of the hellhound's path, stabbed wildly with a knife at its side before it could jump at Lloyd, while Ilsa attacked it from behind. Her hands glowed with blue light, her face pale and scared. Her Gatekeeper talent was mostly helpful against ghosts, not solid monsters. To be honest, the same could be said for the rest of us, too. But between the three of them, the hellhound was trapped, leaking blood from a dozen wounds.

At the sight of the blood, the other hellhounds moved in, growling louder than the eerie whining noise still audible in the background. Then two of them collapsed on the spot with pained growls. Before I could see who'd managed to get a hit in, a heavy body crashed into me from behind, flattening me to the ground. I swore and kicked out, trying to roll onto my front. The hellhound's teeth snapped inches from my skull, and panic roared through me, Evelyn's magic riding the wave. The whip reappeared in my hands, rippling with magical energy, and sliced over my head, causing the hellhound's dead weight to sink onto me.

I groaned and kicked out, blue-red blood splattering the ground beside me. Hellhound blood wasn't deadly, but their drool contained a poison that caused death within a few hours if it got into an open wound. I kicked again. Drool hit the floor inches away, sizzling and deadly. I rolled to avoid it, managing to push the hellhound's weight to the side. Death by hellhound drool would be an undignified end, and one near-death by poison was enough for a lifetime, thanks.

The hellhound's weight lifted a little as Lloyd gave it a firm shove, a blood-slick knife in his hand. "You okay, Jas?"

"Sure." I kicked at the hellhound's body until I could wriggle free. "A little bloody, but I'll live."

"Hey!" Morgan shouted. "Get over here, Jas—it's Mackie."

My heart lurched. I sidestepped the hellhound's body

and ran to where Morgan and Ilsa crouched between two graves. At their feet was Mackie, who lay limp, covered in blood. *No.*

"She used her psychic attack on two of them," said Morgan, his face pale. "But another got in behind her. Have you got a healing spell?"

"Psychic attack?" I echoed. *Oh—that's why they collapsed.* She must have found a way to attack them without jolting the whole spirit line and knocking out any nearby necromancers. "Yeah, I have—somewhere—"

I frantically searched among the spells on my wrist, but the darkness made it near-impossible, and the fog appeared to have reached ground level. Movement stirred within, and a pair of huge eyes blinked. The two remaining hellhounds were twice the size they'd been before. *How's that possible?*

"They feed on death energy," Ilsa said. "Hang on. Morgan, don't—"

A sword flashed, bright blue light igniting the gloom. Ivy Lane dived over the graveyard wall, her blade slicing upwards into the nearest hellhound's flank. As she did so, I drew on Evelyn's magic again, forming a whipcord that caught the last hellhound around the neck. Despite its size, its head came free with ease, and its heavy body slumped to the ground.

Ivy jumped to land next to the fallen bodies.

"Thanks," I said. "None of us were armed enough to deal with so many."

"No kidding." Ivy shook her blade, which gleamed with luminescence beneath the blood. "Please tell me one of you has a spell to get rid of those monsters. I don't know the number for the local clean-up crew and I reckon they'd have a few questions."

"I have a spell, but—Mackie's hurt." I grabbed a candle from my pocket to shine the light over my wrists, found a healing spell, and tossed it to Morgan.

Ilsa watched him activate the spell, biting her lip. "We have to destroy those bodies before they attract more Unseelie."

"Gotcha." Ilsa knew all about Faerie and its assorted monsters. Grabbing a dissolution spell, I threw it at the nearest hellhound's corpse, which immediately dissolved into ashes. I'd caused a few accidents trying to get that particular spell right, but now I was glad of the hours I'd invested.

When I'd destroyed the last hellhound's corpse, I ran back to the others. "Mackie?"

Her eyes half-opened. "Bastard," she said.

"She's fine," said Morgan, a note of relief in his voice. They might bicker a lot, but in the last month, he and Mackie had made a lot of progress.

I sagged against the nearest headstone in relief. "Thank god. I should have known it was a setup." I'd have thought the boss would have, too, but the five of us could have handled almost any other threat. Even Lady Montgomery wouldn't have expected hellhounds.

"What *were* you doing out here to begin with?" Ivy wanted to know. "I know you're necromancers, but this place isn't exactly hospitable."

"We kept getting complaints about a howling ghost who appears here every night at midnight," I explained. "Evidently, someone mistook a hellhound for a ghost."

Not that we ever did find the source of the weird eerie wailing noise.

Ivy's mouth thinned. "Did you see the ghost? Hellhounds aren't intelligent enough to prank humans. Someone brought them here."

"Nope. I looked in the spirit realm, too."

"Same here," Ilsa said. "Nothing was there."

"Where did those bastards come from?" Lloyd asked, frowning at Ivy. I'd not had the chance to introduce the two of them yet, and Ivy looked downright scary with her huge bloodstained sword.

"Hellhounds are independent," Ivy said. "They used to belong to Faerie's Wild Hunt, but now they roam between this realm and the liminal spaces working for anyone who'll feed them fresh corpses. They make good attack dogs."

"And can grow to the size of a tank," Lloyd added.

"We're on a spirit line, so they must have come from a liminal space," Ilsa said decisively. "We should go in and check, Jas."

"Sure." I turned on my spirit sight, and Ilsa joined me. Considering her unusual magic, I'd wondered if Ivy might be able to see the spirit line herself, but then again, she wasn't a necromancer.

After thoroughly scanning the cemetery, I blinked back into my body. "Nothing. Dead, undead or otherwise."

Ivy swore. "Right, I'm going to make sure there aren't any more of those nasties roaming around. You guys should probably head back." She jerked her head at Mackie, who'd managed to sit up against a headstone.

Ilsa said, "Morgan, help Mackie back to the guild. I want to have another look around. Just a quick one."

Morgan turned to her. "You think I'm leaving you alone out here?"

"I'll stay with her," I said. "Just one minute. Lloyd—"

"I'll go back with them," Lloyd said, to my surprise. "But only if you promise you'll be back in ten minutes, no more."

"Promise," I said.

The others left the cemetery via the gates—or in Ivy's case, by jumping over the wall.

"See anything?" I asked Ilsa.

"Nope, but I don't think it's in the spirit realm." Ilsa dropped her voice. "It's actually possible to summon hellhounds, accidentally or deliberately, through blood magic."

My stomach turned over. "Blood magic. You said you used it before?"

"In an emergency," she said. "I think using blood in a summoning is like a kind of signal that attracts anything that happens to be hanging around between the worlds. Those hellhounds appeared directly in the middle of a city without being seen or trampling on any humans. I'd say it's likely they were summoned here."

"And if that's the case, there's got to be a place the person did the ritual," I said, nodding. "The howling ghost —if it exists—can't have done it, though. Must be someone living."

"It's got to be close." She moved around the graves, and I followed, my skin prickling.

Blood magic. The last fury attack hadn't been due to someone summoning them with blood magic. Instead, they'd come through the spirit line of their own free will when the Soul Collector had torn it open.

I almost hoped it *was* blood magic, rather than the alternative.

There was a church at the end of the graveyard which seemed an obvious site for foul play, but the door was locked, and hellhounds couldn't walk through walls. Figuring it'd be easier to search as a ghost, I tapped into the spirit realm and found myself face to face with Evelyn Hemlock.

I nearly jumped out of my body. She floated beside me, her dark brown hair streaming behind her ears, her eyes glowing blue-grey, entirely too alert for someone who was supposed to be in hibernation. How long had she been hovering next to me, listening to every word I spoke?

"There's no ritual here," she said to me.

I frowned at her. "And you'd know?"

"Our magic would." She spoke matter-of-factly. "Always."

"So… they came out of a liminal space. The hellhounds."

It wasn't Leila Hemlock. Her soul was gone. But only a witch could have conducted a ritual, right?

"The walls are coming down," she said in that same calm tone. "Especially here."

"What does that mean? Did the Soul Collector cause permanent damage?"

Her body was already fading, leaving nothing behind but grey smoke. I sighed, blinking back into my body.

Ilsa stood close to me, her shoulders tense. "That was her? Your… your other soul?"

"You saw her?"

"I did." She gave me a brief glance. "I thought you weren't speaking to one another, considering she… you know. Tried to possess you."

"She didn't summon the hellhounds," I said. "No, I think they came from a liminal space if anywhere at all. She mentioned the walls being thin here."

"Because of the Soul Collector," she said. "Have you travelled on this line before?"

"Not this one," I said. "Just—"

"The Hemlocks' one," she finished. "I think that's the one I used when I first travelled on a spirit line. So… does having two souls give you a boost? My Gatekeeper's power stops me from being separated from my body, so I'm guessing it's like that for you, too."

Ilsa made no secret of her academic interest in my second soul. She'd probably been saving up questions to ask me over the holidays, but the last thing I wanted was to chat about shades while standing on a spirit line beside the ashes of a half-dozen dead hellhounds. "Yeah, being bound to Evelyn makes us both stronger. I think my magic lets me cross between realms, too. But I don't know how to check if there's a liminal space here."

"Not worth the risk if there's more hellhounds over there," Ilsa said. "We're better off reporting to the guild so they know not to send patrols this way without backup."

"Good idea." Liminal spaces were invisible to sight, but for all I knew, maybe my magic *could* find them.

Since Evelyn wasn't in a chatty mood, there was one person to ask: Cordelia Hemlock.

6

The following morning dawned as dull and grey as the previous day. I hadn't slept all night, too shaken by the experience with the hellhounds and Mackie's close call to relax, and ended up leaving at the crack of dawn for the Hemlocks' forest just to get it over with.

Evelyn remained as taciturn as ever, making it difficult to tell if she approved of my plan or not. I wasn't sure I believed her claim that hellhounds had jumped out of the spirit line of their own accord, but Ilsa and I had found no signs of any ritual activity. Maybe something else had drawn them to the cemetery. Either way, I needed to consult the Hemlocks to know whether it was possible for me to track down liminal spaces with or without my body.

Reaching Waverley Bridge, I turned on my Hemlock magic and felt my way through to the forest beyond this realm. A moment later, the chill air disappeared, replaced with relative warmth. I'd worn my necromancer coat so nobody would question why I was wandering near an abandoned train station early in the morning, but climbing over tree roots in a long coat was a disaster waiting to happen.

"Hey," I called into the trees. "Come on, Cordelia, you must know I'm here to see you. You can't stay mad at me forever."

Silence filled the space between the thick oak trees. I lifted my cloak off the ground, and trod forward a few steps. "Evelyn and I wanted to ask you something important about my magic."

"We did not," Evelyn muttered in my ear, but I'd said the magic word. The trees disappeared, to be replaced with a huge cave. The back wall was covered in shimmering green glyphs, holding a hole in the universe together. All around, faces stared from the rock, and from the stone sculpture in the centre, Cordelia Hemlock's craggy face and pit-like eyes appeared.

"Evelyn," she said.

"Yes?" Evelyn responded, through my mouth. Oh, great.

"I'm glad you decided to return to us," Cordelia said.

Unbelievable. Even if I believed that Evelyn hadn't been out to destroy the world as we knew it, Cordelia knew perfectly well that she'd forced me out of my body on more than one occasion, assaulted my fellow guild members, and pretended to help Leila Hemlock in a scheme that might easily have backfired on both of us. Yet for all that, in Cordelia's eyes, Evelyn was the true Hemlock heir.

"It was my idea," I said, elbowing her aside. "We'd like to know if it's possible to use the Hemlock magic to cross into liminal spaces and other realms, and how to do it."

Cordelia blinked her pitch-dark eyes. "That's far beyond your level. You have no training."

"Tossing the Soul Collector into a rift between worlds is way beyond my level too, but I still did it," I said. "A bunch of hellhounds attacked us at the cemetery last night. They appeared from nowhere. No evidence of a ritual, so I assume they're hanging out in a liminal space somewhere. Thing is, it's the same spirit line the Soul Collector tried to break."

"That line?" she said, in surprisingly dismissive tones. "Hellhounds have been roaming the liminal spaces since the invasion, if not longer."

"It was a calculated attack. Also, are hellhounds related to furies?"

"Not in the slightest," Cordelia responded. "They're from Faerie. Furies are not."

"They can both scare people half to death by looking into their eyes," I said. "They can also be summoned using blood magic."

"Who told you that?"

Ah, crap. Ivy and Isabel might have met the Hemlocks before, but Ilsa definitely hadn't. Her Gatekeeper family had their own repository of knowledge, though, straight from the Council of Twelve.

"Everyone knows about blood magic," I said. "The guild might not allow it, but rumours get started for a reason. It's also how the first fury attacks happened last year. You know that."

"Yes, but I assumed you'd have the sense not to involve yourself with people who practise illegal magic."

I narrowed my eyes. "Do you hear yourself? You can't paint yourselves as the exceptions to every rule. You know perfectly well what'll happen to me if I'm caught red-handed with an extra soul. Frankly, I think a little blood magic is tame by comparison."

"Jacinda," Cordelia said warningly.

"I'm not *actually* doing blood magic," I said. "For the record. But either someone else is, or those hellhounds came from a liminal space. Our magic allows me to cross realms, with or without my body. Right?"

"Anyone can enter a liminal space if they know where it is," she growled. "I would advise you to keep your head down until the aftermath of the Soul Collector's attack has faded."

"It won't fade," I said. "You know that, right? You might live in a bubble, but the rest of the world doesn't. Things change, they have side effects. The mages think the Ancients will strike again and are trying to rewrite the laws because of it. Sane, rational people are panicking and thinking there'll be a war. Lady Harper did, too."

At the mention of her name, all the air seemed to leave the cave. Cordelia's tree-sculpture *moved,* and a few cracks appeared in the ceiling as the glyphs shifted, luminous patterns moving before my eyes.

I took a step backwards. "You... you're mad at her, not me. Right? She believed the worst of you."

Cordelia said nothing. My heartbeat seemed uncomfortably loud in the silence, and for once, I wished Evelyn would speak up.

"You were allies," I said. "So... how did you end up fighting? Where'd it go wrong?"

No response came. Oh, she was mad at Lady Harper

all right. But why? Okay, my former mentor had believed Evelyn was the person who'd helped the Soul Collector, but then, so had I at first. That was reason enough for them to spurn me, but if my secret was exposed, the Hemlocks were all I'd have left.

"Where did it go wrong?" Cordelia repeated. "Alice Harper and I disagreed on most fronts. She was no Hemlock witch, and couldn't truly understand our cause."

"You were distantly related," I said. "But you've never let Wanda or any of your other distant relations into the forest."

"A lot of supernaturals might claim a distant link to our coven," she said, in tones that suggested if she was physically capable of shrugging, she would have. "We were, after all, the first."

"The first coven?" At this point, I'd suspected the Hemlocks predated every other surviving coven in the UK. No other coven I knew of depended on bloodline for succession, and it struck me as the sort of antiquated approach that would have died out decades ago if not centuries. Something different ran in the blood of the Hemlock witches—a force no other witch possessed. And not in a good way. "You know, your superior attitude sounds awfully like a certain wannabe-god."

"Don't you dare compare us to them," she hissed. "The Ancients have tried to destroy us countless times."

"Don't I know it," I said. "Look at the Soul Collector. He hid out in Edinburgh without anyone ever finding him. Any others you forgot to mention?"

"The Soul Collector had no body or physical manifestation," said Cordelia. "Nor a weapon until he stole ours. If the Ancients survived in your realm, they'd be in a similar form or worse. Most died off, or were sealed away —by us, or by the mages' predecessors. I'd advise you not to go looking for liminal spaces, Jacinda. You might not like what you find."

I threw up my hands. "You're still trying to pull the wool over my eyes? I've seen you at your most vulnerable. I know this place isn't gonna last forever. War or no war, if I'm to stay on your side, I deserve the truth. And not when it's too late for me to do anything about it."

"The truth about what, Jacinda?"

Where to bloody start? "How did you bind Evelyn and me? Why not give us a way out? You knew it was forbidden and that the mages would probably execute us for it if they found out."

That type of magic had been forbidden for the last hundred years at least, according to what I'd read in the archives. Even though they'd been stuck in the forest for decades, the Hemlocks had known.

"We had no choice but to act in the moment," Cordelia said. "Evelyn was dying. Every other heir was dead. There was a good chance we wouldn't live to see the dawn. Hundreds of mages perished when the Sidhe came. I little expected their pedantic human laws would persist."

"Well, you thought wrong." Damn. I'd *hoped* they'd built in a get-out clause, but unfortunately, her words matched up with what I'd heard of the day-and-a-half of hell that had been the faeries' invasion. Half the Mage Lords in the country had died. Laws hadn't mattered, only survival. "Is there a way for me to, uh, bind Evelyn into the forest the same way you are?"

"No," said Cordelia. "The curse on us is unique, and

can't be replicated. Only when we expire will this power pass onto the heir. Both of you."

"I won't be sealed away," Evelyn said through my mouth. "Never again." Magic sparked at my own hands. I got the message—and so did the cave, which warped around us, the glyphs spinning like a merry-go-round.

"That's making me dizzy," I said, but the words never left my mouth. "Come on, I was kidding."

Honestly, if Evelyn wanted to serve her coven as badly as she claimed, you'd think being bound into the cave along with her fellow witches would be an honour.

"Evelyn," I said, but no sound came out. "Evelyn, let me—"

"You're fools," said a voice. Lady Harper strode into the cave. Her face was a little less lined than it'd been in the time I'd known her, but she leaned on a walking stick and wore the irritable expression I'd known her for in life.

Oh, crap. I was in one of the forest's visions, or memories.

"This place claims more of your sanity by the day," Lady Harper said. "Why should I alert the council to your delusions?"

"Not delusions," said Cordelia's voice from behind me. "I see only the truth."

"What am I to tell them?" Lady Harper asked. "That one of your nonsensical prophecies is coming true? They might believe me, but they'd never believe you. You removed yourself from the council too long ago."

"The council sees only the realm before their eyes, not what lies beneath and beyond," croaked the old witch.

"The Gatekeepers don't believe there's a threat," Lady Harper said. "And they'd know. I'd say you've spent too long in this forest, watching battles old and new. It's made you paranoid."

You're one to talk.

"Luck favours the prepared," whispered Cordelia. "Please, Alice, tell your son that his daughter may carry the gift. If she does, we'll need her."

Lady Harper's mouth tightened. "There are no Hemlock witches in my family, Cordelia. You are the last of them."

"There are others," said Cordelia, speaking quickly. "In Edinburgh, in hiding. Contact them, I beg of you. Warn them. Warn the Briar witches, too. Warn them they're coming."

Lady Harper's brows rose. "Survivors?"

"Heirs," Cordelia said. "My heirs."

The scene dissolved. I became aware that I was on my knees on the bridge back in Edinburgh, breathing heavily. Why had the Hemlocks chosen to show me that memory? To prove Lady Harper had been in the wrong?

Taking in a steadying breath, I asked Evelyn, "Do you remember that?"

Evelyn didn't answer. I shook my head at myself. Of course she wouldn't remember. She hadn't actually been there in the forest, she'd been with her family.

Not long after that scene, if it was when I thought it was, she'd died.

The Hemlocks had seen it coming. But Lady Harper? I hadn't known she'd outright denied the Hemlocks' warnings. Had she done as Cordelia asked and warned the other Hemlocks in Edinburgh? She'd been too late to save her son, I'd worked that much out. The daughter mentioned in the vision was Wanda, but she'd never been born with the gift.

And... Cordelia had implied *all* the Hemlocks had been in Edinburgh, meaning I must have been born here. Like Evelyn, and Leila. I had no recollection of the first year of my life, but it explained why Lady Harper hadn't come here and dragged me home after I'd run away. I'd lived here as a baby, before the faeries came.

I wrapped my arms around myself, shivering uncontrollably. Even the supernatural council hadn't believed the Hemlocks' warnings. No wonder the witches had cut themselves off from the world.

I wouldn't have believed them either.

"Evelyn," I whispered. "Tell me there's not going to be a war."

Silence answered.

"Jas, you look like hell warmed over," Keir said across the table at Cassandra's Café.

I sipped my extra-strength coffee and shrugged. "Still the best-looking living Hemlock there is." I gave a laugh that probably wasn't very convincing. "I was gonna text you last night, but let's just say our graveyard shift didn't exactly go as planned."

I told my tale of last night's attack and this morning's revelations in the forest.

Keir let out a low whistle. "How do you manage to find a new way to get into trouble every time?"

"At least I didn't utterly disbelieve a warning about the end of the world."

"It wouldn't have made a difference," he said. "The invasion would have happened no matter what. Lady Harper might have regretted ignoring the warning signs, but it sounds like she saved your life."

"Or endangered it. I really need to track down this Briar Coven. I know they saved my life when I was poisoned, but I was kinda dead at the time."

Not to mention I'd thought they were in Lady Harper's pocket. I'd avoided asking anyone about them for that reason alone up until her death. But now I knew they'd met Evelyn when she was still alive—not to mention my blood family, who'd died before I'd ever known them? If I'd gone looking for them rather than being a stubborn arse, I might not feel so utterly adrift.

"Then we'll find them," he said decisively. "There's nothing else you can do about those hellhounds."

"No..." I bit into my bacon sandwich. "I just find it suspicious that it happened on the same spirit line the Soul Collector attacked."

Keir took a long sip of coffee. "No signs of any ghosts, either?"

"A weird disembodied howling, but it might have been the hellhounds." I chewed another mouthful. "No sign of who summoned them. I have to get back to the guild and fill out a billion reports later, but I have an hour or two free. I mean, if you want to look around the graveyard in daylight in case I missed the site of the summoning, we can do that. Or we could go after the witches."

"I expect the guild will already have sent people to the graveyard at the first light of dawn," he said. "The witches, however... it sounds like they might be important."

"Not enough to actually leave me a message saying

where they live when they saved my life." I put down my unfinished sandwich, my appetite fleeing. "I can't believe I was born here and I don't remember. And Lady Harper knew."

It was the least of what she hadn't told me, but even the half-empty café looked different to my eyes now. Though I was the one who'd changed. The city was the same as ever.

Keir reached and took my hand across the table. "I'd say it's worth tracking these witches down."

"Right." I crumpled a napkin in my hand. "I don't actually have an address. Would you believe it? I was so pissed at Lady Harper that I never asked. But someone at the market will know. I might have to break out a disguise spell."

"Disguise?" he echoed. "Why, you don't think there are still witches out to get you?"

"There are always witches out to get me," I responded, downing the remainder of my coffee. "I'll text Isabel, but I won't drag her out of bed if I don't have to."

Besides, if these witches had known me as a baby... I wanted to meet them alone, at least for the first time.

I snapped on my disguise spell as we approached the witch market, turning into a tall blond woman with nondescript features and definitely no necromancer cloak. Stalls lined the cobbled street, selling everything from bottled and powdered ingredients to specialist handmade spells. Since the market wasn't regulated, buying spells there always carried a risk, but the witches were generally pretty good at running hoaxers out of town. I hoped Evelyn would keep her mouth shut this time.

"Hey there," I said to a young woman who looked like she might be part faerie, who stood behind a stall selling jarred potions for beauty and anti-aging. "I wondered if you could tell me where to find the Briar Coven?"

"The Briars?" She raised a perfectly plucked eyebrow. "They're gone. Left town over a month ago."

"What? That can't be right. I, er, met with them in November." Or my unconscious almost-corpse had, anyway.

"Lots of people have left." She gave a shrug, getting in a toss of her luscious dark hair. "Some bad elements around lately."

"Oh?" I asked, not needing to feign interest. "Like what?"

"You know. People disappearing off the streets. It's been going on for months now. Just ask… hey, Callum."

"Oh, I know what you mean," I said quickly, not wanting to draw anyone else into our conversation. "Can you tell me where the Briar witches used to live?"

"I think they rented that place in Silverwood Street," she said. "But as I said, they packed up and left. At least six weeks ago, now."

"Thanks anyway." I backed away from the stall, frustration bubbling in my chest. *Dammit, Jas. Why* hadn't I gone looking for them before? They'd saved my life, for god's sake. On the other hand, if they'd left over six weeks ago, then it was possible they'd only stuck around for a week or two at most after they'd saved my life. I'd been so preoccupied at the time that the thought of tracking them down had never crossed my mind.

Keir and I walked the short distance to Silverwood

Street. Bitterly cold air whipped my face, and even Keir's hand in mine didn't banish the chill in my bones.

"I don't think there's anyone here," Keir said quietly.

A row of terraced houses faced us. Their windows were almost all boarded up, their doors locked and without the signs of protective wards common to witch establishments. I tapped into the spirit realm, seeing only grey, and left my body, floating from one door to the next.

Empty rooms, bare of furniture. Empty bookshelves. Dust. And no note, no farewell from the coven who'd saved my life.

I jumped when someone put an arm around me, but it was only Keir. "Jas? You okay?"

I turned to him, hovering in the middle of the deserted street. "I was born here. My parents lived here—my whole family might have. And nobody *told* me." Ghostly tears fell from my eyes, not leaving a trace. "I should have asked. Why didn't I ask?"

Keir hugged me, resting his chin on my head. Not feeding on me. Just holding me.

The buzz of my phone in my pocket jolted me back into my body. I grabbed it with numb fingers. "Hey, Isabel," I said, wiping my eyes. "What's up?"

"There's been an incident at the hotel," Isabel said. "I wondered if you heard."

I gripped the phone tight. "No… no, I didn't. Shit, what happened?"

"Shifter attack."

7

"Another shifter attack? On who?" I was already walking away, the phone pressed tight to my ear.

"The mages," Isabel said. "Three of them were seriously injured. And it's worse than before—the shifter who attacked them was an ambassador to the Council."

"Shit." I quickened my pace, Keir falling into step alongside me. "I'll be right there."

I hung up the phone, swearing under my breath. *Not again.*

"All my friends are staying at that hotel," I said to Keir. "The protective spells—I put them on the whole building. The attack must have happened outside."

Because of the wards my Hemlock magic had accidentally put on the hotel, the magical equivalent of an earthquake could hit the place and it'd remain standing. Nothing could breach those wards. *Right?*

I slowed down as we got closer to the hotel, and Keir

stopped walking. "I don't think it's a good idea for me to come inside with you."

"Maybe now's not the best time for you to meet my friends," I acknowledged, spotting Ivy standing beside the hotel doors with her sword out and a scowl on her face. "I'm supposed to be reporting to the guild on the mission last night. I'll ask Lloyd to tell the boss that I'll be late." I'd owe him for it, but one look at the crime scene banished all my other worries. Streaks of blood, matted with what looked like fur, covered the area in front of the hotel, while the taint of a spell caught in my nostrils.

Keir took a step backwards. "I think your boss will make an exception, considering the attack. You okay here?"

"Sure. Just—be careful." The mages might be the targets of whoever was behind this scheme, but if these wards had broken, too, I was the one who'd supplied the security on Keir's apartment block. Not to mention the necromancers' guild.

It's impossible. I thought nothing could outdo my Hemlock magic.

"I'll call you later." Keir embraced me, earning a raised eyebrow from Ivy, who'd finally spotted me.

As he walked away, Ivy approached. "Necromancer?"

"Vampire."

"Not the same vampire who attacked you the other week?"

"Uh…" I'd completely forgotten that Ivy had witnessed the aftermath when Keir had sent a vessel after me to get at the Hemlock Coven, and Isabel and I had destroyed it.

Ivy shook her head. "You're determined to play with fire, aren't you? Isabel was right."

"Where is she, in her room?"

Ivy's mouth tightened at the sight of all the blood. "She's brewing up some tracking spells. The mages have the shifter in custody, but they aren't letting any of the rest of us sit in on the questioning. There's no doubt he was sent to target the mages and nobody else."

"The attack took place here, right?" I moved a little closer to the glass doors, but I didn't see any bloodstains in the lobby. "Because, uh, I'm the one who warded the building."

Her brow furrowed. "Isabel didn't mention that. The shifter never got into the building—we know that much."

"So what exactly happened?" I asked. "Isabel said the attacker was an ambassador? Was he acting alone?"

"Apparently," Ivy said. "As far as I can work out, he was hanging outside waiting for the first mages to come out of the building. Vance and I didn't get downstairs fast enough to stop him. One of the mages had already restrained the shifter by the time we caught up." She waved at Vance as he pushed open the glass doors to join us. "Just updating Jas. Isabel will be down with the tracking spells."

"Use a cleansing spell immediately afterwards," Vance said, indicating the bloodstained ground. "The other guests are already talking. The attacker picked a public location for a reason."

"So you don't think the shifter was acting alone either?" I asked.

"I think the evidence speaks for itself," he said, an irritable undertone to his voice. "As for tracking spells, send word to me if you find out anything new. I'm heading to the guild."

"Can you—" I broke off, resisting the impulse to shrink away from the wrathful look in his light grey eyes. "Can you check if he was carrying any witch spells?"

"Everything he carries will be confiscated and destroyed," he said, as though I was an idiot for asking. *Mages.* You wouldn't think a lone shifter would have the nerve to attack one of them, let alone several.

"Yeah, we know," Ivy put in. "But Jas is right—there's no way a council ambassador would turn on the mages on a whim. Either someone put him up to it, or he wasn't in his right mind."

"I'm aware of that," he said. "I'm intending to find out if the two shifters knew one another. Will you be coming to the guild, Ivy? I'd prefer it if you waited before going hunting for hellhounds again."

Ah. He probably wasn't happy that Ivy had wandered into our mission last night.

"More hellhounds?" I asked.

She raised her sword. "I was going to snoop around the spirit line, but I should stick around here as long as there are still mages in the building. Jas, you said you set the wards?"

Ah, shit. Vance looked in my direction, and I gave an entirely unconvincing shrug. "I did, but it was a while ago. Besides, it sounds like the shifter waited for the mages to leave the building before pouncing."

Now I thought about it, that was unusual. A shifter on a rampage had a one-track mind and would run headlong into a warded gate if their enemy was on the other side.

Vance's phone appeared in his hand. "I'm off. Ivy, are you coming?"

"You think they'd let *me* sit in on the questioning?" Ivy

made a sceptical noise. "Nah, I'm best staying here and making sure nobody else is planning an ambush."

"Call me if you find anything," Vance said, and disappeared in a whirl of air.

The hotel doors opened and Isabel came out, her hands full of tracking spells. "Hey, Jas. Ivy, the mages didn't let you into the questioning?"

"I don't need to see it," Ivy said. "They won't get anything more than a confession out of him before they kill him."

I frowned. "Did you see him after the attack?"

"I saw him shift back into a human when they caught him," Ivy said. "He didn't even struggle. It's like he wanted them to catch him."

"Or someone else wanted it." *I felt I had to come here*, the last shifter had said. "He was a council ambassador? What exactly does that mean?"

"He carried messages between the mages and the shifter community." Isabel adjusted her spells on her wrists and selected one. "You know the shifters, you can rarely get them to commit to sitting in meetings, so they use intermediaries."

"Or they *did*," Ivy said, crouching on the bloody pavement. "Try here, Isabel. I think this is the shifter's blood."

"If he's dead, the tracker won't work," I reminded her. Tracking spells didn't work effectively on the dead most of the time. "But I could summon his ghost if they did kill him."

"Why would you want to?" Ivy's brow puckered.

Ah. I hadn't told anyone else about the shifter ghost's appearance the other night. Partly because it felt like I'd imagined it, and partly because of the lingering guilt that I hadn't reported it to the guild. But Lady Montgomery would have been irked to say the least if I'd led her on a wild shifter-ghost chase that turned out to be an alcohol-induced hallucination. Wouldn't be the first time a drunken necromancer had raised a false alarm, but still.

"Just a thought." I joined Isabel as she crouched on the pavement, activating a tracking spell.

Green light flashed. The hotel doors reappeared in black and white, and I jumped when a tall, rangy figure appeared right next to me. His gaze was blank, looking into the distance as though in a trance.

That's our shifter.

The hotel doors opened, three mages walked out, and a flash of light engulfed the shifter. Claws flashed out, blood spurted, and the mages moved into a defensive formation. One of them conjured what looked like a ball of water, striking the shifter down, but he was on his feet again a second later.

Not fast enough. Lightning sizzled, knocking the shifter flat onto his back. The mages closed in, and the spell cut out, leaving me reeling on the pavement. A residual white glare made spots dance before my eyes.

Isabel swore under her breath. "The spell didn't show where he came from."

"Or who sent him." I rubbed my chilled hands together. "He… he kinda looked like he was in a trance." I hadn't thought to look for witch spells, but surely he'd have dropped everything when he shifted anyway.

"Who knows?" Ivy threw a cleansing spell over the pavement and the blood and fur disappeared. "It's not like it's a big secret that the mages are staying at this hotel.

They have enough enemies to survive daily assassination attempts."

"Generally not from shifters, though, right?" I blinked repeatedly to clear the glare from my eyes. That violent flash of light I'd seen in the vision… it looked like the flash I'd seen when I'd watched the replay of the first shifter's attack at the mages' guild. But where had it come from?

"I can try another spell somewhere else," Isabel said, holding up another green band.

"Worth a shot." I brushed spell residue from my palms, which tingled lightly, reminding me of the powerful wards wrapped around the building. Wards I'd created with my Hemlock magic.

Isabel activated the tracking spell, and I leaned in, tapping into my Hemlock power. She let out a quiet noise of surprise as my hands touched the circle, causing it to vibrate with static. "Jas, what are you doing?"

"Testing a theory."

Magic hummed in my palms, mingling with the circle's green light. Tracking spells had limitations no matter the power of the person who made them… but maybe the Hemlocks would say otherwise.

One way to find out.

The scene expanded, filling my vision with a vivid image of the street surrounding us. The shifter appeared before me, so suddenly that my heart jumped into my throat.

Holy shit. Not only was the scene in colour, the shifter's footsteps on the pavement echoed as though he walked right next to me. He padded forwards, his gaze fixed on the hotel. His eyes were pale grey, and his hands were clenched into fists. A faint gleam surrounded both his hands. *That* hadn't been visible through the regular tracking spell.

He's wearing witch spells. But even my Hemlock magic couldn't pluck a witch spell from a vision and identify it.

The hotel doors opened, and a blinding white glow flashed. I swore, blinking rapidly to clear my vision, and when I next looked, the man had shifted, colliding with the mages in a blur of claws and blood.

The spell cut out and I fell backwards from the circle, my hands trembling. *It worked.*

Isabel and Ivy gaped at me in open astonishment.

"What did you *do?*" Ivy said.

"I enhanced the spell," I said. "Sorry, Isabel, I should have warned you first."

"Don't apologise." Her face lit up in fascination. "I've never seen a tracking spell so clear."

"What did you see?" Ivy asked.

"He was definitely wearing spells on his wrists." I nodded to Isabel. "But I didn't see what type. That white flash, though... no idea what it was." Damn. I'd hoped that if we saw it up close, we might be able to figure it out.

"Nor me," Isabel said. "I didn't see him actually activate the spell in the vision, did you?"

"It happened too fast," I admitted. "Guess even enhanced witch spells have their limits."

"Guess so." Ivy pursed her lips, and I saw her mind ticking with questions.

Before I landed myself in hot water, I said, "The mages must have taken his props, if there was anything left of them. Are you sure you don't know what the flash was,

Isabel?" In the time I'd known her, I'd never witnessed her encounter a spell she couldn't identify.

"Unfortunately." She fixed her gaze on the spot where the tracking spell had dissolved. "It flashed right before he shifted, but I've never seen a spell with a clear white flash before."

"You and Ivy are Council of Twelve members, right?" I said. "The mages know you have expertise. Maybe they'll let you help."

"They're a little tetchy at the moment," Ivy said. "But I'll talk to the mages on your behalf if you promise to tell me what in the bloody hell you with that spell, Jas."

Oh, boy. Ivy wasn't the rule-following type, so I was at least confident she wouldn't turn me in to Edinburgh's mage council, but unlike Isabel, she didn't know about Evelyn.

Then again, Evelyn hadn't done a thing out there. I'd enhanced the spell all on my own.

Without the ability to teleport like Vance, Isabel, Ivy and I had to walk to the mages' guild on foot. I ended up leading the way because the others hadn't spent long enough in the city to know all the routes.

When we came to the gates, Ivy strode ahead, for all the world like we were about to storm a fortress down. Her sword was strapped to her waist, her hair tied out of her face, and faint streaks of blood remained on her clothes, maybe from last night's encounter with the hellhounds.

The apprentice mage guarding the gates shrank away from her blade. "State your names," he growled.

"Jas, uh, Lyons." Crap, I'd almost said *Hemlock* then. "I'm with Edinburgh's necromancer guild."

"Ivy Lane," Ivy said to the mage, not bothering to sheathe her weapon. "You know, I've passed here a dozen times since they stuck you on duty. Asking my name every time doesn't make you look tough, it makes you look slow."

The straw-haired apprentice scowled. He was the same guy who'd told me to get lost when Isabel and I had tried to check out the wards after the first attack.

Isabel stepped forwards. "I'm Isabel, also from the council. Did they bring the shifter here?"

"None of your business."

"We're both members of the Council of Twelve," Ivy said. "Which is more than I can say for you."

"*She* isn't," he said, eyeing me.

"We have important information for the council," I told him. Being snarled at by a kid barely out of his teens was the last thing I needed when the mages had potentially thrown away all the evidence. "About the shifter attack."

"He confessed to attempted murder already," said the mage.

"Are they going to execute him?" I asked.

"They should," said the apprentice smugly. "Riffraff like him should never have been allowed on the council to begin with."

"He was an ambassador," Isabel said. "Appointed by your superiors."

The apprentice's face turned bright red all the way to his hairline. "He's going to spend the rest of his life in prison, and he deserves it."

"Did they confiscate anything from him?" I asked.

"I'm not in charge of the questioning, so I wouldn't know," he said haughtily.

"Then I'll ask," Ivy said. The mage moved to block her path, and her hand slipped down the hilt of her sword. "I wouldn't. I'm one of the Council of Twelve's founders."

"I'm not supposed to let anyone—"

"I'll be the judge of that."

"I'll head back with Jas," Isabel called to Ivy, before shit hit the fan.

Ivy nodded over her shoulder. "All right, I'll catch you up later."

Defeated, we turned our backs on the mages' guild and retraced our steps to the hotel.

"Sorry," Isabel said. "That guy is a twat. He's been giving Ivy trouble ever since we showed up."

"I figured," I said. "I've dealt with a few mage apprentices before, trust me. They're that cocky until they get out in the field." Not that different from necromancers, really, though it was a pain in the arse that I'd had no chance to see if the mages had retrieved any unknown spells from the shifter. Sure, they had their own team of witches, but I had my doubts that any of them could amplify a tracking spell.

The hotel doors were closed, the ground scrubbed down with cleansing spells. No traces of the attack remained. I halted by the door, recalling the way the shifter had just *moved,* transforming in a literal flash. Was it a coincidence that he'd shifted at the exact same moment that flash had gone off? Shifters didn't need spells to help them shift. Even at their least controlled, it was always a voluntary response to an attack, unless the full moon was involved.

I pushed open the door, and a glint caught my eye in the shadows beneath the hotel's front.

Letting the door close, I moved closer. Crushed into the ground was a faintly gleaming band. The remnants of a witch spell... but not one that'd activated. The shifter must have dropped it in the struggle.

"Hey, there." I picked it up. "Now we're talking. Isabel, want to take this thing to pieces?"

She grinned. "Challenge accepted."

———

Not five minutes after Isabel and I had set down the collapsed spell on the chalk-stained carpet of her hotel room, my phone began buzzing. I ignored it at first, helping Isabel sketch out a fresh chalk circle. The faint swirl of glyphs on the walls was a constant reminder of the time I'd inadvertently amplified a simple warding spell to cover the entire building and nearly blown my cover. At least the shifter hadn't been able to bypass the wards this time around.

Evelyn hissed in my ear, "Answer the damn phone, Jas."

"You don't have to listen to it," I told her. "Er, that was Evelyn," I added to Isabel.

"Thought so." Isabel brushed chalk from her knees. "Who's calling?"

"It'll be the guild," I dug in my pocket for my phone. "I owe them a report from last night's mission."

"You can head back if you like. I'll take care of this." She waved a hand over the circle. "I can identify the ingredients and text them to you."

"And then you can work out what type of spell it is?"

"Half of it's crushed, so probably not," she admitted. "I mean, I can guess, but identifying the owner's signature should at least be do-able."

"If you're sure," I said. "I mean, it's safe to say it's a custom job, for sure. Not a market one."

Like the spell that'd conjured the weird white flash. A shifting spell? Was there such a thing? I didn't know. Not only was there no 'official' textbook of witchcraft like there was for necromancy, the Hemlocks didn't exactly do things by the book. They'd probably known it was possible to enhance a tracking spell beyond its limits all along. Hell, that memory-reading forest was almost a living example of the same type of spell.

"Sure, but once I've identified the base ingredients, I'll be in a better position to track down the owner," Isabel said. "Then I can find their coven."

"What if they're not part of a coven?" I said, thinking of the Briar Coven—who'd left the city without a trace. "I mean, when we were trying to find who was working with Leila Hemlock, they targeted witches off the street or just vulnerable people. Maybe the same is happening now."

"Maybe, but it's impossible to make a handmade custom spell like this without leaving *some* trace of the caster. Every witch has a signature."

My phone was still buzzing. Resigned, I answered. "Hey, Lloyd."

"Jas! The doorman won't let me in."

"Oh, you're here at the hotel? I'm not surprised, there was an attempted murder this morning."

"Yes, and I thought you were next. Answer the bloody phone next time."

"Sorry, I was with Isabel. Got distracted. I'll be down in a second." I hung up. "Sorry, gotta run."

Isabel looked up, already elbows-deep in the spell circle. "No worries. You go and tell the guild you're not dead."

"Will do."

I checked the time on the way out the door. The guild's shifts started in less than an hour—no wonder Lloyd had panicked.

I found him waiting outside the doors to the lobby, hovering anxiously on the balls of his feet. "Let me guess—you had urgent witchy business?"

"Kind of. Isabel and I were taking a spell apart and lost track of time."

"I figured," he said. "So—another shifter attack? The novices are all talking about it."

That's not good. Who'd been blabbing at the guild? "An ambassador this time."

I gave him a quick rundown of the morning's events as we walked back to the guild. "Let me guess, Lady Montgomery's gonna tear me a new one."

"Actually, she's concerned about you, Jas. Someone attacked your family?"

"Well, not directly," I said. "I don't know if they were sent after one person in particular or just the mages in general. Isabel's trying to track the culprit by taking apart a spell we found at the crime scene, but the mages aren't being very cooperative."

"I'm not surprised, considering someone's trying to bump them off. When's the next council meeting?"

"Ah—tomorrow." *Oh, damn.* I'd forgotten it was that

soon. "Assuming the boss doesn't stick me on toilet-cleaning duty."

***

Lady Montgomery gave me a stern look across her desk. "Well?"

"Well what?" I said warily.

"What exactly do you mean by hassling the mages?"

Oh, damn. That straw-haired little shit had tattled on me to the guild. "My family was attacked. Isabel and I wanted to speak to the mages about what they found at the crime scene, that's all."

"I understand that you were concerned about your family, but the mage council has strict rules about who's allowed into their headquarters in times of crisis," she said. "The last thing we need is to create tension between them and the guild."

"Ivy and Isabel were with me," I said, holding my tongue about the obnoxious apprentice. "Uh, do you need me to take notes at the council meeting tomorrow? It's going ahead, right?"

"I haven't heard any different." She paused for a long moment, her expression unreadable. "You aren't on the patrol rota for today. Please try to stay out of trouble in the meantime."

No patrols? Maybe she really was concerned about me. But her pause carried a weight that landed squarely on my shoulders. Did she think the shifter attacks would lead to the mages shunning their allies, even the guild? Surely not.

I walked out of her office to find Lloyd waiting with Ivy Lane, of all people.

"Hey," Ivy said. "You owe me for this."

She handed me a wristband, turned on her heel, and left.

"Where in hell did she come from?" Quickly, I stuck the wristband in my pocket before the boss came out and saw it.

"She just strode in," said Lloyd, in half strangled tones. "She asked if I knew whereabouts you were, and when I said the boss was probably reading you the riot act, she kind of… invited herself upstairs."

I walked away from the boss's office. "Sounds like Ivy. I thought the mages would kick up a fuss, but I guess they gave her what she wanted after all."

"Huh?" said Lloyd, still looking dazed. "I'm lost."

"She was supposed to be sweet-talking the mages into handing over the witch spells the shifter was carrying on him when he shifted and attacked," I explained.

"Sweet-talking?"

I gave him a look. "I didn't know your type was fierce warrior women, but you're wasting your time. She's engaged to Mage Lord Colton."

He blinked. "I'm not… attracted to her. She took me by surprise."

"She does that. I should take the spell back to Isabel." I stuck my hand in my pocket to ensure it was still there, and my Hemlock magic tingled in response. *Oh, it's a witch spell, all right.*

"I'll come with you," he said. "I don't like the idea of you going back to the hotel alone."

"Sure it's not because Ivy's staying there, too?" I quipped.

"No!" he said, more vehemently than I expected. "I'm not accustomed to women covered in blood and carrying giant swords marching into the guild without the boss's permission."

"You should have seen what she said to the stuck-up twat the mages had guarding their gates." I grinned despite myself. Thanks to Ivy, I had the shifter's mysterious spell. One problem solved, a million more to go. "C'mon. Isabel will want to see this."

8

"Nice going," said Isabel, taking the spell with an eager expression as Lloyd and I entered her hotel room. She'd drawn even more chalk circles since I'd last been in here, filled with half-dissolved ingredients. It was a good job witch chalk cleaned off easily, otherwise she'd have racked up one hell of a bill from the hotel.

"Any luck with the other spell?" I asked her, pulling out a chair so Lloyd had somewhere to sit without accidentally treading in a spell circle. "I don't know why Ivy came to the guild to give this one to me rather than heading back here. I think she freaked out a few novices."

"The guild was closer, I'd guess. Anyway, I'm almost done." Isabel put the spell down on the desk and indicated the chalk circle she'd been working on, which simmered with transparent flames. "Just needs a bit of fine-tuning and I'll have our witch's signature."

"Nice." Lloyd reached forwards to pick up the wristband I'd put down on the desk. "This is shinier than any witch spell I've seen before."

"Shiny?" I leaned to look closer. While the band shape was familiar, one edge was fused with what appeared to be some kind of luminescent white material. Lloyd tapped the edge with his fingernail and it made a hollow ringing noise. I'd never seen a stone embedded in a witch spell before. Most ingredients were herbs, powders and plants.

"Don't blow anything up until I'm done with this," Isabel said.

"Relax, I'll use my own circle." I dug out my stick of chalk, clearing a space to sketch out a spell circle. "Lloyd, can you pass me the spell?"

He did so, and I turned it over, running my own fingernail along the edge. "Pretty sure it has some sort of precious stone embedded in it."

"Stone?" Isabel echoed. "Not iron?"

"I don't think it's a ward." I put the spell in the chalked circle and re-drew the lines, while Lloyd watched.

"That thing doesn't look like it's gonna come apart easily," he observed.

"We'll see." I waved a hand over the circle. Resistance pressed back, and the spell remained in one piece. "Ah. I think it's glued together. I'll need a stronger force."

"I'll keep my distance," Lloyd said.

"Come on, I haven't blown anything up in weeks."

"That's a sign that you're not being inventive enough, then." Lloyd ducked when I threw a handful of leaves at him. "I joke."

"All right, duck." I plunged my hands into the spell circle and tapped into my Hemlock magic.

A blast like a firecracker went off, bouncing from the

circle up to the ceiling. Isabel ducked her head, somehow managing to keep her hands inside her own spell circle without letting go of whatever spell she was casting. Lloyd dove underneath the desk, while I fell backwards, my hands aglow with Hemlock magic.

"What the hell, Jas?" Lloyd yelped from under the desk.

"What he said." Isabel withdrew from her own circle, her hands glowing green. "What did you *do?*"

"Nothing," I said, nonplussed. "I don't think Evelyn liked that stone very much."

"How'd I guess it was her?" Lloyd unfolded his lanky frame from underneath the desk. "What's she trying to do, blow the ceiling off?"

"I was only trying to pull it apart." I scanned the floor for the wristband, which had been thrown from the circle when it'd burned out. "Damn. That was one hell of a reaction. It doesn't even have a scratch on it."

Isabel glanced at me. "A reaction to what, exactly?"

"All I did was turn on my Hemlock magic," I said. "I just wanted to pull it apart, but I think it might be superglued."

"Let me see that in a second." Isabel peered into her own circle. "I think I got the signature."

"Whose is it?" I asked.

"I'd need to show it to a witch who knows the local covens." She stood and walked to the wristband on the floor, picking it up. "Huh, you're right. It's unmarked. Feels pretty heavy for a witch charm, too."

"Hmm." I frowned at the wristband, not quite daring to tap into my magic again in case Evelyn really did blow the roof off this time. "Evelyn's magic's never reacted to any other witch charm. Any idea what type it is?"

"Nope," Isabel said. "I'll see if I can break whatever's holding it together, provided you keep Evelyn at a safe distance."

Isabel sketched out another circle and put the wristband into it, while Lloyd and I watched. Leaning over the circle, she whispered under her breath, occasionally tossing handfuls of powder into it. The wristband, however, remained intact.

"It really is like superglue," she said. "I think I've got it, though."

"Tell me when to duck," Lloyd said.

There was a flash of light, and I grabbed his arm, pulling both our heads down. A crackling noise sounded, and dark flames licked at the edges of the circle but didn't spill over. Isabel lowered her hands. "Not to worry. It's done."

I coughed as smoke billowed out from the circle. "You did it?"

Isabel picked up the shard of white stone gingerly. "I can identify the other ingredients, but I haven't the faintest idea what this is."

"I wonder if the mages know?" I asked. "I assume Ivy got their permission before swiping it, but maybe not."

"With Ivy, who knows," Isabel said, turning the gleaming shard over in her hand. "I'll check with her when she gets back."

I moved over to the slightly singed bit of carpet where she'd set up her circle. "The other ingredients... looks like a binding spell. Binding what, exactly? Just the spell, or..."

Isabel's eyes met mine and I knew she'd had the same thought—maybe the binding hadn't been for the spell to use, but so that the wearer couldn't get it off. If nothing else, that fact alone proved the shifter hadn't been the one to voluntarily pick up the spell. Someone had forced it on him.

"I'll tell the mages," Isabel said, laying the stone down on the desk. "The market hits rush hour at noon and I'd rather not be there when it's too packed."

"You're not taking that with you?" Lloyd asked.

"Best not risk it," Isabel said. "Not until we know for sure what it is."

As much as it pained me to admit it, we'd be better off handing the stone to the mages. They had way more experience with rare magical artefacts than we did. As for Evelyn's reaction… was that what she'd reacted to in the room where the shifter had killed the mage? I hadn't seen if he'd been wearing a similar wristband, but if he had, the mages would have confiscated it when they'd hauled him off.

"I can head upstairs and ask Drake and Wanda," I suggested. "If you wanted to go to the market alone."

"I probably should," Isabel said. "And in disguise, too. The fewer people who know I'm staying at the same hotel where the attack happened, the better."

"All right," I said. "Maybe I should ask the Hemlocks if they know what that stone is. Anything that sets Evelyn off is worth asking them about."

Lloyd got to his feet from the desk chair. "Wait, you're gonna introduce me to your creepy relatives?"

"Pretty sure I can't bring anyone else with me into the forest who isn't a witch," I said. "They're totally disinterested in anything that happens in this city, besides. Maybe I'll try to find Ivy."

"I'll text her," said Isabel. "I don't *think* she'll have taken that thing from the mages without permission, but it's worth checking with Drake or Wanda."

"Not much left of it," said Lloyd, picking it up. Without the rest of the wristband, it looked smaller, barely the length of my little finger. "Wonder if it's worth a lot?"

"Hang on," I said, and tapped into the spirit realm. The stone's glow didn't follow me there, so I blinked the grey away. "Never mind. I wondered if it reacted to Evelyn because it's linked to the spirit realm, but it's not. We should leave it behind, warded." As much as I wanted to take it with me, I didn't trust Evelyn not to react again.

"You bet." Isabel activated a protective spell over the piece of stone, hiding it under the desk. "I'll let you know if I need you."

"Give me a call if you see anything suspicious at the market," I said to her. "Ivy hasn't texted you, has she? Has she run into trouble?"

"Honestly, trouble is probably running from Ivy." Isabel rolled her eyes. "I'll see what the other witches have to say about this signature."

———

Lloyd and I left her room and made for the stairs to the second floor. "You know, it's a good job the boss isn't keeping tabs on you today," he commented. "When's the next patrol, tomorrow?"

"After the council meeting. Evening shift. Don't look at me like that, it was the best I could get. Besides, we won't be with Mackie this time. How is she, anyway?"

"Back on her feet and giving the Lynns grief, same as usual," he said.

"I'm glad." I took the lead, climbing the stairs. "Those hellhounds… we never did find out where they came from. Did the boss mention any theories? I forgot to ask her. She didn't even bring up the mission when we spoke this morning." That seemed odd, now I thought about it.

"Nope," he said. "Honestly, I'm surprised there's another council meeting tomorrow. What's this one about?"

"Pretty sure it'll be about the future of the Council of Twelve, considering an ambassador tried to murder one of their representatives." I heaved a sigh. "I'm barely *on* the council, but Lady Harper was, and I don't think she planned for everything to fall apart barely a month after her death. I just wish I knew if she wanted me to take her place or not. She left nothing behind to give me directions."

Lloyd placed a hand on my arm comfortingly. "Don't worry, Jas. It's not all your responsibility. It's up to her next of kin to figure it all out, right?"

"That'll be Wanda." I reached the top of the stairs and turned left. "Lady Harper didn't leave her any instructions, either. But maybe you're right."

"Sometimes I surprise myself," he said, with a grin.

"Don't let it go to your head." I paced down the corridor in search of the right room. "Not sure if they'll know about that stone either, including whether or not Ivy got hold of it legally—"

There was a sudden blast of air, and Lloyd and I jumped away from a spray of rainwater as Ivy and Vance materialised right in front of us.

"Sorry, Jas," said Ivy. "Told you you should have looked before jumping."

Vance scowled. "The wards on this place confuse my mage power."

Oops. "Where've you been?" I said, shaking rainwater off my sleeves.

"The Highlands." Ivy sneezed.

"Back to Lady Harper's place." Vance activated a drying spell, and the rainwater vanished from all of us. "I moved some more boxes to Wanda's room."

"She's going to love that." I found the right door and knocked.

"Hey." Wanda waved us in. "Drake's out. Come on in."

While Ivy and Vance strode in, Lloyd lurked awkwardly by the door as though not sure if he was welcome or not. I grabbed his sleeve and tugged him into the room behind me, closing the door.

"I thought you'd gone back to the mages' place," I said to Ivy.

"Nah, if I had, I'd have hit that snot-nosed apprentice over the head." She leaned her sword against the desk. "Besides, how could I miss the opportunity to search more of Lady Harper's worthless priceless junk?"

"These new boxes are from the basement," said Vance. "Jas, what were you saying about a stone?"

Ah, crap. He'd caught the tail end of our conversation when he'd teleported in. "Huh?"

"I distinctly heard a sentence involving the word 'Ivy' and the word 'legally'."

Oops.

"Don't worry," Ivy said. "I just *borrowed* a spell that the mages confiscated from the shifter who attacked us this morning, since they were done with it."

"And you handed it to Jas?" His tone was sceptical.

"She and Isabel are good at pulling spells to pieces," Ivy said. "Right?"

"It nearly blew up in my face," I admitted. "That's what I wanted to ask—is there such a thing as a binding spell with a piece of stone as the base? I figured you guys would know more than I did."

"What did the spell do?" Vance asked.

"Uh…" I hesitated. "I'm not absolutely certain, but when Isabel and I watched a replay of the attack through a tracking spell, there was a bright flash before the shifter transformed. I saw a similar light when I tried to work out what the stone was."

Vance's brow furrowed. "I'll see what the other mages have to say. I'm heading over there now."

"Again?" said Ivy. "All right, but don't tell them Jas nearly blew up the stone. And warn me if you run into trouble."

"Of course." Vance briefly touched his hand to hers, then disappeared.

"He's off again?" asked Wanda, rolling her eyes. "Doesn't really get the concept of a holiday, does he?"

"No, but the council's giving both of us crap," Ivy said. "Where's Drake?"

Wanda walked through the maze of boxes on the floor. "He was going to take me sightseeing again, but he said he has a hot date at Arthur's Seat."

Ivy blinked. "In the rain?"

"You know what he's like," said Wanda. "Er, hi, Jas's friend. I don't think we've met?"

"No, I'm Lloyd," he said. "Hi."

"He's come to help us go through Lady Harper's crap while Isabel's at the market." I moved to the newest box, not feeling optimistic. You'd think, given the important role of the Hemlock heir, that she might have left me a little more direction. Maybe she thought the other Hemlocks would tell me everything eventually.

I lifted a heavy, leather-bound book out of the box and opened it to find yellowed pages of spidery handwriting. "Whoa. I think this is Lady Harper's journal."

"Damn, that handwriting is something else," Ivy said. "Looks like a piskie got into a fight with a fountain pen."

Lloyd snorted. "She's not wrong. What's that, a tome of your mentor's secrets?"

"Let's see." I turned the page. "Monday. Terrorised a group of five-year-olds, jabbed someone with my walking stick, complained about country scenery from the windows of my lakeside mansion... I'm joking, I can't read a word of this."

But it was her journal, all right. My skin tingled, my heart rate kicking up. Finally, a clue.

"I can't read it," whispered Evelyn.

I glanced sideways, seeing her through the spirit realm. "Can't you?"

"Can't I what?" Wanda blinked at me. Oh, bugger.

"Can you read this?" I said clumsily. "It's not much use if it's indecipherable. I can't even read the date."

"Thirty-one years ago," Wanda said, leaning over. "Nine years before the invasion. I wonder why she hid it in the basement."

"Paranoia," I said. "Maybe she and Lord Sutherland had a passionate affair a few years ago and she didn't want anyone to know."

"Thanks for that mental image," Evelyn said, making sick noises. *Knock that off,* I silently told her.

"Hey… old council documents," said Ivy, digging through another box and pulling out a stack of yellowing papers, which promptly disintegrated. "Oops."

"Can you be more careful?" said Evelyn, through my mouth.

She'd taken control without me even noticing. *Hey! What the hell, Evelyn?*

Ivy raised an eyebrow at me. "Sorry. Didn't know that would happen. Why, are you looking for anything in particular?"

I shoved Evelyn aside and said, "I wouldn't mind knowing how she got to know the Hemlock Coven and became their ambassador. She wouldn't tell me a thing while she was alive."

Ivy shifted the remaining papers onto her lap. "Well, she started working for them when she was a lot younger. Like, fifty years ago. This stuff isn't that old. Even the journal isn't, but you might find something in there."

Thirty-one years seemed long enough ago… hang on a moment. Wasn't that the same year the Hemlocks had been confined to their forest?

A shiver ran up my spine and I turned back to the page, wishing I had a magnifying glass. And a translator. Admittedly, Lady Harper might not have actually witnessed whatever had led to the Hemlocks' permanent imprisonment. Maybe if she had, she'd have been caught in the spell, too.

I leaned over the page, then pulled out my phone to shine its light onto the fading lines. Then I looked closer at the scrawling handwriting. It wasn't English. Nor any other language I recognised.

I dropped the book. "The bloody thing is written in code. No wonder I can't read it."

"Lady Harper the Paranoid strikes again," said Ivy.

I swore, resisting the impulse to hurl the journal out the window. "Great."

"Sorry, Jas," Ivy said. "Where's Isabel, anyway?"

"At the market," I said. "Asking if anyone recognises the signature on a spell we found near the scene where the shifter attacked."

"Oh, that's what her message was about," Ivy said. "No signal in the Highlands. It wasn't the same spell I gave you?"

"Nah, we haven't identified that one yet," I said. "The mages really let you take it?"

"The shifter had two of them," she explained. "One on each wrist. Lord Sutherland didn't seem all that fussed, to tell you the truth."

"He should be." I glanced at Lloyd, who sat on the desk chair, texting someone. "Lloyd, you can head back to the guild if you like. I don't think we're gonna have much luck deciphering this journal unless she hid the code-breaker document in the same box."

It was about as likely as the woman herself walking back in here from beyond the grave to give us answers.

My phone buzzed with a message from Isabel.

Found an informant who might know who the signature belongs to. Meet me at the market?

———

Ten minutes later, I hurried to the market to meet Isabel. Lloyd had gone back to the guild while Ivy had departed in search of Vance. Icy rain drenched me as I walked, despite my liberal use of rain-proofing spells.

Isabel met me at the market, standing underneath an umbrella.

"Which coven?" I asked her in a low voice.

"Not sure yet, but I got the details of a local witch who's an expert on signatures," she said. "I didn't want to go and see him alone. Did the mages have anything to say about the you-know-what?"

"It didn't sound familiar to them," I said. "Vance and Ivy found more of Lady Harper's junk, including a journal from the year the Hemlock witches were imprisoned, but she wrote the damn thing in code."

"Seriously?" Her eyes widened. "Trust her to pull a stunt like that."

"Tell me about it. Where's this informant?"

"Asher? He lives just down there." She pointed at a narrow alley between two shops. It ran downhill, rain sliding off the cobblestones. "I wanted to check you were okay with him seeing your face first. He can see through any disguise spells, apparently."

"Really?" Damn. I hoped he was trustworthy, then.

"He has no link to anyone untrustworthy," she added. "Half the market can vouch for him. What d'you reckon?"

"All right," I said.

We trod the short distance down the alley, moving carefully to avoid slipping, until we reached a rusty wooden door with a crooked sign saying 'Asher's Witch Charms'.

Isabel pushed the door open. Within was a typical witch shop—walls decorated with ingredients hung in haphazard rows, shelves stacked with battered books, and a slight man sitting behind a desk, presumably Asher. His harsh breathing was the only sound in the otherwise quiet little shop. The smell of herbs filled the air.

Asher looked up at us through watery eyes. His light brown skin tone suggested mixed race or maybe Middle Eastern heritage, but a greenish tint overlaid his cheeks and a sheen of sweat stood out on his forehead.

"Are you… okay?" asked Isabel uncertainly.

"I ran into an accident a few years ago," he said. "Back-firing spell. I'm fine."

He didn't look fine. He looked like he was about to drop dead on the spot.

"Can I help you two with something?" he asked.

"I need your help identifying a coven symbol," Isabel said, lifting a piece of paper from her pocket and handing it to him across the desk. "I'm told you're the best person to ask."

He leaned over the page. His hands clenched on the desk, trembling a little.

"*That* symbol?" he said. "Where did you find that?"

"When I ran a test to find the signature of a hostile spell," Isabel said. "You know whose it is, don't you?"

"That symbol is out of use," he said hoarsely. "The coven it belonged to was destroyed by fanatics. Nobody uses it actively anymore."

"Fanatics?" I echoed. "Like who?" *The Hemlocks?*

"Humans," he said. "In the world before, there were a number of… I suppose you could call them cults. Anti-supernatural ones. They'd capture any of us off the streets, given the chance. They wiped the entire Blood-root Coven out." He tapped the symbol with a finger.

"They're gone. Whoever is using this symbol is covering their trace."

"How?" I asked. "How do you know the person who did this isn't from that coven?"

"Because that coven died," he said harshly. "They were forced to turn their own spells against one another and participate in dark magic rituals until there was nothing left of them."

My heart lurched. *Dark magic... like blood magic?*

"*Humans* forced them to do that?" said Isabel, looking as sickened as I felt.

"I'd hardly call them human," he said. "But yes, they did, until the coven died out. The Bloodroot Coven is no more."

"Then why would their symbol show up when I tried to track down the signature on a spell?" asked Isabel.

"Because, clearly, the caster wanted to mask their trace," he said. "Or perhaps they wanted to taunt us... to remind us of what we lost, of what they took from us."

He couldn't have been more than a child at the time of the invasion, since he didn't look much older than me. Maybe Isabel's age. But his tone suggested the matter was personal to him.

"You... knew them?" I asked.

"Not well enough to remember," he said, coughing. "No, but my own coven sheltered the last of them. They died cursing the Orion League's names."

I blinked at the unfamiliar name, but Isabel's hands clenched at her sides. "The... Orion League?"

"They're long dead," he croaked. "But this—" He slapped the desk, and the scrap of paper where Isabel had drawn the symbol—"is a reminder of what they did. What spell bore this mark?" Asher coughed into a handkerchief, which came away red.

"I have a healing spell," Isabel said quickly.

"There's no point," he rasped. "Healing spells are temporary. I hoped—I'd have more time—"

Without warning, a rush of magic came to my fingertips. *Evelyn, what are you doing?*

Asher continued to cough, his body heaving. My spirit sight flashed on, showing me his spirit fading. My hands moved of their own accord, the light brightening.

"I can help," Evelyn said through my mouth.

Magic surged from my hands, bathing the room in a bright glow. Isabel exclaimed in alarm as Asher fell back in his seat, his eyes sliding closed. I stepped back, abruptly in control of my own body again. My hands fell to my sides, trembling.

What did she do to him?

Isabel reached his side first, lifting his hand to take his pulse. "He's alive."

"Oh, thank god for that." I checked the spirit realm and confirmed he was still in the land of the living. "What the hell, Evelyn? Warn me next time."

She might at least have given me two seconds to use a smokescreen spell so he wouldn't see my hands heal him without even touching him. His head had been bowed, but if he'd seen her—*what was she thinking?*

"I vote we leave before he wakes up." I didn't know how long he'd be unconscious for, and I dearly wanted to have words with Evelyn.

"Agreed," Isabel said, opening the shop door. Her hands were shaking so much, it took two attempts to get it open. "The Orion League… I have to tell the Mage Lords about what he said."

"What *is* the Orion League?" I asked.

"A group of fanatics," Isabel answered. "They wanted to wipe out all supernaturals. They mostly died out in the early days of the invasion, but a couple of years ago, it was some of their surviving members, working with witches, who stole the details of the fury-summoning ritual from somewhere."

"What?" I said, my heart sinking. "They… are they the people who passed on that information to Leila Hemlock?"

"It wouldn't surprise me," Isabel said. "Good job he didn't recognise your magic."

"He wouldn't. He doesn't know us." But he *did* know the coven whose magic had been used in dark rituals against their will. "So it was this Orion League who tortured that coven he mentioned into helping them? Only a supernatural can even use a witch spell."

"Precisely," she said, grimly. "Forcing shifters to attack the mages and destabilise the council sounds like a League thing, but someone imitating them is bad enough on its own. Either way, we're up against something seriously nasty."

I walked out into the alley behind her, my hands still tingling with residual magic. "So's whatever spell was trying to kill him. I hope he'll be okay."

"So do I." Isabel turned up the cobbled alley. "The enemy covered their tracks, all right. Sneaky bastards."

And they'd used the symbol of a dead coven to do it.

9

I walked into the council meeting the following day with the resolve to tell the mages exactly what they might be up against—even if it meant revealing more than I'd have liked. Isabel and I had parted ways yesterday after agreeing that we'd share what we'd learned without mentioning my Hemlock magic. As for Evelyn, she'd remained stubbornly quiet. I bloody hoped she'd keep her mouth shut today. Isabel had brought the drawing of the symbol and the list of ingredients she'd extracted from the enemy's spell with her to the meeting, with proof that the signature on the second spell also matched the first one. Like we'd suspected.

The same person had created both—but was it a coven, or a lone witch?

I stifled a yawn as we took our seats at the table. Lloyd hadn't even been awake when I'd left for the meeting. Some people got to sleep in… and some of us got to help prevent the supernatural council from imploding. No pressure.

The first thing to implode would probably be Lord Sutherland's beautifying spells, from the way he kept twisting them. A muscle ticked in his jaw, and his sharp eyes followed each person who entered the room and sat down. The table trembled whenever he touched it, his mage power hovering at the surface. As an earth mage, he could cause an earthquake when he was pissed off, and I sincerely hoped he wouldn't take out his rage at the shifter on the rest of us.

The instant the last of the mages took their seats, Lord Sutherland immediately began to speak. "As you're aware, there was an attack on one of our own from a council ambassador yesterday. Our task today is to decide on our future steps."

He cast his gaze around the room, lingering on the handful of shifters who were members of the Council of Twelve. The mages more than outnumbered the other supernaturals, because Lord Sutherland invited Edinburgh's entire council to attend every meeting, even those who weren't actually members of the Council of Twelve. Probably to remind us who was really running the show.

Isabel cleared her throat. "Yesterday, Jas and I used a tracking spell at the scene of the attack. Based on what we saw, it's clear that the shifter who attacked the mages was not in his right mind. Someone used a hostile spell to control his actions."

"The attacker already confessed to his crime," the Mage Lord said. "As for the attacker not being in his right mind—how exactly do you prove that, with shifters? They're often unable to control their animal urges."

A rumble of anger went through the small group of shifters on our side of the table.

"I would think more carefully before you speak," said Vance, his voice so icy that the temperature in the room seemed to drop. "Do not forget that you're in the company of the Council of Twelve."

"Two people are dead," said Lord Sutherland.

Oh, shit. One of the victims of yesterday's attack must have passed away overnight. Which meant the shifter ambassador was dead, or would be before the day finished.

"All the evidence shows that the shifter meant to harm as many mages as possible," Lord Sutherland continued, breathing fast. "The first attacker behaved in a similarly destructive and unrestrained fashion. Even our own shifter members transformed here in this very room, to the extent that we were unable to distinguish them from the enemy."

"You don't think the enemy was counting on that?" I said, my voice rising. "The shifter wore a witch spell—more than one—which influenced his behaviour. Even the wards were broken using a spell."

"They're using the signature of an extinct coven to hide their traces," Isabel said, her voice barely wavering when Lord Sutherland narrowed his eyes at her. "I checked the signature. Any other witch can back me up."

"She's right," Ivy said loudly. "Isabel's tracking skills are second to none."

Isabel dropped her gaze, fidgeting with embarrassment. The other witches were more likely to believe her than me, but the symbol alone wasn't enough proof.

"Exactly," I said. "It sounds like the perpetrator is using the signature of an extinct coven to hide their traces."

"And which coven is this?" queried the blond female mage on Lord Sutherland's right.

"The same coven that was captured and forced to help the Orion League," said Isabel.

Mutters broke out among the council. Lord Sutherland leaned back to speak to his neighbour. Vance looked like he wanted to hit someone, and even Drake looked unusually serious.

"That is a serious accusation," said Lord Sutherland. "Are you implying the League still exists in some form?"

"Lord Sutherland," Vance said. "You're aware of the report that my fellow mages and I encountered several witches imitating the League's methods only last year, are you not? They were targeting supernatural leaders, and they still had their old weapons. It's not unreasonable to assume other artefacts of theirs have survived. Those spells the shifters used—"

"Nothing of the sort has been found," snapped Lord Sutherland. "The League's members were humans. The conspirators in this case are clearly shifters, aided by witches, and they will not go unpunished. We will question the leader of each coven until we find who has committed this heinous crime."

"But it might not be a coven—" Isabel started.

"In the meantime," he said, drowning out her words, "in the event that the witch turns out to be acting alone, I propose we resurrect the idea of a register. It would certainly prevent situations like this from occurring."

"Putting everyone's name on a list wouldn't stop them being mind-controlled by a spell," I said heatedly. "Also, do you know how hard it is to imitate another witch's signature? Most witches couldn't do it. Let alone create a spell that can control a supernatural's mind and affect their decisions."

"Are you sure it was a spell responsible?" asked the blond mage on Lord Sutherland's right. "I hear the necromancer guild has recently acquired some psychics."

All eyes turned to Lady Montgomery.

"If you're suggesting *my* people are involved in this, then I'd advise you to learn a few basic facts about psychics first." Her tone was acid. "The psychics in question would never use their abilities against others, but it's not possible for a psychic to influence anyone except for another psychic."

"One of them was involved with this Soul Collector," Lord Sutherland said. "Correct? I seem to recall she brought him to the city herself."

Mackie. "He was *already* here," I interjected. "As I told you in my report, he was in hiding in plain sight. Maybe it's *his* people involved in this, but it's not the psychics. They can't mind-control non-necromancers."

"What about those vampires?" the blond mage put in. "They're not registered. Not even to the guild."

Oh, for god's sake, not again. Apparently, the mages had come here to accuse everyone except for the actual perpetrators.

"No vampires were involved in this," Lady Montgomery said. "They can possess dead people, not mind-control the living. I would have expected you of all people to do basic research before making accusations, Lady Anders."

Ha.

Lord Sutherland's fists clenched, and the beautifying spells threatened to snap off his wrists altogether. "The fact remains that we cannot trust anyone outside of this building. The witch markets have allowed far too many unstable elements to run around unchecked."

"I thought our purpose here was to discuss the attacks, not throw mindless accusations at every supernatural who strikes you as suspicious," said Lady Montgomery. "As it is, I fear you're wasting your time. The necromancer's guild keeps track of our people far more efficiently than the mages' guild. Isn't your second-in-command currently on holiday playing golf?"

Drake snickered loudly, while Ivy gave a satisfied nod. "There you have it."

Lord Sutherland's face reddened. Despite his loss of control over the situation, it was hard to feel triumph when it couldn't be plainer that the mages wanted one rule for themselves and another for everyone else. And what if they *did* haul the psychics in for questioning? Not to mention the vampires, whose safety depended on anonymity? It wouldn't help them catch the person responsible, that was for sure.

"I think we've heard enough," the Mage Lord said. "No shifters will serve on our council until we get to the bottom of this. That includes ambassadorial positions."

As one, the shifters rose to their feet, and a wave of tension swept through the room.

"Why should we be punished for the actions of others?" asked a stocky male shifter. "Has no mage ever committed a crime? What about the witches—will they be removed from the council as well?"

"The witches are necessary allies for us to get to the bottom of this violent and depraved attack on our council," Lord Sutherland snarled. "However, unless we can find conclusive evidence that the spells were entirely responsible, both of the killers confessed to their crimes and were executed for it. That is reason enough to put a temporary ban on shifters entering our headquarters until this sorry business is cleared up."

My hands clenched, my temper brewing. Evelyn rose to the surface, and I was on my feet before I'd quite grasped that she'd taken over. "This is witchcraft," I said loudly, or Evelyn did. "They aimed to destroy us from within. Have you forgotten your history so easily? Have you forgotten that you were almost destroyed?"

Whoa. Hey there, Evelyn. I'm not old enough to know that.

Lord Sutherland whirled on me. "And you feel better qualified to speak on the matter than those with much more experience than you have, do you?"

"I'm—related to the mages," I said, wishing I could yank Evelyn back in control to explain herself. "I know some of their history."

Thanks a bunch, Evelyn. Having lived in a limbo state for the last twenty-one years meant she was technically older than a fair few of the mages and probably *did* know more than they did. About the world before the invasion, certainly.

"This meeting is over," Lord Sutherland said. "Council, come with me."

Translation: he wanted to hold a secret meeting only for his own mage council, without the rest of us.

The shifters left the room first, and a group of mages immediately followed, probably to escort them off the premises. Lord Sutherland might claim the ban was temporary, but it was one step from there to a full ban on any non-mages from serving on the council at all. And if they intended on interrogating every coven leader in the city—what about Asher?

I have to do something. I watched the room clear, one eye on Lord Sutherland, but when Ivy moved to waylay him, Evelyn rose to the surface again. I bit my tongue and half-ran from the room, turned sharply to the left and ran through the entrance hall until I found an alcove under the stairs to duck into.

Tapping into the spirit realm, I turned to Evelyn, who floated beside me.

"Really?" I said to her. "I know you have opinions, but nobody in that room knows you're alive. Stop risking both our necks because you can't keep your mouth shut."

Her eyes narrowed, her hair streaming back in a non-existent breeze. "You have no idea what you're talking about."

"Try me. You know who's behind this?"

She shook her head, her mouth tight with anger. "Not a Hemlock. And by the way, we're not alone here."

I turned on the spot, seeing two spirits not far away from me, hidden behind a closed door. Two very familiar spirits. Frowning, I opened the door, and two people fell out in a tangle of limbs. The first was Morgan, the only Lynn not invited to the meeting, and the second was Lloyd.

"Hey, Jas," he said. "Thought I heard your voice."

"What the hell?" I peered behind them into what looked like a broom cupboard. "What are you doing eavesdropping on secret council meetings?"

"It wasn't deliberate," Morgan said, disentangling himself from Lloyd. "We had to hide when people started leaving the meeting room."

I narrowed my eyes at him. "Of course it was your idea. How did you get in here to begin with?"

"Shadow spells," said Morgan. "We followed a couple of the mages when they went through the gates. I heard a noise in the spirit realm. You guys didn't seem tuned into it, so I thought I'd check it out."

"You heard *what* in the spirit realm?" I asked. "What was Lloyd even doing here?"

Lloyd looked down, his ears reddening. "I was going to wait outside for you anyway, Jas. But we had to hide when everyone came out of the meeting room. Are you sure they're gone?"

"For your sakes, I bloody hope so. What exactly did you hear?"

"A noise," Morgan said. "Kinda like howling. I think there's something dead in here."

"Do you want to be the one to tell the mages their headquarters is haunted?" I shook my head. Then it hit me. "Shit. They killed the shifter who attacked the mages."

And his ghost must have stuck around.

"Killed him where?" said Lloyd, looking faintly perturbed.

"In the jail or wherever they were holding him." Damn. After Evelyn, the last thing I needed was to give the mages another reason to target me and my friends. "I expect this nonsense from Morgan, but you should know better than to piss off the council. You know they expelled all the shifter ambassadors?"

"Damn, really?" said Morgan. "I'd have thought the boss would have put her foot down."

"The mages make the rules," I reminded him. "Fine, I'll

find us an empty room. One quick look, and if there's no spirit in here, we're getting out. Deal?"

I took them to the library, where I sealed the door shut with a locking charm, hoping the mages had already started their top-secret council meeting and wouldn't come barging in. Then I set up some candles, mostly for Lloyd's sake. *I can't believe I'm doing this.*

Then again, if the shifter's ghost was haunting this very building and had unfinished business? Technically, it was my job to look for the wayward spirit.

I plunged into Death, looking around the blurred greyness. "Where did you hear the howling?"

"Uh… over there," said Morgan, pointing ahead. "I think."

"Really helpful." I turned on the spot, ghostly figures drifting past us, and turned off my spirit sight to get my bearings. The problem with Death looking exactly the same everywhere was that it was hard to pinpoint a specific ghost, especially if you'd never met the living person. I'd seen the shifter in the vision, but it wasn't the same. "If he's actually haunting the place, we'd have better luck searching on foot."

"Except for the part where we're screwed if we get caught?" said Lloyd.

"Exactly," I said. "That's why you should have texted me so I could *ask* the boss to search the place—"

A howling noise came from the grey fog. I quickly tapped into the spirit realm again, floating out of my body through the closed door into the entrance hall.

The shifter appeared. It was him, all right—the same guy I'd seen through the tracking spell, right there in the middle of the mages' entrance hall.

"Hey," I said to him. "You—"

The shifter looked up at me, his pupils dilating. Then a horrible howl tore from his throat, chilling my blood, and scales rose to cover his arms, his hands becoming clawed.

In one bound, he turned and sprinted towards the doors of the mages' guild, disappearing the instant he passed through them.

"Hey!" I shouted after him. "Come back."

"And you nag *me* about taking risks," Evelyn hissed in my ear.

I ignored her, and blinked back into my body. "He's gone."

"Was he, like… possessed?" Morgan frowned, staring through the door with the vacant expression that indicated he still had his spirit sight turned on. "He didn't look like he shifted on purpose."

"Same as the other guy," I said. "But—what the hell is going on?"

"I think we all want to know that, Jas," said Lady Montgomery's voice from the spirit realm.

10

"What were you thinking?" demanded Lady Montgomery.

Lloyd, Morgan and I faced the boss, who'd thankfully elected to wait until we'd left the mages' headquarters before she launched into yelling at us. It was a small miracle none of the Mage Lords had seen us doing the walk of shame out of the building.

As a top-ranked necromancer, of course Lady Montgomery could sense if anyone else decided to go for a wander around the spirit realm if she paid close attention. I should have known she'd have one eye on me after the meeting. At least she hadn't heard me talking to Evelyn.

"The shifter's ghost was in there," I told her. "I don't know where he ran off to, but he moved in and out of this building of his own accord. A ghost shouldn't be able to do that."

"Not only did you find a ghost and decide not to tell me, you let him free to roam around the building?" she asked.

"He wasn't tied to the place," I said. "Not like a regular ghost. I didn't see him pass through the gates, either. He was just… gone."

"And you invited your friends to help, despite their not being official council members?"

"It was me who heard the ghost first," Morgan said. "I heard howling from the spirit realm. That's why Lloyd and I came in to tell Jas."

"Howling?" she said, in tones that suggested she thought he was talking bollocks.

"I wouldn't have gone in there, otherwise," he said defensively. "I know we're not on the council—it was my idea, not Lloyd's."

Lady Montgomery's mouth pinched. "As you might have gathered, the peace I've worked to maintain for my entire career is in danger of collapse, and breaking into the mages' headquarters to use necromancy without guild permission was a foolish and selfish move."

Morgan's face flushed. "I came to meet Ilsa after the meeting. And Lloyd came to meet Jas. We're not on duty until later, so—"

"You're not on duty at all," she said. "Morgan, you're to clean the training room. Lloyd, you're to clean the summoning chambers. And Jas, you're on archive duty until this evening. No arguments."

There were none to be had. The shifter's ghost had disappeared without a trace, leaving yet another basket of unanswered questions behind.

———

Three hours into my stint in the archives and I was about ready to scream. I normally found archive duty fairly relaxing, but the dusty books seemed to mock me with their reminder that I still hadn't found out anything about the shade *or* how to undo the curse binding Keir and me.

Evelyn sighed. I tilted my head, turning on my spirit sight to see her floating beside me, her blue-grey eyes darting around.

"There are some disadvantages to being conscious," she muttered. "I can't get away from the boredom either."

"Hey, Evelyn," I said. "You were alive thirty-one years ago."

"Well observed," she said dryly. "I was a child, but yes, I was alive then."

"You wouldn't happen to know where Lady Harper might have hidden the code for her journal, would you? She wrote it the same year the Hemlocks ended up stuck in the woods."

"No," she said. "And before you start asking probing questions, let me reiterate that I was a thirteen-year-old child at the time. Leila was four."

"You lived in hiding in Edinburgh, right?" I said, mentally calculating. That meant Leila had barely been a teenager in that vision I'd seen of her in the forest during the invasion. "Hang on—but the Hemlocks weren't stuck in the forest for all your life, then."

"They spent enough time in there that they might as well have been," she said sourly. "The rest of us lived in hiding long before the invasion. That's why we weren't able to access the full extent of our power. And that's why I will free our magic, so we can become what we deserve to be."

"Okay, that's enough," I said. "I let you create a scene in front of the mages—which almost got me into a lot of trouble, I might add—but you have got to stop acting like both of us won't be deep in the shit if the mages find out you exist. You *know* that. Do you really not care if they lock us up?"

"Soon there will be no prisons to contain either of us," she said. "The mages are heading full-tilt towards their own extinction. They barely believe the Ancients still exist."

Yeah, she's probably not wrong there. "I thought it was witches doing this. Or the Orion League. Have you had personal experience with the League?"

"Before the Sidhe came, everyone had heard of them, and everyone feared them. The one good thing the faeries did was wipe them off the face of the earth."

"Now you're praising the faeries who destroyed the world?" I said incredulously. "All right, I'm done."

I tapped out of the spirit realm and turned back to the mountain of files on the desk. No rest for the disgraced.

After a few silent minutes passed, the door opened and Keir walked in. At this point, I was so relieved of the distraction I didn't care that he was probably breaking the rules by being here.

"Hey, Keir," I said. "I'm in the doghouse."

"Looks like the archives to me."

"Ha." I put my head down on the desk. "Would you believe I got stuck on probation for attempting to find a ghost at the mages' headquarters?"

"A ghost?" he echoed. "Of who?"

"The shifter, who they executed for attacking them. I take it you're actually allowed to be in here?"

"I came to talk to your boss, actually. She wanted to… well, warn me about what was said at the meeting. The registers, and vampires."

"Ugh." I lifted my head. "And she told you I'm in disgrace?"

"More or less, but I want to hear it from you."

"You probably heard it already. Shifters banned from the council, witches probably next, Isabel and I got dismissed, and the mages had the shifter who attacked them at the hotel executed. Then his ghost showed up after the meeting and ran off, and the boss caught me." I heaved a sigh. "In fairness, it's as much Morgan and Lloyd's fault as it is mine, but this is the second time I've seen a shifter ghost run around in shifted form and then just disappear without being banished."

Keir frowned. "I can't say I've ever heard of a shifter ghost transforming, either. Did you tell the boss that?"

"I did, but she's pissed beyond measure at the council and probably concerned we'll be next," I said. "Besides, I can't say I've ever banished any shifter ghosts before. Not in shifted form, anyway. They always look human."

Keir rested his hands on the desk. "Maybe we could poke around later."

"Keir, I'll lose my apprenticeship if anything else goes wrong."

"All right," he said. "How about I take you out after your shift and we conveniently wander in the right direction?"

"What direction?" I asked. "That's the problem, I don't know *where* the shifter ghost went. He wasn't tethered to the mages' guild at all." Which would make him a high-ranked ghost. Pity the boss didn't believe us.

"Hmm." He lifted his hands, stepping back from the desk. "I don't know, then. Were you near a spirit line?"

"Nope," I said. "The only explanation I can think of is that it might be an aftereffect of the spell someone used on him to make him attack the council. But that's a stretch. There's no proof."

Keir tapped his fingers on the desk. "Why would a witch want to start a war with the council?"

"They might not have had a choice in the matter," I said, thinking of Asher.

His brows shot up. "Oh?"

I told him what Asher had shared about the signature, the lost coven, and the link to the Orion League.

Keir's mouth thinned. "I can't say I ever had the pleasure of meeting anyone from the League in person, but they're one of the reasons my family lived in hiding before the invasion."

"Really?" It shouldn't surprise me. I might not remember my own early childhood or my family, but it sounded like the League had been the bane of the supernatural world at large before the Sidhe had come along.

He dipped his head. "The invasion wiped most of us out, but the League picked off the remains. There was an attempted revival once, but that was when I was a child."

"Might it be linked to what's happening now?"

"I couldn't say." He turned to the map of the UK on the wall, a distant look in his eyes.

"I think they terrorised my coven, too." I thought of Evelyn's words, the expression on her face when she'd said they'd forced my family into hiding. There was guilt in there, and shame. Not emotions I saw from her often. "I wouldn't know, because Lady Harper decided to write her journal—written nine years before the invasion—in a code with no translator."

"Seriously?" He pulled his gaze from the map. "Where'd you find this journal?"

"Under the floorboards in an old country house balanced on a cliff in the Highlands. There's paranoia and there's being downright impractical." I rolled my eyes. "Anyway, it's not much help now. She worked for the Council and the other Hemlocks didn't, so I assume she'd be ticked off if it did collapse. On the other hand, the original Council all died. Maybe this one will, too."

"I wouldn't assume she wanted you to do anything at all," he said. "She made one choice, the witches made another. It's up to you, Jas."

"I think it's more up to the mage council," I said. "You should probably leave before Lady Montgomery catches us gossiping and assigns me to the night shift. But we'll figure something out, okay?"

"Sure," Keir said. "Who was the witch Isabel met with, do you know? The one who identified the signature?"

"He's called Asher," I said. "Oh, and… well, I accidentally saved his life by healing him with Hemlock magic. Long story."

"Damn," he said. "You don't do things by halves, do you?"

"Nope. That… that was Evelyn, actually."

She kept on surprising me lately, and the conversation we'd just had reminded me how very little I knew about her, and the world she'd grown up in.

"Maybe you're a good influence on her," Keir said.

"Or bad. She's getting way too bold." Maybe I should

have re-bound her to the forest after all. But running from my problems had only boxed me into a corner.

"I think it's worth speaking to this witch again," he said. "To make sure he hasn't told anyone else what you did."

"Yeah. I don't think he's the villain, but maybe I should warn him the mages are planning on interrogating every coven leader, too."

"If he doesn't already know. Word travels fast."

That's what I'm afraid of. "I won't let them do the same to the vampires," I said. "Even—if the worst comes to the worst, Lady Montgomery will protect anyone who comes here."

"There are a lot of people who wouldn't take the risk."

I swallowed. I'd been afraid of that, too. "I know. If you want to leave—"

"I'm not going anywhere, Jas," he said. "If it comes to it —we'll deal with that later. We've survived worse."

Yeah, but as long as our souls are bound, you have no choice but to stick with me if it kills you.

———

I met Keir outside the guild as soon as Lady Montgomery gave me the go-ahead to escape the archives. On the plus side, since I hadn't actually banished the shifter ghost, I had no paperwork to file. The minus side was bloody obvious.

"Asher doesn't belong to a coven," I said to Keir as we walked. "His people used to shelter survivors of the Orion League. I don't think he's villain material."

"Did he ask you any questions that suggested he might know about the Hemlocks, or anything else?"

"Nope. He seemed quite taken with Isabel, though," I said. "I mean, he was probably shocked that I used my magic on him, but there's no way he can possibly know where it came from. Even if he met Leila. She didn't have any magic of her own."

"Good point," he said. "Tricky. Where's his shop?"

I pointed at the alley… except it wasn't there. A blank stretch of bricks faced us, as though the narrow alleyway had never existed.

I turned back to Keir, bewildered. "His house was there. Just yesterday."

"I think," Keir said, "he may have been forewarned."

Or attacked. Had he sealed the alley off himself, and left the city? Or had the enemy got to him first?

11

I couldn't sleep. Apparently, Evelyn couldn't either. When I tapped into the spirit realm in the hope that my body would rest while my spirit wandered, it was to find her staring back at me.

"What?" I grumbled. "Ghosts don't need to sleep, right?" Some top-ranked necromancers actually left their bodies resting while they wandered around as a ghost, wide awake. Not many people knew that trick, but it was a useful one.

Evelyn, however, was out of my body and onto the spirit line already. If she went off alone, it wasn't like anyone could actually see her—except necromancers, who might get a bit confused about the resemblance between her and me—but after her restlessness today, who knew what shenanigans she'd get up?

"All right, let's go for a wander." I floated out of my body, through the ceiling, then right up through the roof of the guild. The veil of the spirit realm covered the world in shimmering fog which made Edinburgh's Old Town look like a mystical otherworld. The castle was visible, too, wreathed in an eerie mist. Floating north on this spirit line led to the train station, and it'd take one quick shift to enter the Hemlocks' forest. South, I knew, plunged through the countryside and wound up in London somewhere.

The *other* spirit line, though... I never did find out where those hellhounds had come from. But the only way to get there from here was to hop off the spirit line and over to the next one.

I took a step over the edge.

"What the bloody hell are you doing?" Ivy Lane of all people appeared. "Trying to get yourself killed?"

I withdrew my foot. "Trying to find a liminal space."

"And *where* is your body?"

I pointed downwards in the general direction of the guild. "Safe. I know what I'm doing."

"Talking to ghosts," she said, looking at Evelyn. "Ghosts who look exactly like you do. I thought the guild frowned upon making friends with the dead."

"She's not haunting me," I said. Oh, crap. Well, Ivy knew most of my secrets already, and it wasn't like the geas would hold now she'd actually *seen* Evelyn. "We're bound. Spirit to spirit. The Hemlocks did it using a ritual."

"The Hemlocks..." Ivy looked from me to her, then back again, as though to determine we definitely weren't the same person. "Fuck me. Well, that explains a lot."

"Unfortunately," Evelyn said.

Ivy raised an eyebrow at her. "I didn't know that was possible. She's... alive?"

"In the bodily sense, nope," I said. "Don't look at me like that, Evelyn, you know it's true. The Hemlocks needed an heir to survive and I have no magic, so they bound her to me so I could use hers."

"Lucky for both of us," said Evelyn.

Ivy's brow pinched. "You know… that makes sense. I did wonder how they planned to survive when they're stuck in that forest. They're not immortal."

"Nope," I said. "Yeah. I know that kind of magic is illegal, but I didn't volunteer. Evelyn did."

"It is?" Ivy frowned.

"Wait, you don't know? You're on the council."

"The Council of Twelve doesn't lay out the rules for magic. That's on the Mage Lords."

"There's a rule specifically saying binding two spirits together is forbidden. So's blood magic. And magical rituals. Basically, the Hemlocks think they're the exception."

"Ah." Ivy's lips pursed. "I see. Normally, that law is enforced because of the risk to the participants' lives, but you're clearly still alive and kicking. When did it happen?"

"Evelyn nearly died in the invasion and the only way to pass her magic onto me was to bind us. Nobody else survived."

"Ah," said Ivy. "I'm on my way to give Ilsa a lesson, and you might as well come along, too. She has the same ability."

"Travelling on the spirit lines? How can you do it? You're not a necromancer."

"Most necromancers can't do it either," she said.

Good point, but Ivy was something else entirely. I'd heard a rumour she was part faerie, but faeries' only relationship with Death was to stay as far away from it as possible.

We floated south of the guild, and found Ilsa hovering

expectantly on the path, her forehead gleaming with the Gatekeeper's mark. Her eyes widened. "Jas, you told her?"

"She saw me," I said. "I guess she's in on all your secrets, too?"

"Yep," Ivy said from behind me. "Do you have a power source, or does your magic come from within you?"

"It's from… Evelyn," I said. "We can both use it, though. As for travelling on the spirit line, it's because we're both shades. Meaning we both died and survived it."

"Damn." Ivy glanced at Ilsa. "You know all this?"

"Some of it," Ilsa said. "I guessed the rest. The Soul Collector stole the Ether Converter from where the Hemlock witches hid it, right, Jas?"

"*They* had the weapon?" Ivy's gaze sharpened. "That makes way more sense than the cover story. But it is gone, right?"

"Absolutely," I said. "The Soul Collector is gone, too. Except he didn't tear the worlds apart and fall into the void of his own accord. I did it."

"Well, fuck." Ivy shook her head. "You know, I figured you were hiding something, but I'd never have guessed… is that what your Hemlock magic can do, then? Tear a hole in the universe?"

"Apparently." I resigned myself to running through the events of the last two months, finishing with the Hemlocks' ongoing war with the Ancients.

"Isabel knows," I added to Ivy. "I told her not to tell anyone, including the mages. You understand why, right?"

Her hand tapped the spot where her sword's hilt would have been in the real world in an apparent unconscious movement. "Yeah, I do, but Vance will probably guess."

"And he'll tell the rest of the council in the interests of safety." I gave her a pleading look. "Then I'll be locked up. You saw how quickly they kicked the shifters off the council when they must know perfectly well that they're being manipulated."

"Exactly," Ilsa said. "We're keeping it quiet at the guild, Ivy. Jas is looking for a way to separate her soul from Evelyn's without doing any damage to either of them. Have you made any progress with that, Jas?"

"No time," I said honestly. "It's not in *any* of the necromancers' books, including the ones you swiped from the boss's office. Because most shades don't survive. Unless the Hemlocks know, but I'd have better luck asking the bloody Ancients. I bet the Soul Collector knew. Pity he'd rip my head off for asking."

"You should know," said Ilsa. "Not all the Ancients are, or were, evil. They used to be regarded as gods by the Sidhe. Until they drove out or killed them all."

"How do you know that?" I frowned. "I didn't think the Gatekeepers… oh, right, you deal with Faerie. I guess the Sidhe probably remember, since they're thousands of years old."

So were the Ancients. They made the Hemlock witches look like children.

"They do," said Ivy. "I didn't know the Hemlocks went to war with the Ancients, though."

"Nor me," Ilsa said. "I guess some of the Ancients wound up on Earth and got into a fight with the supernaturals already living here."

"Sounds about right." The Hemlocks didn't like to share, I knew that much. "Ivy—how did you even learn about the Ancients?"

Ivy reached down, as though pulling out a weapon, and whipped a surprisingly realistic-looking sword out of thin air. Its outline was less substantial than in the real world, but its blue shimmering edges marked it as the source of her own magic. She lifted the weapon, revealing glyphs shimmering on its hilt and up the length of the blade.

"This contains the power of an Ancient. It's a talisman, but not a faerie one."

My mouth fell open. "Seriously? Like—the Ether Converter?"

"Not exactly," she said. "The Sidhe made it, not the Ancients, and the god whose power is in here didn't give it up voluntarily. Reckon I did them a favour by taking it off their hands. Ilsa…"

"I inherited mine." Ilsa reached into her pocket and pulled out a square leather book. "It doesn't look like much, but it's the source of the Gatekeeper's power. The Gatekeepers worked with the Ancient who loaned us his power to conserve the peace between the realms for years. He wasn't evil."

"Still." I hardly believed they spoke so casually. *Talismans.* Fragments of the Ancients' magic. Like my Hemlock magic—powerful enough to bypass even Death itself. "So that's how you can both wander around the spirit realm?"

"I think the Ancients must have travelled between realms all the time," said Ilsa, tapping the mark on her forehead. "This is the god's symbol."

"It is?" I squinted at the swirling silver glyph, but I couldn't make heads or tails of it. It wasn't like when I looked at a witch symbol and instinctively understood what kind of spell it indicated. "Do you two think another Ancient is involved in the attacks on the mages, then? It'd play into their hands if the council fell to pieces. They'd have an open shot at this realm." Not a cheery thought.

"Maybe." Ivy lowered the blade. "There was another Ancient I met, who... well, who the shifters used to worship as a god."

I nearly fell out of the air. "Shifters? They worshipped —the Ancients?"

"Some of them did," Ivy said. "Just one Ancient, though, who took the form of a dragon shifter. He's dead, but he has a few descendants left."

Ilsa stared at her. So this was news to her, too. "Wait, so the *shifters* are descended from the Ancients?"

"Maybe," said Ivy. "I reckon the Ancients interbred with humans a few thousand years back and the shifters are the result. But not many people know that theory. Even the local shifters back home thought I was nuts when I tried to tell them."

"Damn." I looked at the glowing sword in her hands. *That contains the power of a god.* No wonder it had a physical presence, even in Death. The Soul Collector had seemed the same. "Do you think it might be linked to whatever's happening now?"

"I can't see a clear link." Frustration furrowed her brow. "When the Ley Line broke open in the invasion, it caused a lot of shifters to get stuck in animal form, so I thought the spirit lines might be involved. That's why I was at the cemetery the other night. But the attacks didn't take place on a spirit line."

No... but the shifters were in half-shifted form even as ghosts. "Ivy, you know that wristband you took from the mages? The stone inside it—it flashed in the vision when the shifter transformed. I was sure the stone was at the centre of the spell."

"Huh?" Ivy frowned. "I thought you said it was a binding spell."

"That's what Isabel and I thought at first," I said. "But it also reacted against my Hemlock magic when I tried to take it apart."

Ivy turned on the spot, her hand clenching on her sword's hilt. "Vance's family is part shifter. From the same bloodline as the dragon shifter I met. I'll have to tell him about this."

"He's descended from the—" Holy crap. "Seriously?" I'd thought he was mage through and through. That explained his strong reaction to the shifters being kicked off the council.

"He doesn't go shouting it from the rooftops, but it's hard to hide," Ivy said. "He planned to speak to the shifters directly tomorrow. At least we know to look for those stones."

Might Vance end up being affected by the person manipulating the shifters? It seemed unlikely that anyone would be able to get close enough to try anything on the Mage Lord. Vance had been avoiding assassins since he was a kid, from what I'd figured. Somehow I'd missed the part about him having shifter relatives, but he didn't talk much about his family. A lot of the mages didn't, but being related to the shifters was a hell of a secret to hide.

A link between the shifters and the Ancients surely couldn't be a coincidence. And that stone? How many more were in the enemy's hands?

12

"It's dawn," Evelyn told me. "Are you going to hang around here all day, too?"

"You don't have to stay in the same place as me," I said, hovering on the thin grey line. After I'd said goodbye to Ivy and Ilsa, I'd stayed in the spirit realm, watching the city from the sky. Not only did I get to watch a sunrise more stunning than any I'd witnessed in my body without having to drag myself out of bed for it, I'd spent the night swooping around the city like someone from one of Lloyd's comic books. I wouldn't lie, it was pretty amazing.

Less successful were my attempts to find liminal spaces. The Hemlocks hadn't lied when they'd said that anyone could find one by accident, but I'd floated around the spirit line over the cemetery for hours without finding so much as a single crack in the universe.

Evelyn sighed. "Are you planning to let your boss lock you in the archives all day again?"

"With any luck, she'll decide I've been punished enough." I turned on the spot. "I owe Keir a call, though."

"I'll keep my distance," Evelyn said.

Now I knew how to get rid of her… make out with Keir. Rolling my eyes, I reached out for his familiar presence. A moment later, I found him hovering in the fog of the spirit realm.

"Jas," he said. "What's up?"

"If I'd known you were awake in here, I'd have come to find you earlier."

"You've been in the spirit realm all night?" he asked. "Your body's probably turned into an ice block by now."

"I'll survive," I said. "I'm at a loose end. Is it a bad idea for me to go and talk to the shifters?"

"Depends which shifters. Why?"

"I know what to warn them to watch out for now," I said. "The mages won't listen, and I want to do something useful."

"Hmm. I do know a shifter," Keir said. "A friend… I'm not sure he'll be awake this early."

"Keir, don't take this the wrong way, but some of your contacts turned out to be less than reliable. More hazardous."

"Relax, he isn't a vampire," he said. "What exactly did you want to warn the shifters about?"

"I'll tell you on the way. Want to meet at the café?"

———

By the time I'd woken up—having to employ three warmth spells to get sensation back into my frozen limbs

—showered, dressed and hurried to the café, I'd filled Keir in on last night's events.

"Clancy doesn't know any more about the Ancients than I do," Keir said. "But he does know they took my brother. He was the one who took me in for a while, actually."

"He did?" It shouldn't surprise me that he knew at least one shifter—those who weren't part of a pack were loner types, like vampires.

Keir and I crossed South Bridge, heading for Princes Street. "Do you have the stone with you?" he asked.

"No, I left it with Isabel. A spell that can force shifters to lose control outside of the full moon, though—if it's true, we have to warn the other shifters they might be next. And I bet it's not a priority to the mages. They're more concerned with saving their own skins."

"Agreed." Keir took the lead, and we stopped outside a mechanic's shop. The shop was called "Auto-Magic."

I raised an eyebrow. "Who can even afford a car these days?"

"Rich people, obviously," he said. "Clancy works for the mages mostly… another reason he doesn't live with the other shifters. But they're good business. Looks like he's awake—the light is on."

"Good," I said.

"One thing.' Keir caught my arm before I opened the door. "Don't bring up the register if you don't have to. He's like anyone who was a kid during the invasion. He won't react well to the idea of having to go into hiding again."

"I'll just ask him about the stones, that's all."

We entered the shop, which was staffed by a big man

whose muscular arms implied he'd once been a wrestler or something similar. Now he resembled more of a cuddly teddy bear—softer, but no less dangerous-looking.

"Hey, Clancy," Keir said. "Sorry we're here so early. This is Jas—"

The man lifted a hand. A hand that was suddenly scaled.

"Oh, *shit.*" I took a step back.

There was a blinding flash of white light. I leapt for the door, but he moved *fast,* swiping at me with a claw. I dove to the ground, narrowly missing being skewered, and Keir jumped onto the desk, grabbing a piece of metal and hitting the shifter in the back of the head. Clancy blinked once, dazed, then recovered. I grabbed a chunk of metal from the floor and hurled it at him, ignoring the prickle of Hemlock magic at my fingertips. Keir wouldn't appreciate me killing his friend, even if he was out of his mind. I couldn't even tell what animal he was—some kind of wolf-like creature, covered in thick grey fur, but with *scaled* hands and claws.

Keir crashed into him from the side and the shifter staggered, off balance. I glimpsed a gleaming band on his wrist, so tight that it'd melded into the scaled skin deeply enough to draw blood. *I knew it.*

I activated a shield spell, angling it so the shifter flew backwards, crashing into the desk in a heap. Before he could recover, I threw a trapping spell at him. Red lines criss-crossed the desk, pinning him down.

"Get that wristband off him!" I yelled at Keir.

Both of us scrambled over the collapsed desk, and I grabbed the shifter's clawed hand. The shifter roared, clearly in pain.

"He'd have to shift back to get it off," Keir said.

"Hang on." I searched the spells on my wrist. "This might work. Unlocking charm."

I found the right spell and threw it at the shifter's flailing claw, but nothing happened. The red lines of the trapping spell strained as he fought to break free.

Keir swore. "I can't drain him, not like this. And he's too strong for a vampire to bring down."

Damn. "Fine. Evelyn, you'd better behave this time. Keir, can you hold his arm still?"

Keir grabbed the shifter's arm. "Jas, what're you—"

"You might want to duck." I tapped into my Hemlock magic and pressed my hand to the shifter's wrist.

The band exploded, throwing both Keir and me off our feet. Keir was up first, catching the piece of stone as it flew through the air, while the shifter slumped over sideways.

Then his fur receded and so did his scales. In seconds, a man lay panting in the trapping spell circle, behind the wreckage of the collapsed desk.

"Sorry about that," I said to him.

The man's eyes rolled back in his skull and he passed out.

"Wonderful." I deactivated the trapping spell with a quick flash of my Hemlock magic. "He'll be sore as hell when he wakes up, but I'll be seriously pissed if it turns out he put that thing on deliberately."

"He won't have." Keir turned the stone fragment over in his hand. "Someone did it to him."

"I know." I sent a silent thanks to Evelyn for not causing more harm to him than she had to. "Guess we should wait for him to wake up so we can find out who did it."

"Might as well fix the place while we're at it," he said, lifting the end of the collapsed desk.

By the time the shifter returned to consciousness, his workroom was almost back to normal.

"Keir," said Clancy, crawling to his knees. "What... mate, what's going on?"

"You shifted and nearly skewered us to death," I told him, still feeling less than charitable towards the guy. My whole body hurt, while Keir bore scratch marks on his face that he refused to use a healing spell to get rid of.

"Who are you?" He scrambled to his feet. "You... you attacked me."

"Jas—Lyons." What was it with me tripping up over my name lately? "Do you remember who put that wristband on you?"

"What wristband?"

"This was part of it." Keir held up the gleaming stone. "Where'd you get it?"

Clancy frowned, his brow wrinkling. "I... it's vague. Someone came into my shop last night..."

"What did they look like?" Keir asked.

He shook his head. "I don't remember. It's all a blur. I was supposed to... there was somewhere I was meant to go."

I glanced at Keir. Both of us were thinking the same: the enemy couldn't possibly have known that Keir and I were coming here today. They hadn't targeted him through his connection with Keir and me—but he *did* work for the mages. My blood went cold.

"You were 'meant' to go somewhere?" I asked. "According to whom?"

He shook his head. "I don't know."

"You don't remember anything?" I asked. "All right, would you object if I used a tracking spell?"

It might not work, considering we'd made a mess of the place, but Clancy nodded. "Go ahead. I'd like to see what the fuck happened. I think I hit my head."

"I hit your head," Keir said. "To stop you from trampling Jas. You might have a headache for a bit."

He waved a hand. "Never mind that, I'm just glad you're not hurt."

I found a clear spot on the floor to use the spell, glad I'd brewed up a new batch of trackers.

Crouching down, I activated the spell, and immediately, the shop appeared in black and white. Then I pushed some of my Hemlock magic into the circle.

The scene snapped into colour, and I jumped when the door clattered open behind me. I turned around to see the newcomer, a youngish man with a freckled face. He wore a waterproof coat with the hood pulled up, and walked slowly, his feet dragging.

"Excuse me, can I help you?" Clancy said from behind the counter. "We're closed."

There was a flash of white light, and Clancy's hands shifted to claws, dropping the pieces of metal he was fiddling with. The man shuffled to the desk, leaning forwards to grab Clancy's hand. A gleam lit up the air and he shoved the wristband onto the bigger man's rapidly shifting wrist.

"The next time you see a mage," he said. "You're to activate that band. You hear me?"

"I… hear you," Clancy said, his eyes glazed.

The newcomer turned and shuffled away. Not slowly, but in weirdly off-balance steps. *Is he being controlled, too?* My mind reeled. Not only had my worst fears about those stones been confirmed, but the intruder had also forced the shifter to partially shift without even touching him.

The spell cut out, and I looked up at Keir's frowning face.

"What did you see?" He crouched at my side. "Jas, you okay?"

"I can draw a picture of the person who came in," I said, becoming conscious that my hands were shaking. "But—Clancy, he told you to activate that band you were wearing the next time you saw a mage. It'd have forced you to shift, and…"

Clancy fell back into his chair, looking aghast. "Someone wanted me to act as their personal assassin?"

"Whoever it is, they're working against the shifters as a collective," Keir said, as I got my notepad out. "There have been two other attacks this week. Each of them has involved a shifter under some kind of mind-control spell, attacking the mages seemingly of their own free will. Now we know for sure what form those spells take." He put the stone into his pocket.

I sketched the man from the vision onto the notepad page, while Keir gave Clancy an abbreviated explanation of our suspicions about the stones' role in the enemy's plan. I'd blown the rest of the wristband to pieces when I'd used my magic on it, but the stone was bad enough on its own.

"This place is warded," Clancy said. "Heavily. I got the spells from the market. But he just walked in."

"You know him?" I held up the notepad to show him the picture. "Would you be able to pick him out of a crowd?"

"It's fuzzy. Until—you broke the wristband." He looked down. "Then my thoughts became clear again. But I don't know that man. Should I report this?"

"No," Keir said quickly. "Not with the mages as trigger-happy as they are at the moment."

"But—" I bit my lip. The mages wouldn't believe any of us, but if Clancy hinted that he planned to attack them, they might lock him up as a precaution. "Do you know anything about that stone?"

"No bloody clue. I fix cars, not magic." He slapped a palm on the desk. "Bloody cheek of them, destroying my wards. I didn't spend the last fifteen years building this place from the ground up only to be forced into hiding again."

"I can redo your wards," I said. "But that's not to say the enemy won't break through them again."

He eyed me. "Witch, are you?"

"Yeah, I am." What the hell. The enemy would probably know I'd been the one to remove the wristband. I was pretty sure no regular witch magic could have done it.

If I hadn't come here with Keir, he might have killed someone and been executed like the others.

I went outside to reset the wards, adding a few trip-wire security spells for good measure. I hadn't actually seen how the intruder had undone the wards, but that seemed the least pressing issue.

After I'd thoroughly warded the place, Keir and I left. As we walked, I pulled out the notepad to examine my drawing of the man's face. "I wish I could track someone through the spirit realm using this. It'd be much more efficient."

"We know he's a witch," Keir said. "That's a starting point."

"Even then, he might have been wearing someone else's face," I said. "Would Clancy object if I told Vance, at least? He's part shifter. He won't turn him in."

Keir's brows rose. "I suppose if I'm going to be forced to put my name on a register in the near-future, I might as well make acquaintances of the mages."

"Keir—" I broke off. What could I say? He might well be right. "The mages I'm friends with aren't local, and they oppose the very idea of a register. If they can work out what this stone is and track down who created it, we'll be able to stop it."

But Vance and the others had no say in what Edinburgh's Council of Mages thought was best for the city.

He gave a short nod. "For everyone's sakes, I hope you're right."

I messaged Isabel and Wanda telling them I was on my way to the hotel.

Wanda replied first, so when we reached the hotel, Keir and I went to her room.

The smell of burning wafted out when she opened the door. "Come in. Drake and I are burning Lady Harper's old crap. It's fairly therapeutic."

"Uh, it's not the useful old crap, is it?" I said. "Not the journal?"

"No, of course not," said Wanda. "Oh—it's your... friend?"

"I'm Keir," he said. "The vampire."

She blinked. "Vampire?"

"You didn't tell them about me?" Keir gave me a mock hurt look.

"It slipped my mind."

"I'm devastated." He made a big show of turning around, and I grabbed his shoulder and yanked him into the room.

"Keir, this is Wanda, a childhood friend. That's Drake, a pyromaniac."

"She means the most badass fire mage in all the realms." Drake held a piece of paper over a flame in his palm. "Should I burn the map, or have you not ruled out buried treasure?"

"Leave the map. And the journal. Is Vance in?"

"Is he ever?" said Drake. "I don't think he's stopped for a minute outside of a council meeting the whole time we've been here."

"I need to talk to him. Urgently," I said, beckoning to Keir. "You still have that stone?"

He pulled it out of his pocket, and I took it. "Isabel has the other one in her room. This is what's causing the shifters to lose their minds."

"Let me see that." Drake walked up and picked the stone out of my hand. "This looks valuable."

"Can your fire damage it?" I asked. "I couldn't put a dent in it."

Blazing orange flames engulfed the stone, but it remained in one piece. "Shit, it's fireproof." Drake shook his hand and the fire went out. If anything, the stone gleamed brighter than before. "Where'd you get it?"

"The shifter who attacked us was wearing a wristband with that stone embedded into it," I explained. "When it flashed, he shifted. He said the dude who put the spell on him told him to attack the next mage he saw."

Wanda had gone white. "That's sick. Who put the spell on him?"

I held up my notepad. "This man. Recognise him? He's a witch."

Drake's mouth twisted. "Nope, doesn't look familiar. What the bloody hell is this stone?"

"I kind of hoped one of you would know," I said. "A stone that affects shifter powers… surely someone's encountered it before."

There came a knock on the door. I got there first, and opened it.

Isabel stood on the threshold, wild-eyed and staring. "Jas, get out of here. All of you. There's a—"

The whole hotel trembled, and the lights went out.

Then, howling came from outside.

13

Flames burst into life behind me, illuminating Drake's hands. "Isabel, *what* is chasing you?"

Isabel's eyes were wide, her pupils dilated. It was rare enough that I saw her terrified that I knew what it was before the howling started again. The air chilled, and greyness began to filter in.

"Ghosts," I said. "Is it them? Shifter ghosts?"

I knew the answer. The chill was unmistakable.

"One of them appeared in my room," she said, her hands clenching. "My spells went right through him. I know it sounds absurd, but when his claws almost touched me, they *felt* real."

"I'm going to check it out." One glance at Keir's distant expression told me he'd already left his body behind. I did likewise, plunging into Death.

Grey fog unfolded, swamping the room and furthering the chill that permeated the building. Glowing lights marked the presence of the others close by, and as I blinked, Keir's spirit came into focus. He hovered at my side, frowning into the grey.

A tall man appeared, his hands covered in grey-black scales and claws.

Another shifter ghost.

He threw back his head and howled, and two other howls answered from elsewhere in the building. Crap. More shifters must have died.

"Hey," I said loudly. "Get out. Go beyond the gates of Death."

The shifter's gaze snapped onto me, then he pounced.

As a ghost, dodging was harder, and he landed on me, his huge paws knocking me over in mid-air. I flipped over, wincing. *Ow.* I shouldn't be able to feel pain as a ghost.

"Jas!" Keir shouted.

I flipped the right way up, alarm flickering through me. He shouldn't be able to hurt me, but my chest stung where he'd swiped. Sure felt real to me.

Luckily, so was my magic.

I drew on my necromantic power and gave him a firm shove, knocking the shifter back a few inches. He roared, the noise echoing through the spirit realm, and I spotted Keir grappling with another. Like the first shifter, he looked solid, even though they shouldn't be.

Something is seriously wrong.

Hemlock magic surged to the surface, forming a whip in my hands. I lashed the shifter ghost around the neck, holding him still. "How are you here?" I snarled at him. "You're not supposed to be able to touch me."

The shifter struggled, fighting against the whip around his neck. My Hemlock magic was clearly hurting him—

but he remained in one piece. He had no reason to fear physical threats.

"Tell me!" I said urgently. "Tell me who sent you—"

Claws stabbed me in the spine, protruding from my chest. Red. Glistening.

Keir shouted my name.

And then I was flying backwards, into oblivion.

Death called, but someone caught my hands before I could fall into its jaws. I held on tight, unsure if the screaming in my ears was coming from me or the shifter. The hotel room seesawed, my ears ringing with screams, crashes, the sound of breaking glass. The spirit realm came into view again, and in front of me, Evelyn blasted the shifter with Hemlock magic. The shifter flew back a few metres, then lunged at Evelyn.

"Don't!" I croaked, but my body and spirit hurt so much, the words were barely a whimper.

Death faded once more and the grip of a hand on mine solidified. "Jas, hang on! I've got you." Isabel took both my hands and I clung onto her, her healing magic flowing over the wounds in my chest. Through the haze of pain, I saw Wanda's hands glowing blue as she aimed her icy magic at—

Holy shit.

The back wall of the room had *gone,* the window reduced to nothing but shattered glass. My wards—the shimmering glyphs that'd covered the entire building... they'd vanished. The floor trembled beneath us, threatening to collapse.

No.

I gritted my teeth, pushed the pain aside, and focused hard. My magic ignited, and Isabel gasped. I was still holding onto her hand, but I couldn't stop the Hemlock power flowing from me, pushing against the room's boundaries, stopping the destructive magic threatening to tear the place apart.

Creaking sounded from all around me as the hotel shook to its foundations.

"Get out!" I yelled at the others. "Isabel—let me go, I'll be fine. Get Keir out of here!"

"I'm right here!" said Keir's voice from beside my ear. "Jas, hang on!"

I screamed as he lifted me, fresh pain piercing my chest, and death rose to meet me.

———

Nine lives, Jas.

You have nine lives.

I'd better. Being stabbed to death by a ghost wasn't how I'd have chosen to go.

I blinked, once. A familiar row of hand-stitched puppets faced me. My head pounded. Definitely alive.

Keir stood with his back to the wall. He was white as a sheet and covered in what looked like plaster dust.

"Keir," I croaked. "Wow, that hurts. That ghost officially wins the prize for the most violent spirit I've ever met, including the poltergeist who threw me into a river."

"You nearly died twice over," he said quietly. "I had to bring you here—the entire front of the hotel collapsed, and your spell only stabilised it for a few minutes."

"Shit." I closed my eyes, a tremor shaking my limbs. "Did everyone get out?"

"Thanks to you," he said. "The place was half empty anyway."

"Isabel?"

"She's helping with the clean-up."

Relief swept through me and I opened my eyes again. "Does she know what broke my wards?"

"Never mind your wards," Keir said. "You nearly lost your *life*. Those ghosts were too strong to be mere spirits."

"I bloody hope the guild knows, then." I twisted around, trying to reach my back. "It's healed?"

"Isabel used a healing spell on you just in time. It didn't cross my mind that your injuries might follow you from the spirit realm to the real world."

"It's not supposed to be possible." I rested my head back on the pillow. My insides felt hollow. *My Hemlock magic failed.* My wards had gone out. Had the ghosts somehow done that, too? "Who—who were the shifters? They weren't the same ghosts as last time."

"There was a fight this morning," he said. "A brutal one, on shifter territory."

I sat upright, gripping the edges of the bed as my head swam. "Where are the bodies? I bet they're wearing those wristbands. Those stones—it's got to be the stones causing it all."

My phone buzzed in my pocket.

"I think your boss is trying to get hold of you," said Keir.

I groaned and flopped back against the pillow. "I don't have time to get stuck on archive duty again. I have to figure out what's powering those ghosts. Did anyone banish them?"

His mouth pressed together. "I can answer your phone and tell her you're still unconscious. Stall for time."

"Go for it." I dug in my pocket and tossed him my phone. "Ask if she's sending any of her people in."

"That place is way too unstable for anyone to go inside." He tapped my phone screen. "Hey, it's Keir. Jas was injured in the hotel's collapse. She's fine, but unconscious, and I'm taking care of her until she wakes up. I take it she's excused from the doghouse for a bit?"

I gave him a warning look, which he ignored.

"Yes… you heard. Good." He moved away from the bed, lowering his voice. "Yes, she's fine. I know there's a procedure—"

From the way he cut off, Lady Montgomery was speaking too quickly or loudly for him to interrupt. I smiled for a moment, then pushed the covers off me, activating a cleansing spell on my torn and bloody clothes.

He ended the call and dropped my phone back on the bed. "She cares about you."

"She values her employees." I climbed to my feet. "And now I'm going to make a miraculous recovery and go and poke around at the hotel. Whoever managed to undo my Hemlock magic wards is not the sort of witch I want an unwitting necromancer patrol to run into."

"No kidding." His mouth turned down at the corners. "Nor is whatever let those shifters gain physical form in Death."

"Might it be a side effect of that stone?" I said. "You can't make a witch spell that turns the dead solid, that much I know. That stone is the only unknown element. And it can override a shifter's will in a way that shouldn't be possible outside of the full moon. I can't think of anything else that might have done it."

"Yes, I think you're right." He dug a hand in the pocket of the new coat I'd got him, and pulled out the fragment of stone. "I do have a few contacts who deal in rare artefacts—"

"Nope," I said. "A fury tore a hole in your wall only a couple of months ago. I'm not waking up to find ghostly shifters have attacked you in the night."

A grin quirked his lips. "You really care."

I gave him a thwack in the chest. "You just worked that out?"

He caught my arm before I could pull it back, yanking me against him. "You know, I could insist you stay on bed rest right here rather than risking your neck again."

His vampire's touch caressed me, slipping down my spine. "Keir." The word was more of a moan as his lips captured mine.

"Yes? Didn't quite catch that." His touch deepened, and though I knew he was feeding on my soul, it felt more like he was giving something back to me. Shivers danced to my fingertips, and my nails dug into his shoulders.

I knew I was probably pushing it too far, considering my fragile state, but I didn't want to let go. He groaned against my mouth as I pressed against him, body to body, spirit to spirit. Part of me wanted to strip off my clothes, the other part was conscious that when our spirits touched, it was as intimate as skin against skin. More like soul against soul. And it felt so good.

"Keir!" I moaned. In the real world, his hand slipped between my legs, but his vampire's touch was all over me, head to toe, drawing, giving, pressure building until I hardly knew whether I was in the spirit realm or the real one. Both were reduced to nothing but the pleasure of his touch, vampire and human.

And then his hand was between my legs again, his fingers moving delicately. Riding the aftermath of his vampire's touch pushed me right over the edge. I gasped aloud, shudders racking my body from head to toe.

He kissed me once again, lighter this time, and I held onto his shoulders for balance.

"Need to sit down?" He sounded amused.

"You're forgetting I just got stabbed to death." My voice was shaky, but this time in a good way. None of those ancient tomes on vampire magic had mentioned they were capable of giving someone an orgasm through the spirit realm. "The textbooks didn't mention that one."

"You're quite receptive in the spirit realm," he murmured into my ear. "I'd have thought you might have tried—"

"No, I've never had sex with a ghost," I said. "Don't spoil it by bragging about your conquests, please."

"I always thought guild necromancers had no imagination." He grinned, and I gave him another thwack. His hand closed around my wrist. "We could do this all day."

"Most ghosts want to whine at us, not screw us." I released a breath, the real world pushing its way back in. "And as nice as that sounds, there's a bunch of angry shifter ghosts on the loose who're capable of stabbing the living. I need to find my friends."

Keir shook his head. "If you go to the mages, they'll know you're not unconscious."

"And they'll tell tales on me to the guild, I know," I said. "I'll call Isabel, then."

I rang her, and Isabel picked up the phone instantly. "Jas," she said. "Are you okay?"

"Better than I was before. Keir and I are on the way back to the hotel."

"Don't go to the hotel," she said. "There are mages everywhere. They're taking the place apart trying to figure out how the wards came undone, and… there's a chance they might figure out how there came to be such strong wards on the place to begin with."

My heart plunged. "Oh. Damn."

"Exactly," she said. "Don't worry, you're not gonna be the first person to come to mind considering you're not actually staying there at the moment, but I figured I'd warn you. Want to meet at the market?"

"I'll be there with Keir. You sure you don't know how they broke the wards? Was it the shifter ghosts, or someone else?"

"I thought ghosts couldn't break wards."

"I thought they couldn't stab people either," I said quietly. "This is different."

Whatever magic is driving them is stronger than my Hemlock magic. There's no other explanation.

I *really* needed to figure out how to destroy those stones.

14

Isabel met us at the market. Plaster dust still covered her arms and face, and her eyes widened at the sight of me. "Jas. I'm glad you're in one piece."

"Same here, believe me." I dug in my pocket and pulled out my notepad. "I don't know if this helps, but this is the face of one of our enemies. He's the witch who put the spell on Keir's friend. If we can find him, we might be able to find out where they're getting those damned stones."

Isabel examined the sketch. "He doesn't look familiar to me. I wish I'd put on a disguise spell to come here, but they won't let me back into my hotel room to fetch the rest of my stuff."

"Shit, I forgot." I'd left half my ingredients in her room, too, but I was just glad my friends had made it out. "Well, considering the shifter ghosts have seen me through the spirit realm no fewer than three times now, it's safe to say the enemy knows I'm onto them."

Nobody had any answer for that, so I marched over to the nearest stall, the one with the beautifying spells.

"Hey, there," I said to the young woman staffing the stall, yanking out the notepad from my pocket. "Have you seen a witch who looks like this? He's wanted in connection with official necromancer guild business."

I wasn't even in uniform, but I put on my best 'official' voice. The dark-haired witch blinked at my spiel, her mouth dropping open. "That guy? What's his hair colour?"

"Ginger."

"Sure, I saw him," she said, pointing down the cobbled street. "Ten minutes ago, maybe."

I didn't particularly want to ambush an innocent person if it turned out the guy was wearing a mask, but it couldn't be helped. I made my way back to others, thoroughly regretting the whole operation. "Apparently he was here ten minutes ago. If it's true, there's probably a catch."

"Maybe we should have asked Asher," Isabel said.

Might be tricky if he's pulled a vanishing act. "I'll look, but I'm not expecting to get lucky."

I took the lead anyway, weaving between the stalls. The market was less crowded than usual. Maybe word had made it over about the collapsing hotel. Or the mages had scared everyone off, if they'd already started interrogating coven leaders. Twice, I followed someone out of the market only to realise the face was wrong, or the hair.

As I entered the market for the third time, Keir grabbed my arm and pointed urgently over my shoulder. I looked past a group of student-aged witches gathered beside a stall selling bottled potions, and saw a familiar ginger head pop behind the crowd.

There was our guy, all right.

I twisted a shadow spell on my wrist and approached,

using the group of students to provide cover. My footsteps trod carefully, slowly, my spine prickling when the man turned on the spot. Like before, there was something about the way the man walked that wasn't—right.

Hang on a moment. He's...

I tapped into the spirit realm, looked past the bright blur of the students' spirits—and saw nothing but grey.

Crap. He was a walking corpse. A vessel. But he looked alive in the waking world, and I didn't see the tell-tale blue glow of a vampire's presence or even a necromancer.

Keir stepped out in front of him. "Hey, mate," he said. "You shouldn't be walking around here."

So he'd seen his lack of a soul, too.

"You shouldn't, either, vampire," said the man.

Keir smiled. "Well, now."

A loud bang went off and the students scattered with shouts of alarm. A nearby stall toppled, jars smashing on the floor, and the dead man moved so I could see his arms were loaded with spells.

Keir swept his legs out from underneath him in one smooth movement. The dead man toppled, and I grabbed his arm, wrenching it behind his back before he could activate another spell.

"Help me get those spells off him!" I gasped to Keir—I didn't want to find out the hard way whether or not my Hemlock magic could counter a dozen spells at once.

A blast hit the dead man full in the face, and he collapsed, his arm going limp in mine. Smoke exploded across my vision, forming a screen in front of us. A smokescreen spell... and not mine.

I peered into the smoke, looking for the newcomer. It was Asher.

"Get him out of here!" he rasped. "That smokescreen spell won't hold for long. Bring him to my shop."

"I thought your shop was closed," I said, completely bewildered. *I thought he disappeared.* I'd also thought he was half-dead, but maybe Evelyn's magic had worked after all.

"Argue later," Keir said, hauling the zombie's body over his shoulders. "Huh—that wasn't there last time we were here."

I looked over his shoulder, spotting the cobbled alley between the shops. It'd reappeared, not at all like it'd been boarded and bricked up yesterday. Asher must have used an illusion charm—a really good one. Smart thinking.

Asher collapsed into a seat the instant we entered his shop, while Keir deposited the body on the front desk. The ginger-haired man looked entirely too lifelike for a walking corpse. Not a vampire, either. He had no soul or heartbeat, and his skin was cold to touch.

Asher leaned over the body and coughed into his hand. "Bastard."

"Are you okay?" asked Isabel.

"Better than him." He jerked his head at the dead man, then his gaze zeroed in on me. "Your healing spell saved my neck. That's the only reason I'm not kicking you out of here. That clear?"

He hadn't seen Evelyn. *Thank god for that.* "You were dying."

"Yes, I was dying," he said. "I'm always close to death. It's why I have this." He took a swig from a bottle on the desk. It was tinted green, preventing me from seeing what was inside it. "You didn't need to help me. But you did."

"Yeah..." Damn, maybe he really didn't remember

Evelyn taking control and blasting him with Hemlock magic. "I came here looking for you yesterday, but your shop was totally shut down."

"Of course it was," he growled. "I'm taking no chances, not with monstrosities like this bastard walking around. What were you thinking, taking him on in public?"

"I didn't know he was *dead*," I protested. "He attacked a bunch of people, besides. Who in hell is he?"

"A proxy." He lifted the dead man's arm, which had flopped off the desk. "I'm no necromancer, but this isn't your typical undead."

He pulled the man's collar down, revealing a symbol was carved onto his upper back. The symbol wasn't familiar to me, but it looked like the ones used in rituals. In necromancy gone bad, and summonings from other realms.

Was he resurrected using dark magic?

Isabel made a faint noise. She looked like she was about to be sick. "What *is* that?"

Asher looked up at her. "Not something I wanted to see again."

"Oh?" I said, not daring to say aloud what was in my mind. *Blood magic. How could it have been used on a person?*

He drew in a ragged breath. "These symbols contain power... and can be used to raise the dead under the control of the person who summons them."

Nobody spoke. My head swam with a sense of unreality, like I'd been stabbed all over again. *It can't be that. The guild would know. There's no way...*

The symbol had been cut directly into his skin. I hadn't known it was possible to do blood magic using a *living* person before. Or a dead one either, except in the sacrificial sense.

I looked up into Asher's eyes. They were hazel, flecked with silver-grey, and much clearer than before I'd healed him. "Asher... you've seen this before. Was it—the same coven? The ones the League forced to help them?"

"It was their trademark," he said. "When you saw those symbols on a body, it was one of theirs. That's how they wiped out my coven."

"*Witches* did that?" Surely even the Hemlocks wouldn't have occasion to use blood magic to resurrect the dead...

My hands twitched, fighting the impulse to check for marks on my own body. *Really.* I'd know if I had a blood magic symbol on my skin.

"It's another Orion League trick," said Asher. "But they usually did it on the living."

"On the *living?*" Isabel recoiled. "How? What does the symbol mean?"

"That symbol means *control*," Asher said. "Control over the living or the dead."

"Almost like necromancy," I said. "But... not guild necromancy. That's *got* to be illegal."

"Of course it's illegal," said Asher. "They did it to all their elite soldiers—tattooed them with marks of the same nature, to make them stronger and faster than regular humans."

"That's... possible?" Isabel shook her head, a dazed look in her eyes. "It's not... it can't be like coven leader magic."

"Where do you think they got the idea?"

Oh. Those symbols that appeared on her skin when

her life was in danger—the League must have tried to create their own version. And succeeded.

"Were they all humans?" I asked. "Not supernaturals?"

"Yes, to my knowledge," he said. "It was an easy way to upgrade their recruits so they could go up against supernaturals without being killed."

"But they'd need supernaturals to put the mark on them, right?" I swallowed bile. "The witches."

"The Bloodroot Coven," Asher said. "Yes, they did. It looks like the art hasn't died out after all. I suppose this man was sent to run errands under the guise of a regular witch."

"He was sent to use witch spells on shifters," I said quietly. "To force them to kill each other and attack the mages. I guess we're not gonna be able to interrogate him. Unless someone knows his name, but I doubt the person who did this to him let his ghost stick around."

"I thought you were a witch, not a necromancer," he said.

"I can be both." He'd seen my Hemlock magic. Yet he hadn't brought it up yet. I was having difficulty caring who knew, considering the warped dead body lying in front of me.

"I can't sense him in the spirit realm," Keir said. Bringing back souls wasn't a vampire's strong point, but I had an inkling even the most powerful guild necromancer would have trouble with this one.

"Let me see." I held my hands out over the dead man's body, turned on my spirit sight, and searched for anything, the tiniest thread of a connection. Nothing was there, just Death. After all, he wasn't possessed by a vampire, but reanimated by a spell. His soul was long gone.

I turned off my spirit sight. "I have to tell the guild. And the mages. If we don't, there's no way they'd ever guess the enemy's creating zombies without using a necromancer." And that wasn't the worst of it. A *witch* had done this—reanimated him, used him to put those other illegal spells on the shifters. A blood magic witch.

"If you tell the guild, that's your prerogative," Asher said. "Not my business."

"But you knew about the symbols," I said. "How long have you known people like him were wandering around?"

"Not much longer than you have." He took another swig from the bottle. "I'm hardly in a position to stop them."

Neither am I. I was in too deep to claw my way back to the surface now. The guild needed to know—no question.

"He must have died recently," Isabel said. "Otherwise he'd have started to decay."

"Undead reanimated in that way are preserved as they were in life," Asher said. "They don't decay."

"Oh, that's bloody wonderful." I turned to Keir. "I'm going to need help carrying this guy back with me. We're taking him to the guild."

"Jas, are you sure?" he said. "Your boss doesn't know where you are."

Right. I wasn't even supposed to be on my feet. "I'll call her, say the dude ambushed us. It's pretty much true." The important thing was figuring out who'd reanimated him. That path would lead me right to whoever wanted to destroy the Council of Twelve.

Asher was still eyeing me suspiciously, so I left the shop before calling the guild's number.

"Lady Montgomery." I pressed my phone to my ear. "I was on the way back to the guild when a zombie attacked me."

"Of course," she said dryly. "Have you dealt with the undead yourself?"

"Uh, I think you're going to want to see the body. He's not like a normal undead."

"In what way?"

"He's a witch, dead, and reanimated, but there are weird symbols on him. I don't know what they are."

"You're with your vampire friend, aren't you? Bring him here."

Ah. I should have known she'd suspect I wasn't alone.

"All right. We'll be there soon." I hung up and went back into the shop. "Keir, she's asked you to help me get that guy back to the guild. Isabel… are you going to find the mages?"

"I guess, but…" She turned back to Asher. "This dead guy's trace is all over your shop."

"It's warded," he said. "They won't find me."

"And he can turn it into a convincing brick wall," I added. "But you should know, the spell this dude put on the shifter broke through a heavyweight set of wards. Several times."

"I'll stay here," Isabel said, glancing at Asher. "Er, if it's okay with you."

I expected him to say no. I mean, we'd barged in here and then caused a ruckus in public, forcing him to blow his cover.

Asher gave a nod and took another swig from the

bottle. "If you'd like to know more about that type of reanimation, I'm not an expert. But I can talk about the Bloodroot Coven."

"Oh, sure," said Isabel, giving me a faint nod to indicate that she'd tell me everything he said later.

Honestly, I was less than sure taking the zombie to the guild was the best idea. But Lady Montgomery had lived through the invasion. Maybe she'd seen this form of illegal blood magic before.

Maybe the Hemlocks knew, too.

15

Keir and I carried the body—or it started out that way. After we'd dropped him twice, Keir took over, giving the dead guy a piggyback under cover of a shadow spell while I walked on foot.

I turned on my own shadow spell. "We usually destroy the bodies, not haul them around."

Keir chuckled under his breath. "Life with you is never dull, Jas."

"Neither is death." I stumbled along the cobbled stones, the shadow spell making it even harder to see the edge of my cloak than usual. It was that or walk along talking to myself, so I put up with the indignity. The boss hadn't seemed surprised at what I'd told her, but it was hard to judge over the phone. A corpse reanimated using witch magic blew all the rules of both witchcraft and necromancy out the window. *I swear, if Evelyn knew, I'll skewer her.*

Evelyn, however, remained quiet, which was probably for the best. It took forever to get to the guild, which only gave me more time to brood on how and *why* someone had thought it necessary to use blood magic on a living person. Even the regular type of blood magic involved using symbols that were too powerful to be controlled with magic alone and demanded an extra sacrifice from the caster. So if the symbols were drawn onto a person, fuelled by their own blood... as much as I desperately wanted to deny what I'd seen, it made sense. That meant the witches must have drawn the symbol on the zombie before his body had rotted, eternally preserving him.

Keir and I turned down the street to the guild, manoeuvred the doors open, and managed to get the zombie inside the lobby. With a relieved sigh, I switched off my shadow spell. "All right, down the corridor on the..."

"Boo," said Lloyd. Then he jumped when Keir appeared out of thin air with the zombie on his back. "What the bloody hell did you do?"

"I'll explain later. The boss didn't say what she wanted me to do with this guy?"

"She asked me to empty a training room. I guess that's why."

At least there weren't many people around. Carrying a dead body through the lobby wasn't *that* unusual here, but the fewer people who knew about this, the better.

"Sorry," I said to Keir. "I'm afraid you might be the one to get the interrogation."

"We have bigger problems." He adjusted his grip on the zombie and followed Lloyd into the corridor, where a door lay open on the right.

Sure enough, Lady Montgomery was in the designated empty training room, accompanied by River. Ilsa stood beside the door and raised her eyebrows as Keir brought the body in.

"You weren't kidding," she said.

"Nope." I moved to let Keir pass with his undead cargo. "Where should we put him?"

"On the floor," Lady Montgomery said. "We'd better see what we're dealing with before anyone uses necromancy."

Ilsa and River both stared when Keir put the body down, exposing the symbol on his back.

"He's definitely dead," I told them. "But he was walking around like one of the living, for days, perfectly preserved. No vampires involved," I added, for Keir's benefit. He straightened upright and took a few steps away from the body as though unsure if he was being dismissed. Lloyd stood behind him, gaping openly at the dead man. Even River, one of the most experienced necromancers at the guild, looked vaguely stunned.

Lady Montgomery moved closer to the body, peering at the symbol.

"Yes, I have encountered reanimates like this before," she said. "But not for a long time. Where did you find him?"

"At the witch market," I said. "He is—was—a witch. I saw his face in a vision through the tracking spell I used at the…" I glanced at Keir, unsure whether or not he wanted her to know Clancy had been attacked.

He gave a nod, granting me permission to continue.

"Keir's shifter friend was attacked this morning," I went on. "And when I used a tracking spell to replay the incident, I saw this man force Keir's friend to put on a spell like the ones the mages confiscated from the shifter who attacked them. He said he'd been ordered to target the next mage he saw."

"And then you went to the hotel to warn your friends?" Lady Montgomery guessed.

"I did," I said. "Then this guy attacked me when I left Keir's place. The moment I checked the spirit realm and saw he didn't have a soul, I knew we couldn't leave him out there."

Lady Montgomery knelt and examined the body. From her silence, she was likely checking the spirit realm.

River moved in behind her. "When you say you've encountered an undead like him before… where, exactly?"

"In the days following the invasion, there were a lot of attempts made to seize power," said Lady Montgomery. "These beings were used by people without necromantic skills, who needed willing puppets."

"Wait, it *wasn't* a necromancer who did it?" Lloyd said.

"Apparently not." I glanced at the boss. Having lived through the invasion, it made sense for her to have encountered wannabe-necromancers who stole witch symbols and used them to reanimate the dead. Maybe Asher's knowledge wasn't so unusual after all.

"No, only a witch is capable of using this type of magic," she said. "So, Jas, this man was sent to ambush shifters on behalf of someone who wished to turn them against the mages? If that's the case, I'll have to call Lord Sutherland."

Despite myself, I felt some measure of relief that he'd be shown undeniable proof that the shifters hadn't entirely been in control of their decisions. Maybe he'd lift the ban on the ambassadors. From the look on the boss's face, I wasn't getting off the hook so easily, but I hardly cared.

"What does that symbol mean?" asked Ilsa.

I didn't say anything. I didn't dare. Not only was it familiar, it belonged to the same language as the glyphs in the forest, and the symbols Lady Harper had taught me when she'd tried to unlock my magic as a teenager. But neither Isabel nor I had recognised the symbol's actual meaning the way Asher had.

"The symbol belongs to the oldest known form of magic," said Lady Montgomery. "It was forbidden by the mage council long before the guild as we know it existed. None of you tell a soul outside this room that you saw this unless I give you direct permission, and you're absolutely not to draw or describe it. The word alone contains power."

I tasted bile at the back of my throat. So similar to the Hemlocks' power. *Control...*

"Of course," River and Ilsa said, and Lloyd nodded frantically.

"The Mage Lords will be informed," she added. "And the Council of Twelve."

I unstuck my tongue from the roof of my mouth. "Would he want to hear it from me, since I'm the witness?"

"I will ask, Jas," she said. "However, for now, I'm ordering you to go to the medical room for an evaluation."

"But—"

"The hotel collapsed on you, from what I heard."

Actually, I got stabbed to death. "All right," I said,

resigned. She'd likely be talking to the Mage Lord for a while, and besides, I needed to update Lloyd on the latest.

Keir caught my arm as I left the room. "I'm fairly sure I was just dismissed. You're going to the medical room?"

"Guess I have to. Thanks for helping me out back there."

"Anytime you need me to carry a zombie, let me know." Keir briefly embraced me, then left.

Lloyd came out of the room behind me. "That's nothing. I can do the same and I have way more style than he does."

I rolled my eyes at him. "Come on, let's see what the nurse has to say."

Shockingly, the nurse dismissed me in two seconds flat as 'absurdly healthy'. I decided not to tell her about the near-death-by-shifter-ghost situation. Maybe I should have told the boss, but she already knew about the first shifter ghost. If she didn't know they'd been at the hotel, it was impossible to keep that type of thing quiet with necromancers around.

By the time I'd brought Lloyd up to speed on the day's events, he was shaking his head at me. "Really, Jas? You had to fight the dude in public?"

"I didn't know he was a zombie until I was about to kick his arse. It's not like I had the faintest idea you could use blood magic to revive them."

"Uh, yeah, neither did I." He shuddered. "Never heard of this Orion League either, though the name kinda rings a bell. Maybe I read it somewhere."

"Since when did you actually read the books in the archives?"

He hit me in the arm. "Funny, Jas. Speaking of the archives, she didn't tell you to get back in there?"

"No, she just told me to report to the nurse," I said. "You're not patrolling?"

"Nope, I'm on cleaning duty in half an hour. Unless you have a witch spell for that?"

"I can make one." I grinned. "Give me ten minutes in my room. I want to grab some food, too."

"And then? We're long overdue a zombie marathon."

"Not to deprive you, but the boss is telling the Mage Lord about those zombies. I need to stick around in case he wants to hear the story from me."

I stopped at the cafeteria to grab a sandwich to go, and Lloyd did likewise. We ate them on the way to my room, where I'd left some spell circles already set up. He raised his eyebrow at the latest set of sketches on the wall, featuring a group of hellhounds swarming the cemetery.

"Too soon, Jas," he said.

"I told you, I like to draw out my nightmares so they don't haunt me when I'm asleep."

"Keir, too?" He indicated the sketchbook I'd left out on the bed, open to a portrait of Keir.

I pointedly closed it and made for the ingredient stash. "If you're jealous, I'll draw you your own portrait."

"He got you these," he observed, picking up the box of paints Keir had given me. "Maybe I was wrong about the vampire."

I grabbed a piece of chalk and sketched a fresh spell circle. "He's not going to clear off again, Lloyd, trust me."

"Because he'll die if he doesn't feed on your soul."

I tossed a handful of leaves into the circle. "That's not why. It's just a complication."

"Just a complication?" He snorted. "Have you made any progress on that front? Or has he accepted he'll be sucking on your soul forever?"

"Have I had a moment's peace lately?" I grabbed a jar of powder and sprinkled some into the circle. "Nope. Besides, what I've learned today has invalidated half the textbooks I've ever read. Shifters can be controlled after death. Bodies can be reanimated without necromancy. At this rate the Ancients will show up tap-dancing on the roof."

"Sometimes I'm glad I'm not in your shoes, Jas." He made a big show of ducking out of the way when the circle lit up with transparent flames. "Cool magic, though. Pity you don't have time to try the fun stuff. I heard there's a new batch of love potions doing the rounds on the university campus."

"What, you want one for the person you secretly admire?" I picked up the newly formed cleansing spell and tossed it to him, and Lloyd caught it in one hand. "Gonna enlighten me on who it is? I've not exactly been paying attention lately, so you could be dating the half-troll cleaner and I wouldn't be any the wiser."

"Not him, no." He slid the cleansing spell onto his wrist. "And now I think about it, I don't want your Hemlock magic anywhere near any love potions."

"Yeah, I wouldn't trust Evelyn with that one." I hid a smile at the horrifying idea of an amplified Evelyn-style love spell.

Then I thought back to his unexpected appearance at the mages' place. "Hang on," I said. "Does the person you like have the surname 'Lynn'?"

A pause. "Maybe."

"Morgan?" I said. "You like Morgan Lynn? Wait… *what* were you two doing in that cupboard?"

"Nothing," he said, his face reddening under its dark hue. "He… doesn't actually know I like him."

"Well, then." I reached for a fresh handful of ingredients. "You're the one who usually plays matchmaker. Besides, life's short, and being a ghost isn't all fun and games. I'd say go for it."

"Yeah, no. You're the risk-taker."

"Risking rejection or risking your life? Pfft." I turned on my magic and once again, flames sprang into life in the spell circle. "How about this? Tell him you like him, or come with me to the Hemlocks' forest."

"What the hell d'you want to go there for?"

"To ask them about those blood magic symbols reanimating the dead," I said. "And if they had past experience with the Orion League, too."

They probably did, but then again, they'd been in the forest for a long time. Besides, Evelyn wouldn't need to use blood magic to resurrect the dead. She had me to do that for her.

Lloyd watched as I picked up the newly formed healing spell. "Jas, it's your choice, but you nearly died today. You have a sign on your head telling every enemy in the city to come and take a shot at you."

"He's not wrong," Evelyn said from beside me.

I jumped. "Shit, you can't eavesdrop on our conversation."

Lloyd's forehead scrunched up. "Er, Jas, you're not talking to *her*, are you?"

"You have zero concept of privacy," I said to Evelyn, then turned back to Lloyd. "Unfortunately, yes, I am."

"Evelyn's here right now?" he asked.

"Technically, she always is," I said. "But she seems particularly restless at the moment. Don't you want to talk to the Hemlocks, too?"

"You can do that without leaving the guild if you want to," she said. "If you really care so much about following the rules."

Shit, I could. If I left my body. "Are you sure you're not trying to get into my body to possess me and run amok again?"

"No, I want to talk to them, too," she said. "About those symbols."

"You're seriously thinking of letting her have her way?" Lloyd said. "You know what happened last time. I'm not up for being strangled by your mad ancestor."

"She's coming with me," I said. "Don't worry, I'll keep an eye on her."

"That's not necessary," Evelyn said.

Lloyd scowled. "Yeah, I don't trust her."

"Relax." I brushed dust from my clothes and stood up. "It's no different to going into the spirit realm."

"Except you might get stuck there again. Or possessed."

"Tell you what, I'll set up a circle, then," I said. "Use one of the protected rooms. It'll only be for a minute, and if the Hemlocks won't help me, I'll get out of there."

"All right," he said. "But I don't trust her. A bit."

Nor do I. But in all my hours exploring the spirit realm lately, I hadn't thought to travel into the forest as a ghost to speak to the Hemlocks. The idea of leaving my body unattended was still as unappealing as letting Evelyn have her way.

Lloyd and I found an empty room and set up a candle circle. Since there were more patrols out in the city than usual, nobody disturbed us, and I put a sealing spell on the door just in case. Lloyd watched me, second thoughts written all over his face, but I gave him a reassuring smile and stepped confidently into the circle.

In one blink, I was out of my body, rising through the ceiling to the guild's roof. Evelyn floated alongside me. Despite her usual closed expression, she had to be enjoying this. The spirit realm was downright fun when you had this type of freedom.

As a spirit, the forest was even easier to find than I expected. One second, Evelyn and I hovered side by side on the spirit line. The next, trees crowded in around us, and darkness closed overhead.

"Hey," I said, not sure if my being here as a ghost would alert the Hemlocks or not. Considering Leila had got into the forest undetected, probably not. "Hey, Cordelia. We're here."

Silence. Not so much as a stirring in the branches.

I turned to my companion. "Evelyn, please tell me you know where the cave is."

"It's not geographically fixed."

Wonderful. Lost in the woods with the ghost of my dead ancestor. I floated down the path, hoping to see a landmark, but there weren't any.

Fine, then. I tapped into my Hemlock magic, and it rose to my fingertips, lighting them in grey and green. The forest warped and shifted, and the next second, we were in the cave, faced with the sculpture containing the form of Cordelia Hemlock.

"You two," said Cordelia. "Where is your body, Jacinda?"

"Don't worry, it's safe," I said. "The guild has me on house arrest, so I thought I'd pop in and visit. And Evelyn wanted to talk to you, too."

"Yes, I do," Evelyn cut in. "Someone is using the old rituals to incite chaos among the local supernaturals. That suggests it's time."

"Uh, time for *what*, exactly? I thought we were here to discuss those symbols." The glowing green glyphs at the back of the cave snagged my gaze. Definitely similar ones, if not the outright same.

"Jacinda knows little compared to you," Cordelia said to Evelyn, completely ignoring me. "It'll take time to bring her up to speed."

"I'm right here," I pointed out. "What I'd like to know is, what's that language in those glyphs, and why the hell can it be used to reanimate corpses? Only necromancy is supposed to be able to do that."

"As I said, your knowledge is limited," she said. "Humans like to hide from what they fear, not embrace it."

"I *am* human," I said. "Let's skip the part where you lament what a disappointment I am and tell me what the bloody language is. Why does it have power over life and death?"

"Because *we* do, Jacinda. The language is ours."

"You mean you created it, or…?" My words trailed off. I already knew. The Hemlocks had created it, humans had stolen it, and now the enemy was using it against us. "You created the base for the witches' language? How is that possible?"

"Because the symbols are nothing more than shortcuts, and what matters is the magic itself," Cordelia said. "If you'd paid attention in lessons, you'd know."

"I knew *that* part," I said. "It's the same with necromancy. But I'm a little lost on *why* you created a symbol that can reanimate and control someone against their will."

"Our predecessors created the symbols, Jacinda, not the means of controlling every decision someone makes regarding how to use them. Yes, that does mean they can be used for terrible deeds."

"That figures," I said. "I take it they're not common knowledge, then. Who might be using them in Edinburgh?"

"Who indeed?" she croaked. "The knowledge trickled out of our grasp long ago."

Translation: Leila might have told anyone. And the symbols weren't restricted to the Hemlock witches. I'd always thought necromancy and witchcraft weren't that much different, but I hadn't known the symbols were the exact same. Most necromancy only used the spoken words which didn't correspond to any existing language.

"They're not just raising the dead," I said. "The same people are creating spells to force shifters to transform and attack the mages against their will."

"Not all shifters," Evelyn interjected. "Specifically, direct bloodline descendants."

"Hey!" I turned to her. "You knew? You were hanging around while I was talking to Ivy and Ilsa, too."

"Of course I was," she said. "We cannot be separated that easily, Jacinda."

Irritation prickled at me. "Look, there are basic rules of manners... never mind."

Direct bloodline descendants. Shifters who were descended directly from the Ancients. Had they been targeted because they were easy targets—or because whatever the enemy used to control them worked more strongly on shifters of that bloodline?

I turned back to Cordelia. "My magic reacted violently when I touched the spell controlling the shifters. Why?"

Cordelia's eyes gleamed like dark pits. "Your magic cannot abide to be near the magic of our ancient enemies."

"That doesn't explain why—" I broke off. "Was it the *stone* that destroyed the wards on the hotel?"

"Perhaps," Evelyn said. "It's as likely as anything else."

If it was true… there were more pieces of stone inside the mages' headquarters, where the others had relocated. And where my friends were right now.

16

Ignoring Evelyn's shout of protest, I faded out of the forest, back into my body. If Evelyn got left behind, it was not my problem. I had to warn the others.

"Whoa," said Lloyd, as I jerked upright, knocking several candles over in the process. "What is it?"

Ice cracked on my hands, and I winced. "I'm ninety percent sure it's those damned stones that brought down the hotel wards. I should have known."

"Seriously?"

"Yep." I grabbed my phone and sent Isabel a text. "Not that it really matters considering those shifter ghosts can get anywhere they like anyway, but I'm the one who left the bloody stone in Isabel's room."

"That's it, I'm coming with you." Lloyd grabbed a couple of candles.

"Sorry, Lloyd, but necromancy isn't much help when you're being clawed open by a rabid shifter, even a ghostly one. Can you take the candles back? If the boss asks, tell her my family might be in trouble again. She can't blame me for going to warn them."

Lloyd let out an exasperated noise. "It's not worth telling you to be careful, is it? Please *try* not to die this time, Jas."

"I'll make a special effort just for you."

My phone buzzed with a call from Isabel as I ran out of the room.

"Hey," I said, accepting the call. "I'm on my way now. Are you still at Asher's?"

"I am, but—I think that's why the shifters went after me first. I had the stone in my room."

"I should have known." My free hand clenched. "I'm going to warn the others. I know the mages will probably yell at me, but whatever."

"I'll message Ivy—no idea whether she's there or not, but she's usually good at convincing people to listen."

"Thanks," I said. "Seriously, be careful with those stones. They need to be destroyed, but hell if I know *how.*"

Even Drake's mage fire hadn't put a dent in them. Nor Isabel's explosives. If they were somehow linked directly to the Ancients, was it even possible to destroy them?

"I'll try to think of something," Isabel said. "And I'll get there as soon as I can."

"Thanks." I turned off my phone, ducking out of sight of a group of passing necromancers. When the coast was clear, I sprinted through the lobby and out into the cobbled street.

Never mind my job—those stones could bring the wards around the guild's headquarters crashing down. And now I'd abandoned Evelyn in the woods. Not that she couldn't join me at any time if she wanted to, but I was setting records for fuck-ups and the day was barely half over.

I broke into a full-blown sprint, my lungs burning, my legs protesting. *Please tell me the mages have guessed what those stones might have done.* Vance must have worked it out, surely. I should have checked the hotel wards when I'd last left, but it had slipped my mind.

I hurtled around a corner and skidded to a halt outside the mages' guild entrance. The wards were back up, the gates sealed, and the same mage apprentice as before stood on guard outside. I nearly groaned aloud at the sight of his impeccably combed straw-coloured hair and polished shoes.

"You again?" said the mage. "What do you want?"

"What did the mages do with the spells they confiscated from the shifters?" I asked, between breaths.

"Why?"

Being direct was probably the best approach. "They're booby-trapped," I said. "They can neutralise witch wards, including the ones right behind you."

"You're having me on," he said. "Who sent you?"

"Uh, I'm friends with several people in this building," I told him. "Ask for Ivy Lane or Mage Lord Colton if you don't believe me."

He scowled and raised his sleeve, tapping a mark on his arm. A mage mark. Mages used them to communicate with one another, usually master-to-apprentice or two partners on a mission who wanted to be able to find each other quickly. The swirling lines made my stomach turn over, recalling the bloody symbol on the dead witch's body. The glyphs the mages used weren't unlike the witch runes. Maybe that type of magic had never gone out of style at all.

"What're you looking at?" he said. "Never seen a mage mark before?"

"Wouldn't it be quicker just to use your phone?" Where in hell was Ivy?

His scowl deepened. "Quit taking the piss. I'm Lord Sutherland's son, and the mark connects me to him."

I blinked, then stifled a laugh. "He doesn't trust you not to wander off alone?"

Usually, the marks were used for members of a team of mages to stay in contact with one another while on a dangerous mission. For Lord Sutherland to put it on his son meant he was either ridiculously overprotective or said son had a habit of shirking his duty.

"Don't you laugh at me!" He flushed to his hairline. "Dad, get out here. Tell her to go away."

"There's no need to shout." Lord Sutherland strode out behind him. "Neil, what are you doing?"

"She insulted me!" he said.

I rolled my eyes. "He's acting like a spoiled child. I told him about a legitimate threat to your security and he didn't believe me, so here we are."

"Threat to our security?"

"Those wristbands the shifters were wearing contained a stone that has the power to neutralise witch wards," I said. "That's how the enemy attacked the hotel. What did you do with the ones you confiscated?"

His eyes narrowed, showing his beautifying spells had slipped, and there were wrinkles in the corners of his eyes that hadn't been there before. "And how exactly did those stones get into the hotel? Was it you who brought them in?"

Ah, crap. "I didn't know. Nor did you, otherwise you'd have warned the other mages… right?"

His gaze went to the shimmering wards on the gates. "If you are correct, I assume that if nobody has been foolish enough to remove one of those stones from the building, the wards remain functional as ever."

Crap. Ivy took one. My hands itched to feel the wards, to see if they were as intact as they looked, but that'd blow my cover.

"So you still have them?" Cold sweat gathered on the back of my neck. I'd have to wait until he was gone to check, but as long as the enemy had those stones, they could break in at any time.

"If you mean the spells the attackers used against us, they're with my own team of witches, who are analysing them as we speak."

"And has anyone tested to see if they break?" I asked. "Isabel's best explosives couldn't put a dent in them. Drake's mage fire couldn't damage them either."

"My team are more than capable of handling the matter ourselves," he said, nodding to Neil. "See to it that Jas leaves the premises immediately."

Neil looked like Christmas had come early. I wanted to punch him in his smug face.

"And the dead body?" I said, not moving. "That doesn't concern you?"

He held my gaze for a moment. "A lot of things concern me. Things that aren't fit for the ears of simple necromancer apprentices."

White-hot anger bubbled inside me. Now I wished I

could punch both of them. "Lady Harper would disagree with your approach." Or maybe she wouldn't. She'd probably give me a tongue-lashing of her own. Damn, I missed her. Who'd have thought it.

"Lady Harper was a remarkable woman, with a remarkably flawed vision."

What does that mean? "You knew her personally?"

"Did you?" He left the question hanging. "I'll be hosting another meeting tomorrow, Jas, the last gathering of the Council of Twelve. Feel free to tell me more about your theories with the rest of the council as an audience."

Damn him. I turned away, my cheeks burning. I should have known the mages would have their own plan to deal with the enemy, but he seemed entirely too unconcerned about the stones. *What is he scheming?*

Then again, Lord Sutherland would be fine no matter what happened. Not just because he lived in one of the most protected places in the city, but because the supernatural world's laws always protected mages first, above all others.

The last meeting of the Council of Twelve. I doubted he'd used that wording by accident. Whether he was right or not, the mages would be going it alone.

And no wards would protect them the next time the walls between worlds came crashing down.

By the following morning, I was a brittle mess of nerves. While Ivy claimed that the stones, if the mages had them, hadn't left the building, Lord Sutherland dand his son's smug words had chased one another around my head all night. Seeing his face as he opened the meeting made my blood churn and my Hemlock magic simmer below the surface. The meeting room seemed emptier without the shifters, and half the witches hadn't shown up either. In fact, only Isabel and two others were present.

The Mage Lord spoke. "We have spent the last day discussing the attacks and the future steps necessary to prevent further conflict. Removing the shifters from the council was the first step, but the attacks would not have been possible without the aid of a witch. Therefore, no witches will serve on our council in future."

"Does that include the person who makes your beautifying spells?" Ivy said, not bothering to lower her voice.

Lord Sutherland gave her a look frostier than the January air. "*No* witches, including your friend, will be permitted to stay in this building."

Isabel shifted next to me, her mouth pressed in an angry line. "I suppose you won't have need of any wards?"

The Mage Lord turned to his council. "It's a necessary precaution, until these dark magic practitioners are brought to justice."

"At least you admit it's dark magic," I said. What the hell—if Isabel was getting kicked out, I might as well go out in a blaze of glory. "And the shifters aren't plotting against you of their own free will."

He narrowed his eyes at me. "All practitioners of dark magic will naturally be sentenced to death."

Uh-oh.

"And how do you propose you'll find them?" Lady Montgomery asked. "As you said to me yesterday, you have no way of tracking the practitioners, particularly if you expel your witches."

"I think it's obvious," he said. "Any witch who belongs to a coven is to sign a register. Any witch who doesn't is no longer allowed to practise magic. That will root out the traitors quickly."

"But—there are already laws preventing anyone from selling spells on the market without a licence," Isabel protested. "How can you police what people do in their own homes?"

"It should be relatively easy, with these." He held up a band-shaped spell. "Any witch who fails to comply will wear one of these. My team has been perfecting them—I suppose at least I can say the enemy's methods have been helpful for our own research."

My stomach lurched, and I was glad I hadn't had time to eat anything before the meeting. The spell was a design not unlike the bands the shifters had been wearing, minus the stones. Before I could reel my own magic in, I found my hands inching towards it, and Lord Sutherland smiled slightly as he pushed the band onto the table. My hands twitched, my magic tracing the spell's edges.

A binding spell. It'd attach itself to any witch who used magic, locking down their power. Who'd made this? One of the same witches he was kicking out?

"This is absurd," said Drake. "What next, tagging all the nonhuman species? Because one of your ancestors tried that and it didn't end well for him."

Lord Sutherland scowled, his cheeks reddening a little as a murmur swept down the row of mages. The mages tried to cover up their histories of cruelty towards the other supernaturals, sweeping them under the rug of the faerie invasion, but Drake had apparently been poking into Lord Sutherland's background. It figured that he'd come from a long line of dickheads.

"What Drake means to say is that our council will not be following your example," Vance said. "As it goes against the principles of our council and the Twelve."

"Naturally, the decision is up to each individual council," said Lord Sutherland. "As for the Council of Twelve, I think the days of cooperation are drawing to an end."

Crap. I'd hoped my suspicions were wrong. Just for once.

"We cooperated in the war with the Sidhe," said Lady Montgomery. "More lives would have been lost if we had not. We would have been driven to extinction."

"I seem to remember the council was designed to *prevent* a war with the Sidhe," Lord Sutherland said, with a sniff. "Plainly, they were not successful in doing so."

"We were blindsided," said a dark-skinned mage further down the table. "If not for our cooperation, we would never have survived. Divide and we won't stand a chance in the next war."

"Precisely," Vance said, and voices rose among the mages—arguments and objections clashing. The other supernaturals seemed too appalled to say anything—and it struck me that more than the shifters and witches were absent. The Summer Gatekeeper was, too, and Ilsa's sister. Had something urgent in Faerie come up, or had the mages tried to discourage the others from attending the meeting? Or just plain not told them about it?

"I think it's clear that something needs to be done about the abundance of dark magic in this city," said Lord Sutherland, when there was a lull in the debate. "If an agreement cannot be reached, then we will proceed with our plan without the need to consult the Council of Twelve. The witch covens have agreed to cooperate. That leaves us with a clear line of action."

"In acting against the city's supernaturals, you're alienating your allies and allowing the true enemy to walk free within the city, unchallenged," Vance said. "If a mage with mind-controlling abilities used them against you, Lord Sutherland, would you require all the mages in the city who refused to submit to have their powers bound?"

"No witch has objected to my decision," the Mage Lord said. "Every coven leader I have spoken to has agreed to have their members sign the register. The shifters have not responded, but I will send them a reminder. The guild of necromancers will receive similar forms, and any rogues will be asked to join a coalition or surrender themselves to us."

The vampires. Keir hadn't mentioned if they'd elected a new king or not, but there was no way in hell they'd consent to join the necromancers' guild. For someone under a curse as Keir was, one slip might be fatal.

"Has *every* mage on your council agreed to do this, Lord Sutherland?" I asked. "Or have you pushed the decision through without consultation?"

"In a state of emergency such as this one, I can do exactly that," he said. "Which register will you be signing, Jas Lyons? Are you a witch?"

"Both witch and necromancer." I took in a deep breath, my heart hammering. "You'll have a job and a half policing people with backgrounds like mine. I'm from a family that's part witch, part mage and part necromancer. I never met most of my living relatives. And what about orphans of the invasion? There are tens of thousands of them in this city alone. Besides, it's possible for humans to develop magical talent without—"

"The human school system already offers magical testing," Lord Sutherland said. "We'll simply formalise it. The cases of someone demonstrating magical capabilities at an older age than the average are negligible."

Bugger. I couldn't give up necromancy, and Evelyn would never allow herself to be bound again. I'd have to leave the guild, leave the city, relocate somewhere the rules wouldn't follow me. I had the money I'd inherited from Lady Harper. That would keep me going for a while… but what kind of future would I have, living as a fugitive?

Think, Jas. Lord Sutherland seemed to have entirely forgotten about the stones, and had his personal team of witches put together binding spells instead of looking for the enemy. How had his team of witches made those intricate spells so damn fast? He'd been planning this for longer than he let on. There was no other explanation.

Seeing me looking, Lord Sutherland picked up the wristband. "It's painless, of course," he said. "From now on, any witch who uses magic without a licence in this city will be cuffed and brought to trial depending on the severity of their transgression."

Using magic was a crime now? I couldn't believe the rest of the council was falling for this crap, but he was the one calling the shots. Nobody had licence to challenge him. The others were outsiders, he'd rejected the Council of Twelve, and I… was nothing but a novice necromancer.

I'd lost. If I didn't figure a way out of this, I'd be cuffed the instant I used my magic. To add insult to injury, the reanimated body was somewhere in this building if it hadn't been destroyed, and the Mage Lord probably had his team taking it to pieces behind the scenes. Maybe they'd start using runes to make their own zombie slaves next. I wouldn't put anything past them.

I waylaid Drake on the way out, since he seemed most likely to pay attention. "Drake, are you still staying here after what he said?"

"God, no," he said. "I'm going to find Wanda and we're getting the hell out. I'd rather find a hotel than stay in the same building as him."

"I don't blame you." I heaved out a breath. "About the stones—"

"They break the wards? I know. Vance knows, we all know. And as far as I'm concerned, the enemy is more than welcome to use them to stride in here and see if Lord Sutherland wants our help then."

"He knows," I said. "He—he's been planning this for ages, I'm sure. The binding spells, at least. Please tell me Vance has a plan."

He jerked his head towards the half-open meeting room door. Vance and the Mage Lord stood in heated conversation. The latter's shoulders were tense and he seemed to be talking as firmly as possible without raising his voice. I admired his self-control. Ivy stood at his side, glaring daggers at Lord Sutherland like she wished she could run him through with her blade.

"Worth a shot, at least." Drake shrugged. "Want to help me and Wanda move out? Vance will be occupied arguing with that dick for a while, and we'll need a witch to set up wards."

I glanced around, seeing Lady Montgomery had gone

outside. Worry twisting in my gut, I nodded. "Sure. I'll help you find a safe hotel, set up wards…"

And then… what? Hand myself in? Run for the hills? The register would be on Lady Montgomery's desk the instant she got back from the meeting. I could beg for Keir's help, but he'd have to enact an exit strategy of his own soon, too. All the vampires would.

Drake led the way upstairs. Curved bannisters ran either side of us, carved with dragons and other mythical beasts. This place was even fancier than Vance's house, if it was possible. The upper corridor was as ornate as the ground floor, and thick carpets cloaked the stairs, red and patterned in swirls.

As we reached the upper floor, I whispered, "Drake, do you know what he did with the stones? We have to figure out how to destroy them. They're the crux of this."

"No clue," he said. "If my fire can't do it—what exactly are they, do you know?"

"I think they're related to the weapon the Soul Collector carried in some way, or a similar type, but shifter-specific. I don't know if Lord Sutherland is totally clued in."

Drake halted mid-step. "You're shitting me."

"Nope. I assume Lord Sutherland and the council at least made the connection, but who knows what he's thinking?"

"He's thinking he's gonna be replaced," said Drake. "He's scared shitless of it. He'll say and do anything to retain credibility. Bloody mages."

"Er, you are one."

"Well observed," he said. "I'm the son of a disgraced

count and Lord Sutherland has been trying to get me kicked off the council since the start."

"I didn't know that." Drake, like a lot of mages, rarely talked about the family he'd lost before the invasion.

He shrugged. "Not just me. He wants rid of everyone who doesn't fit. First the shifters, then the witches, then the rest of us riffraff. Frankly, I expected the necromancers to go first."

"Lady Montgomery won't go for it. Guess that's the end of our partnership with the mages." Her hands were tied, too. Her sole responsibility was the guild. She didn't make the rules.

Drake pushed open a door on the right. "Hey, Wanda—"

Nobody was in the room. The place was ransacked, bedcovers pulled off, boxes overturned. Lady Harper's boxes.

"Wanda?" He looked around. "She wouldn't have gone off alone."

"Maybe she was eavesdropping on the meeting," I said, my heart sinking unpleasantly.

The wards weren't fool-proof. And nobody had listened to my warnings.

We backed out of the room, searching the corridor. "She can't have gone that way," Drake said, jerking his head at another staircase. "Out of bounds."

"Not in the spirit realm." I stopped walking. "I can search the whole building. Give me a minute."

Grey fog filtered in. I sensed Drake's presence glowing beside me, and more mages downstairs... and Keir. He must have been watching the building from outside.

"Jas?" Keir looked up at me. "What is it, another shifter ghost?"

"Wanda's missing," I said. "She's supposed to be staying with the mages, but she's disappeared from their headquarters. Have you seen anyone leave the building?"

"Aside from now? No. I've been watching all the exits."

"Shit." I turned off my spirit sight. "Drake, when did you last see her?"

"Before the meeting. A few hours ago… I left her sleeping in."

Before Keir showed up here. My blood chilled. "I… Keir didn't see her leave during the meeting. He was watching all the exits."

Drake's scarred face paled. "What? She'd never have left on her own, knowing those bastards are targeting mages." Like Vance, he doted on her—as the baby of the mages, she was like a younger sibling to the older ones.

"Let me check back with Keir," I said quickly, turning my spirit sight on again.

Keir appeared beside me in the spirit realm. "I know what she looks like. I can probably track her."

"Me too, but someone captured her from the mages' guild. They might—"

"Still be here?" a voice whispered, and an arm locked around my neck, yanking me out of Death.

17

I twisted on the spot, breaking free of the ghost's grip. The first shifter—the one who'd killed Lord Forrest—bared his teeth at me. His hands were sheathed in grey scales, and I was damned lucky it was his scales that'd cut my neck and not his claws.

He never left. He was still here all along.

"This is all your fault," he snarled.

"I'm not a mage," I said. "I'm not the one you should be blaming for this."

The shifter let out a chilling howl. Then he turned on his heel, sprinting out of sight. As the last of the spirit realm faded away, the mages' corridor came back into view.

Drake's body lay crumpled and bleeding at my feet.

Shit. Deep claw wounds lacerated his chest, and blood soaked into the thick carpet. I scrambled for a spell, and Evelyn snarled in my ear, "That's not strong enough, you fool. He's bleeding out."

"Don't stand there bitching, then." I activated the

healing spell, then I held my palms over Drake's crumpled body. Hemlock magic flowed from my hands, mingling with the healing spell. Amplifying it, enhancing it, swirling into glyph-like patterns. Drake twitched as the spell engulfed him in shimmering grey-green lines.

Footsteps came from the stairs. Damn. I had to get him out of here.

The light faded, and Drake groaned and sat up, no longer bleeding. "The fuck? What stabbed me?"

"A shifter ghost. They survived Death, thanks to those stones. Drake—someone's coming upstairs."

The footsteps grew louder. Drake looked down at the blood covering his torn clothes and scowled. "I'll handle them. They'll take *this* seriously."

A moment later, two mages ran into the corridor. "What is going on?" one of them demanded, taking in the blood-soaked carpet and Drake's shredded clothes.

"We were attacked by a ghost," Drake said. "And someone kidnapped Wanda. They got in here this morning. Seen anyone around here who shouldn't be?"

"Kidnapped?" he echoed. "Nobody has been up here."

"Clearly they have," Drake said, indicating the blood staining his clothes. "Go and warn your Mage Lord there's been a break-in. Go on."

To my surprise, the mages turned their backs and headed downstairs. Guess Drake carried some clout after all, for all the good it did. Wanda was still gone, and the shifters' ghosts… maybe I should just let them finish Lord Sutherland off. Heaven knew it'd make things easier for the rest of us.

"Let me check the spirit realm," I said. "I *really* want to question one of those ghosts. I bet they know where Wanda is."

"You can do that from here?" Drake let out a low whistle.

"Not according to the mages, but fuck them." I turned on my spirit sight.

Greyness filtered in, but there were no signs of any shifter ghosts. And no Wanda. Hopefully Keir was having better luck.

"I'll break it to Vance," Drake said, when I returned to my body. "Maybe she's not the only person they took."

"But why take her to begin with?"

He shook his head. "Maybe because she's Lady Harper's granddaughter? Or because she was alone? Haven't a clue."

"Shit, you're right." What if they'd stolen some of Lady Harper's things? Though what they want with a lot of old junk, I couldn't even imagine. But she'd made no secret of her disdain for the other mages…

Keir spoke in my ear. "She's out of my range."

"What, out of the city?" I said aloud.

Drake twisted to stare at me. "Are you talking to another ghost?"

"Nah, my vampire friend. He's looking for Wanda and he says she's out of reach. That means…"

She must be outside this realm. *Please say she isn't on the spirit line where the hellhounds were.*

Drake's jaw dropped. "How are we supposed to track her?"

"I probably can," I admitted. "But I'll need the mages *not* to be watching when I do."

"I can divert their attention," Drake said. "As long as

you find her. I don't want to lose you, too."

"Wanda isn't lost," I said. "I'll get her back."

Drake and I made for the stairs once more. The other mages had cleared out of the entrance hall, though Lady Montgomery waited expectantly outside the building. She hadn't gone into the spirit realm to find me this time, then. Steeling myself, I ran to meet her.

"Jas Lyons, what have you done this time?"

"Wanda was kidnapped," I said. "My friend—one of the mages. And a shifter ghost attacked my other friend, just now. Stabbed him."

Her brows shot up. "Stabbed him?"

Oops. I hadn't told her the ghost had stabbed me yesterday. "The affected shifter ghosts can attack people even in death. I know Lord Sutherland doesn't trust me, but I'm not kidding. The shifters' ghosts seem to be able to walk in and out of buildings however they like, too. There's one right here somewhere, the first shifter who died."

"If that's the case…" She swept to the gate, past the mages guarding it, and beckoned to Ilsa and River. She must have asked them to wait outside. "Ilsa, River, Jas tells me there are shifter ghosts on the loose somewhere close by. You're to bring in a team and surround the place."

Ilsa paled. "But the Mage Lord said—"

"This is for his own safety," said Lady Montgomery. "I'm sure he'll appreciate the effort."

Yeah, right. I held my tongue, spotting Keir a few feet away. He caught my eye and nodded.

"Is Ivy around?" I asked Ilsa.

"Nope. I think she's still with the mages."

I swore under my breath. To find Wanda, I'd need to

leave my body and risk discovery, and since I didn't know for sure that Wanda was inside a liminal space, I'd do her more harm than good if I got caught. I needed help.

Keir walked over to me. "Jas, I can't find your friend. We're going to have to move away from this place." His tone implied *away from eavesdroppers.*

I glanced at Lady Montgomery. "I'd help, but my friend is in danger. Can I—"

"Right, go ahead." She waved a hand, her phone in her other hand. "I'm alerting the guild—you are *not* to put your life in any more danger than necessary, Jas Lyons."

Pretty sure I have no choice.

Ilsa caught my arm. "Jas, before you go—if you want to find a specific ghost, you can summon it directly. If that helps."

As River called her name, she ran after him, leaving me standing on the pavement in confusion.

"What did she mean by that? Everyone knows you can summon ghosts by name, it's basic necromancy."

Keir stepped closer to me. "Because you might want to summon the shifter?"

"Shit, of course." Some necromancer I was. "Hope the boss can handle the others. First she has to deal with the mages' draconian registry crap and now this. C'mon, then, let's summon a shifter ghost. Wait, I don't even know his name."

"It's Vaughn Sanderson," Keir said. "I eavesdropped on the mages in the spirit realm."

We ran around the corner, finding a nearby alley. I didn't bother with candles, jumping right into the spirit world. Then I shouted, "Hey! Vaughn Sanderson, I summon you."

The air flickered, and the shifter reappeared before us, his hands covered in blood, scales creeping up his arms.

"What are you doing?" Vaughn growled. "Can't you leave me be?"

"Not until you tell me what that stone is," I said. "Can it be destroyed? How can it affect you after death?"

He swore, his hands shifting to claws. "The Moonbeam—it's a piece of the Moonbeam."

Keir grabbed his arms from behind, stopping him from lunging at me. "What the fuck is the Moonbeam?"

The shifter struggled, guttural snarls escaping. "It's too late for us," he said. "It's too late—we're in the Moonbeam's thrall. Let me go before I'm forced to—kill you."

"You won't kill me." My hands glowed, not with Hemlock magic but with the ghostly blue light of a necromancer. "I banish you beyond the gates of Death."

The shifter roared, and Keir struggled to hold him still, shouting the banishing words in his ear.

"I banish you," he growled, holding the shifter's throat in his grip. "Dammit—Jas, it's not working."

"If I can't banish him, I can at least slow him down. Heads up." Raising my hands, I blasted the shifter with Hemlock magic, willing it to take the form of a binding spell. The shifter stiffened, his body immobilised. Even then, he continued to shift, scales covering his arms. Those stones, pieces of that Moonbeam—they *forced* the shifters to continue existing.

Another howl echoed through the spirit realm.

"There are more of them." Keir released the shifter's limp body. "We have to find this Moonbeam, whatever it is."

My phone buzzed, jolting me back into my body. "Hey —Isabel. Where are you?"

Her voice was high, panicky. "I'm with Asher. Shifter ghosts attacked him. We're barricaded in the shop."

"Damn. They're attacking everywhere at once," I said. "They stabbed Drake and someone captured Wanda—the shifter ghost I just spoke to said the enemy's using pieces of an object called the Moonbeam. Does Asher know what that is?"

A heartbeat's pause passed. "Yes," Asher's voice said into the phone. "The Moonbeam is an item of legend, which once belonged to the shifters. It went missing a long time ago."

"And like the witch symbols—it's being used against them." I clenched my hands. "You'd think the mages would have known that."

"They do," said Isabel breathlessly into the phone. "Asher—" A pause, while the two of them exchanged words. "Apparently some of the mages once owned the Moonbeam themselves."

The truth sank in, far too late. "Then they knew…"

Someone on the inside was involved. Someone who worked for the mages.

Footsteps sounded, and a shadow appeared behind me. A person-shaped shadow—and not a ghost.

A witch, or someone using a shadow spell.

"Keir!" I ended the call, reaching for my magic, but too late. Neil the mage apprentice appeared, a knife in his hand, and lunged at Keir.

Keir twisted around, but not quickly enough to stop the knife sinking into his side. He staggered forwards, his mouth bleeding, a dark stain spreading across his shirt. As he crumpled to his knees, Neil swung the weapon at his neck.

"Hey!" My Hemlock magic lashed out at Neil, and blood sprayed out. Neil collapsed, the knife dropping to the floor.

I was at Keir's side in a second. He half lay there, limp, drenched in blood. *Healing magic, Evelyn.* Never mind that I'd just signed my own death warrant by attacking Lord Sutherland's son—I couldn't let Keir die.

The wound sealed under my healing hands, glowing grey-green, but Keir's spirit remained diminished even as his body healed. He needed to feed.

Evelyn moved before I did, her arms wrapping around Keir's stunned-looking spirit. He stood rigid, then a blue light kicked in as he began to feed on her. I gaped at both of them, unable to believe it. My stomach twisted at the sight even though I knew full well there was no intimacy between them. Since when did Evelyn care if Keir lived or died?

I turned to the mage apprentice lying dead at my feet. No, not dead. Neil's body was lacerated with wounds, the pavement was drenched in blood, but his eyes were open.

"My father will slaughter you, witch," he gasped.

Lightning flashed, blasting me off my feet. He raised a hand and blasted me again, leaving my body trembling with aftershocks. His eyes gleamed, his face a mask of pain—and he pressed his hand to his mage mark. Summoning his father.

Keir rose to his feet and grabbed him around the neck, draining his spirit in the time it took to blink. Neil collapsed into a bloody heap.

"Idiot," I gasped at Keir. "Now both of us will be in the shit when this is over."

"I'm not letting you face them alone, Jas," he said, his jaw tensing. "They're close. The mages."

"Fuck!" I threw an illusion spell over Neil's inert body, though it wouldn't erase his memory of the attack, and sprinted down the alley—

"Dead end," Keir said quietly.

I skidded to a halt. We were goners.

The air trembled. Then a dark figure appeared behind us in a swirl of icy air, and the alley vanished.

In its place was an empty hotel room with plain beige walls and grey furniture. I staggered against the nearest chair, dizziness sweeping through me. I scanned the room for our rescuer and my gaze snagged on Vance—he'd used his teleporting ability to save our necks.

Problem: his arms were scaled, his hands turned to dark claws.

At my side, Keir tensed and moved into a fighting stance. Vance's eyes, however, were clear. "Jas—are you hurt?"

I shook my head, staring at the unfamiliar beige furniture. "Where are we?"

"Somewhere safe. I'm going after Wanda."

"Wait—do you know where she is?"

He shook his head, his claws gleaming. I couldn't take my eyes off them. He was in his right mind—so he mustn't have run into any of the Moonbeam fragments yet.

"Vance, the person behind this is using bits of the Moonbeam—"

"I know they are," he said. "The mages are a lost cause, but Wanda—if we find her, we find our enemies."

"I can track her," I said. "But there's a chance she might not be in this realm and you won't be able to follow her. Also—Neil Sutherland tried to kill Keir and me, and I had to knock him out. Did you know the mages were compromised?"

Vance's eyes gleamed with anger. "I suspected as much," he said. "There was no way for me to prove it—I'm not a member of the local council and I'm treading a thin line with my own shifter abilities. I put measures in place to make sure the enemy can't get near me, but there's a limit, and they've targeted my weak spot."

Wanda. He cared for her like a younger sister.

"Where's Ivy?" I asked. "She can travel between realms, like me, and I could use an ally. I don't know what I might find over there." I was also starting to suspect that the enemy had taken Wanda deliberately to target Vance himself. He was part shifter and mage. Had they wanted *him* to take down the Council of Twelve? Nobody else on the council was vulnerable to the Moonbeam's influence.

"I'll call her." Vance pulled his sleeve up, exposing a swirling mage mark of his own. "If you find the Moonbeam—or what's left of it—bring it straight to me, Jas. I already disposed of several of the other pieces."

"Sure, but—how is it not affecting you?"

"These marks have more than one purpose," he said, and the symbol on his arm glowed bright green. "I'll be one moment."

He vanished. Keir barely had time to raise an eyebrow before he reappeared, with Ivy at his side.

Ivy looked at me. "Lead the way, Jas."

18

Ivy and Keir both watched me expectantly. On top of Vance's intense stare, it was fairly intimidating. Not least because Keir hadn't acknowledged that he wouldn't be able to follow us into the liminal space.

Ivy turned to him as though sensing my thoughts. "Can you travel between realms?" she asked Keir.

"I've never tried."

His brother had, though. Was that why he wanted to come?

"I have no idea what's waiting on the other side," I said. "You might get separated from your body."

"I'll risk it." The stubborn set of his jaw warned me not to waste time trying to persuade him.

"Keir, I saved your neck once today. Don't make me watch you die."

I wouldn't say any more with the others there. Ivy moved in to speak to Vance, dropping her voice to whisper in his ear. He shook his head, once, and took her arm, pushing up the sleeve. Sure enough, she wore a mage mark of her own, identical to his.

"If they use one of those stones on Vance, the mark is set to knock him out cold and call me straight to his side," Ivy explained, seeing me looking. "All right, let's move."

I sat in one of the armchairs—it didn't matter what position I left my body in, but I'd be sore for a while if I remained standing—and plunged into the spirit realm.

It didn't take long to locate the spirit line. Its grey gleam was visible from here, and my late-night adventures in Death had made it easy to track. I called Wanda's face to mind, extending my consciousness in that direction, but found no trace of her.

"A little help, Evelyn?"

Her willowy form appeared at my side. "She's not here."

"Someone is," I said. "The enemy must be on that line— it's the central one, and it was damaged." Pity I couldn't see liminal spaces from this angle. I moved right onto the line until its grey trail was below my transparent feet, and tried to *feel* through, the way I had when I'd entered the forest. I called Hemlock magic to my hands, but still… nothing.

"You need to be on our line to do that," Evelyn said. "I've tried."

I swore. "You're telling me this now? How am I supposed to find Wanda, run around on foot?"

The line went transparent and for a moment, the scene changed to a field, transposed over the city.

And the transparent field was swimming with hellhounds.

"Ah," said Ivy.

Evelyn made a sharp noise of impatience. "Ignore them."

All the hellhounds' eyes turned to us. I stiffened, ready to fight.

"They can't harm us," Ivy said, though she didn't sound certain. "Not when we're ghosts."

"Want to risk that?" I felt my Hemlock magic bubbling below the surface, but if I struck first, they'd swarm us.

Keir moved to my side. "My vampire abilities won't work on creatures like them. They're closer to dead than living, magically speaking."

Ivy raised her glowing sword. "Go," she told the hellhounds. "Go back to Faerie or taste my blade."

To my surprise, their eyes all snapped to her.

"I'll handle them," said Ivy.

"How? There are a hundred of them, easily."

She waved her sword, which glowed with blue light. Magic... the power of an Ancient. They followed the movement as though hypnotised. "Trust me, I've got this."

The hellhounds were connected with her in some way? Ivy wasn't out of surprises. But we were down one ally and hadn't even found Wanda yet.

I backed away from the spirit line. "Keir, can you grab a vessel and have a look around near the key points?"

"I can, but vessels can't see key points."

I made a low noise of frustration. "I suppose if we look for the Moonbeam first, we might find Wanda too. I'll bet they must be keeping what's left of it somewhere nobody can get at." I'd been so certain that I'd be able to find the enemy as a ghost, but Edinburgh was riddled with places which might hide liminal spaces. Searching the city would take hours.

"The Moonbeam," said Keir. "You know—I have heard the name before, a few years ago. I'd forgotten."

"From your brother?" I guessed.

He inclined his head. "I wish I could remember what he said. But I do know one thing… he used to say our gifts originally came from the gods. They're the origin of our powers."

"Gods," I said, staring at him. "You don't think…?"

"Maybe that's why they took him," he said. "Maybe we're like the shifters. Not direct descendants, but close enough. I mean, we can't be affected by the Moonbeam, I don't think, but it's been stuck in my head for a while."

"Fascinating," said Evelyn, appearing at my side. "There's only one way to get through this spirit line—call someone on the other side."

"Evelyn, what are you talking about?"

She didn't respond, floating forwards until she stood directly on top of the line. Her hands glowed with magic. Mine did, too. *What the hell is she doing?*

The glow brightened and spread through her transparent form until every inch of her glowed.

"Evelyn, I really don't think—"

"They will notice me," she said, and her magic ripped down the spirit line.

The vibration sent me reeling backwards, but Keir caught my hand before I went spinning off into space. Magic rippled the air, turning it silver green.

"EVELYN!"

The world faded to grey, and I blinked back into my body.

Ice cracked on my knees as I lurched to my feet from

the armchair in the hotel room. Vance's gaze immediately went to Ivy, who sat in the other armchair.

"She's holding off the hellhounds," I told him, my head spinning. What the hell was Evelyn thinking, making a public display like that? Was she trying to get both of us killed? "Sorry. We didn't find Wanda, or the person pulling the strings."

Keir jumped to his feet and ran to the window. "What the hell is happening out there?"

I hurried over. Behind him, the sky burned purple-red, vivid and sharp. ""Oh... my god." *Evelyn... what have you done?*

Vance briefly glanced that way. His hands had started to gleam with black scales again. "Who is Evelyn?"

I gaped at him. I hadn't spoken aloud, right?

"You shouted her name before you woke up," he said. "Well?"

I closed my eyes, my body trembling. Let's face it, if my attacking Neil wasn't enough for a death sentence, Evelyn setting loose a hail of magic on a spirit line would be.

Opening my eyes, I faced Vance. "Evelyn is my ancestor. The Hemlocks preserved her spirit beyond death, but she has a mind of her own. I don't know what she did to the spirit line, but she seems to think it'll help us get to Wanda."

Vance shifted his gaze to Ivy, then back to me. "I suppose Lady Harper knew," he said, each word precise, deceptively calm. "I suspected that the person manipulating the mages and shifters intended to use me to bring them down, but not that you'd help them do it."

Oh, god. "She's not on their side, and neither am I," I

said. "She's on the Hemlocks'—well, her own side. We're not the enemy. The Soul Collector didn't die by accident —we killed him. Together."

His eyes simmered. Oh, boy.

"Look, you must know why I couldn't tell the mage council she existed," I said quickly. "I need her magic. If we're sentenced to death, the Hemlocks go extinct and we lose the war with the Ancients."

"That explains Lady Harper's fixation, then," he said, stalking towards me. His hands were clawed, his arms scaled, and the air stirred with menace.

"If you lay a hand on her, I'll kill you first," Keir said.

"Oh, for crying out loud." I turned to Vance, exasperated beyond measure. "Leave Evelyn to do her thing. You can't touch her when she's nowhere near my body. Kill *me*, and both of us will haunt you to death. That clear?"

I didn't *want* to leave Evelyn to do her own thing. She'd been so convinced there'd be a war that she'd made it an inevitability. Then again, so had the mages.

Vance narrowed his eyes. "If you have brought about Wanda's death, I will see to it that you regret it for the rest of your existence. Tell me where to take you."

I cast my mind around, thinking hard. "Isabel's in trouble, too. Asher knew about the Moonbeam. Can you take us to the witch market?

If Wanda was on the spirit line, I'd have seen her, so the enemy must have taken her elsewhere. I'd go back for Evelyn later, one way or another, but not before I saved my friends.

Vance moved closer to Keir and me, and in an instant, the hotel room disappeared. The next second, the three of us landed the cobbled street just down from the narrow alley leading to Asher's shop. Before I could open my mouth to speak, Vance had disappeared.

"With friends like yours, who needs enemies?" said Keir, scowling after him.

"Don't you start," I said. "Wouldn't you be pissed off if I got one of your friends kidnapped, even unintentionally? Besides, I never should have let Evelyn anywhere near that spirit line. I don't even know what she did to it."

The sky was still burning red and purple, with flashes of black like ripples of darkness against the clouds. Throughout the witch market, people gasped, staring up at the apocalyptic visual overhead.

Keir hissed in alarm and grabbed my arm, pointing at a group of figures walking jerkily through the market. "The dead. There are more of them."

Shit. Please say Isabel and Asher are okay.

I grabbed a knife, hoping that I could still use my Hemlock magic with Evelyn absent. Keir grabbed his own knife, but his vampire powers wouldn't function against the reanimated dead. It was all on me.

Unlike the first witch we'd encountered, these ones were more obviously dead. Their clothes were torn, their skin streaked with blood and marked with symbols— crudely drawn, as though the person who'd created them had been in a rush. Now they formed a monstrous army even a necromancer would have trouble putting down.

As the group moved closer to the alley's entrance, I hurled an explosive spell, pushing some Hemlock magic into it. The blast knocked the zombies into one another, and several fell over. Keir was there a second later, stabbing at one of the fallen zombies, but the dead man rolled over with surprising speed, aiming a vicious uppercut.

Keir deflected the blow with his forearm, his eyes widening. "He's too fast. They're under another spell."

"Crap." I called my Hemlock power, whipping at the oncoming dead. Limbs fell, severed, and screams rose as the shoppers in the market scattered, fleeing the dead and the glowing power pouring from my hands.

Even as I cut them down, the army of the dead still moved too fast. They weren't just marked with *control* symbols—their creator had given them super-speed, too. Not only were they as impervious to pain as any undead, no vampire could drain them either. The perfect weapons.

Not enough to outdo my magic, though.

A whipcord appeared in my hands once again, yanking an undead man off his feet. Keir kicked him down as he tried to rise, and a scream ripped through the spirit realm. Not a ghostly howl, but a psychic's shout.

Mackie?

19

Another undead lunged at me, but Lloyd got there first. He kicked the undead in the knees, causing it to pitch forwards, then swept its legs out from underneath it.

"Need help, Jas?" Lloyd said. Morgan came running up, with Mackie behind them.

"What are you doing out here?" I asked in disbelief. "I thought you were at the guild."

"Saving your neck," Mackie said. "I screamed, and it stopped the shifter ghosts from spawning for a bit. Finally found something they're not immune to."

"Damn, good thinking." I backed away from the zombies, towards the cobbled alley between shops. "Asher and Isabel are holed up in his place. The dead are hunting them—"

"She's not there," Keir said. "Or him. The shop's empty."

My stomach dropped. "I should have come straight here."

I ducked into the alleyway, finding Asher's shop door open, blood splattering the entryway. *Isabel. No.*

An undead lurked in the doorway. This one was barely marked, the only clue about his undead nature indicated by the lack of a soul when I tapped into the spirit realm. Keir struck first, throwing the dead man over his shoulder into the wall, exposing the marks on his neck and collarbone.

I clenched my hands. "Hold that bastard still. I'm gonna try to find his master."

Keir hauled the undead to his feet, pinning the dead man's arms behind his back. "Really hope you know what you're doing, Jas."

Yeah, me too.

The *control* symbol was visible on the dead man's collarbone, and I pressed my hand to the mark, feeling for the magic inside it. White-hot power surged against me, my hand burned with pain, and I recoiled. "Ow. Hang on."

I tapped into my Hemlock magic, holding my hand inches from the mark without touching it this time. Power lapped against my palm, sharp and hostile. *Think, Jas.* I'd tracked a zombie once before, to find Keir, but that had been a regular undead without any sinister witch marks.

All right. Drawing in a breath, I tapped into the spirit realm. While this zombie might not have blue threads connecting to its summoner, it wasn't possible to raise one of the dead without leaving a trace.

Rather than Hemlock magic, I called necromantic power to my fingertips and pushed it towards the dead man, demanding that he rise and obey me.

Magic whipped at me in retaliation and I quickly drew

on my Hemlock power, forming a shield between me and him. Keir struggled, holding the dead man still as his body vibrated with the power humming inside the glowing mark on his collarbone.

My teeth clenched, rattling with the clash of magic against magic.

"Take me to your master!" I yelled, throwing everything I had at that twisted mark—necromancy and witchcraft both. The dead man writhed, Keir tightening his grip.

Then the mark began to bleed, thin rivulets streaming down the dead man's chest. Keir released him, and the body decayed before my eyes—bones protruding, skin sagging. A foul smell emanated from the corpse, and I coughed.

Keir stared down at the rotting body. "Jas, what did you *do?*"

"I think I broke the witch mark. He's just a vessel now."

Which meant I could control him.

I shoved necromantic power at the corpse, and said, "Take me to the one who raised you."

The undead jerked upright, staggering to his feet. I held my breath at the foul smell, following the zombie uphill, out of the alley.

Lloyd and the others all stared when Keir and I emerged from the alley behind the zombie.

"This guy will take us to the enemy," I said. "You guys… how are you even here? I thought you were with the guild."

"We've been chasing those shifter ghosts," Morgan said.

"Then we heard about the zombies," Lloyd added. "I thought you or Isabel might be at the market."

"She's—gone. They took her." My throat closed up. I didn't want to lead the others into danger either. Even on the slim chance that we escaped alive, the others might be arrested for helping me when the mages caught up to us.

The zombie fell sideways, his rotting legs barely supporting him. I yanked him upright again and followed close behind, with Keir at my side.

"I'll be pissed if he just leads us back to the mage guild," I said. "Wanda's not there, that's for sure."

"The mage guild?" asked Lloyd. "We heard the meeting broke up and someone went missing…"

"The leading Mage Lord is a traitor," I said. "I attacked his son with Hemlock magic, so I'm as good as dead."

His mouth dropped open. "What? You can't be serious."

"I am. It was self-defence, but the mages won't see it that way. Plus, you know, the man in *charge* is the enemy."

"I fucking knew it," Mackie said. "I knew they were all bastards. They'd never help us."

I didn't have the words to reassure her, not when she was dead right. "Lady Montgomery won't stand for their bullshit, but even she can't get me off the hook for an attempted murder charge—" I cut off, realising we'd reached the street where Keir and I had come looking for the Briar Coven. "You've got to be kidding me."

"There's someone living in there," Keir said, jerking his head at one of the houses. "The others are empty."

I ran to the house he'd pointed out and slammed my foot into the door, which bounced off. No surprises—it was warded. Was Wanda behind that barrier? Maybe. We weren't on a spirit line, though—not even close. I pressed my hands to the wall, but my magic didn't respond aside from a faint tremor.

"Hang on," I said. "It must be warded on the inside."

When Isabel and I had been faced with this dilemma before, we'd had to climb in through the window. I doubted I'd be so lucky this time around. Why hadn't I made duplicates of those wall-climbing spells?

Morgan rapped on the door. "Hey, is anyone home?"

"I wouldn't," I warned. "The place is warded on the inside. Let me check the window."

Lloyd was already there. His hands traced the windowsill, and he jumped back. "Ow. Static shock."

I moved to his side and pressed my hands to the glass. My palms tingled with unfamiliar magic, and glyphs swirled behind the darkened glass. I activated one of the spells on my wrist—a destructive spell combined with an unlocking one—and glass shattered, but the wards held. A shimmering barrier met my eyes, covering the whole house, including the broken window.

"Don't touch that!" Keir said, his eyes widening with alarm. "That's not witch magic. It's necromancy."

Sure enough, when I tapped into the spirit realm, the wall of light was there, too. "A spirit barrier?"

"No." He put his hand on my arm, and I felt a tremor under his skin. "I know vampires who use this sort of barrier to protect their vessels. Only the dead can pass, not the living. It's set up via a blood sacrifice."

My throat went dry. "Oh no, we're not sacrificing anyone."

"I'm not keen on being sacrificed, for the record," said Lloyd.

"Not *us*," Keir said. "Nobody who's alive can walk past the barrier at all. Only the dead, and I think he's seen better days." He indicated the dead man, whose legs had fallen to pieces. Bugger.

"Does a vampire count as alive?" asked Mackie.

"Yes," said Keir. "I don't know about shades, but they must have guessed you'd come here."

"Maybe a shade would confuse it," I said. "Could you use a vessel to get in?"

"I think so," he said. "But there are living behind that barrier as well as the dead, and they won't be able to get out as long as the barrier is there."

"Living people?" Crap. The wall of shimmering light in the spirit realm had thrown me, but when I checked again, I did see moving lights behind there. *Isabel? Wanda?*

"Allow me to help you, Jacinda," said a voice, and sharp claws pierced me through the spine.

The pain lasted barely a second before I left my body, floating free into the grey. The others' faces disappeared as the realm of death rose to consume me.

Grey light smothered the world, muting all sound, preventing me from hearing my body hit the ground.

The shifter vanished, leaving me alone in the void.

Ah, crap. I'm dead again?

Slowly, the shimmering barrier came back into focus. This time, there was no resistance. I floated over the barrier and through the wall of light.

The light brightened, dazzling my eyes. Then a room came into focus, below the greyness of the spirit realm, and I gasped.

Dead bodies lay on the bare floorboards, lined up in rows. As I watched, one of them sat jerkily up, crude symbols glowing on his collarbone. He rose to his feet, taking what looked like a permanent marker in his hands, and shuffled over to one of the other bodies. Crouching down, he pressed the marker to the dead man's throat.

If I'd been in my body, I'd have thrown up. Other reanimated corpses moved throughout the room, drawing symbols onto each dead person until they rose, too. The stench of dark magic was overwhelming even on this side of the veil. I floated, unable to look away from the ghastly scene. None of the dead saw me, but then again, they had no spirits to speak of. Someone had set them up to move on autopilot.

As I watched, the undead moved out of the room and into a hallway. I glimpsed a line of them queuing by the house's back door. So that's where the army was coming from.

I have to slow them down. It wasn't like I could actually touch anything, though. I was dead, and when my body revived, I'd probably be yanked onto the other side of the barrier again.

I called on my Hemlock magic, my hands glowing with faint green light.

"That won't do any good," whispered a voice. It was quiet, raspy, and didn't come from any of the dead. I couldn't tell *where* it came from. Not the spirit realm, either.

"Who are you?" I asked of the room. "Dead, alive, related to me? Give me a clue here."

"I am the Whisper," said the voice, which sounded cold, and vaguely feminine. "I walk free, and I hear the call of my brethren."

My non-existent blood iced over. "You're an Ancient."

"They once called us gods, and we remember even now."

"Good for you," I said, unable to hide the tremor in my voice. "Any reason you're collecting dead bodies? Or why you're using witch magic instead of your own?"

"Our magic was stolen from us," rasped the Whisper's voice, which seemed to echo from all the corners of the room. "And you will pay for what you did, Hemlock. We remember."

"Funny story there," I said. "You see, I *don't* remember. Whatever my ancestors did, I wasn't even alive then. I'm not really alive now."

My hands glowed brighter. Screw this. I'd unleash everything I had and blow the doors off this place, bringing down the Ancient's twisted army before they could overrun the city.

"If you use that magic, they die," rasped the voice.

Two heads rose as though their names had been called —Isabel and Asher.

No.

The faint glowing from their bodies told me they were alive, but their hands moved jerkily, wielding the same tools the others did.

The enemy had forced both of them to use dark magic against their will.

"You sick fuck," I snarled. "Show yourself, if you have a body or spirit to show."

"They took my body and mind," the Whisper said. "They destroyed my soul, but part of me broke free. I will not be forgotten."

"You can't have no body *or* spirit," I said to the disembodied voice. *Right?* The Whisper must have something anchoring her here. She couldn't be a voice without a spirit.

The spirit world began to distort. My body must be reviving, which meant I wouldn't be able to stay in here. But Isabel and Asher—

"Isabel, I'm coming!" I shouted to her. "I'll help you get out of here."

"You will never save her, Jacinda," said the Whisper. "Your friend told me all about you… it seems I have you to think for my revival. You awakened the spirit line."

My heart dived. When I'd banished the Soul Collector, she must have escaped. Like him, she was able to influence people without having a body of her own. And like him, I was immune to her power, but my friends weren't.

The spirit realm flickered. The last thing I saw was a great shimmering mirror at the back of the room of corpses, gleaming with silvery light. Then I blinked back into my body, lying on my back on the pavement. "Dammit!"

"Jas?" Keir leaned over me. "Jas—did you get inside?"

I pushed up onto my elbows. "I did. The enemy has Isabel and Asher. They're being forced to raise those zombies with blood magic. But I didn't see Wanda, nor anyone else."

Lloyd swore. "They're forcing Isabel… that's fucked up. Who's doing that to them?"

"Another Ancient, called the Whisper." I rested a shaking hand against the wall, staggering to my feet. "She claims she has no body. Or a spirit. But she has them under her control and I don't know how to undo it."

"No body or spirit?" Keir said. "That's not possible."

"This is the Ancients we're talking about," I said. "She's

not possessing people like the Soul Collector or a psychic, but she has some kind of hold over them. Not the stones —I didn't see any of them in that room." A sick taste filled my mouth. Isabel didn't deserve to be the puppet of a maniac I'd set free. And I hadn't seen Wanda at all.

"Are you sure you didn't see anything else in there?" asked Lloyd.

"Before I came back, I saw some kind of giant mirror," I recalled. "Otherwise, a load of bodies and that's it."

Mackie cleared her throat. "I screamed and scared that shifter off, but I bet he's still around if you wanna make him talk."

"He killed me on purpose," I said. "To get me over the barrier. But he wouldn't have known I could come back, right?"

Or would he? It wasn't like I could hide my shade nature in the spirit realm.

"We can summon him," Keir said. "But he's likely to attack us again. If he did know you'd survive, Jas, then maybe he's trying to fight the enemy's control."

"Maybe," I acknowledged. "He tried to warn me off before, when he told me the Moonbeam was in pieces. But I don't think… I don't know if he can help us. We know where the enemy is, we just can't reach them."

"We don't know where the Moonbeam is," Keir added. "Maybe with Wanda…"

"Why'd they take Wanda?" asked Lloyd.

"To get hold of Vance, I think," I said. "He's part shifter —and on the mage council. He and Ivy anticipated their plan, but they're counting on him being desperate enough to take the risk. Imagine what the mages will do if one of the founders of the Council of Twelve attacks them."

"Damn," said Lloyd. "Their whole council will fall to pieces, right?"

"If it hasn't already." I swallowed. "The Moonbeam, or what's left of it… maybe if I had a piece of it, I'd be able to track it."

Assuming my magic didn't blow it sky-high.

"What, this thing?" said Morgan, pulling a piece of stone from his pocket.

20

"Where'd you get that?"

Morgan shrugged and passed me the stone. It was cool to touch, humming with power beneath the surface. Maybe not unbreakable, if it was a splinter of a larger stone, but impervious to my magic. Hemlock power brushed against it, and the stone hissed, steam rising from the surface.

"We found it in the street," explained Mackie. "Near those zombies."

"Speaking of zombies," Keir said, "I'll grab a vessel and see if I can get it past that barrier, but I can't guarantee those zombies won't swarm me if I go in there."

"Shifter incoming!" Lloyd warned.

The air shimmered, and a ghostly figure appeared, hands sheathed in claws.

Crap. Had the stone drawn him here?

I gripped the stone, brandishing it. "Hey," I said. "Stop."

The stone glowed bright... and the shifter halted, his

gaze on the stone. His expression was glazed, his transparent form still.

So it's true. The stone could control shifters, but it could be wielded by anyone. Even me.

Now to test my second theory.

I held the glowing stone high, and the shifter's gaze followed it as though hypnotised. "Tell me," I said. "Is Wanda somewhere in there? The female mage your people took? She's about my age. Ring any bells?"

"She..." The shifter's voice was slurred. "She has the mage. The mage is with her."

"Her?" I echoed.

"The witch," the shifter said, his voice fading in and out. "Find the witch. The witch can stop this..."

"What witch?"

The shifter howled, an ear-splitting noise, raising his hands. Claws formed, scales creeping up his arms. "Stop. Please... end this torment, necromancer."

He howled again, his form flickering, madness and fear colliding on his expression. My stomach twisted, and I squeezed the stone tight. In my other hand, I called the power of the veil.

"I banish you," I said to him. "I banish you beyond the gates of Death."

Keir joined me, his voice rising alongside mine. "I banish you, Vaughn Sanderson."

The shifter howled again, but his body was fading, and the shape of Death's gates appeared behind him. In a blink, he was gone.

I turned the shard of stone over, my heart pounding. "Damn... I don't think he was going to tell us anything else, but that's some twisted magic this thing has." The pieces of the Moonbeam entirely took away the shifters' free will. "Lloyd, Mackie—can one of you tell Lady Montgomery and the other necromancers that the only way to stop the shifters' ghosts attacking is to use those stones and banish them?"

"Sure." Lloyd pulled his phone out of his pocket. "Anything that gets rid of those ghosts… but who has the rest of the stones?"

"The mages," I said. "If they aren't behind this, they've definitely known how to banish them for longer than we have. When the necromancers are done with the stones, they should hand them over to…" I faltered. Who could even be trusted now? "Anyone who isn't Lord Sutherland. Lady Montgomery, maybe."

"My vessel is on the way," Keir said, his eyes glowing faintly. "It should be able to get through that barrier."

"Be careful," I said. "The Whisper… I don't know how, but part of her seems to be in that room. I don't know if she'll see you cross the barrier. She said she had no body or spirit, but she knew I was there."

"All right," he said. "The worst she can do to me is stop the vessel or turn it against us. But your friends…"

"I know." I scowled at the sealed barrier. "I should be able to get in if I just leave my body behind… maybe if I possessed someone."

Keir shook his head. "You can't go deeply into a vessel the way a vampire can, Jas. Not to the extent that you become the same person."

"It's that or die again." Wait—Evelyn might be able to confuse the barrier. She actually *was* dead, shade or not. "Wanda's in there somewhere, the shifter's ghost said."

He'd also said to find the witch, whoever it was. I wished I'd asked more questions before banishing him.

An undead man shambled up behind us, Keir looking through his eyes. The vessel moved on towards the door to the abandoned house, pausing beside the barrier. "I'm going in."

"Evelyn!" I tapped into my magic fiercely, drawing her in. "Evelyn, possess me."

"Excuse me?"

I jumped as she appeared at my side. "You were already there?"

"Where else would I be?"

"I thought you were still breaking the spirit line. No, wait—don't go. Only dead people can pass that barrier. Does that include you?"

Her eyes glittered. "Yes, it does. If you're willing to totally break the connection."

Am I? No question. Isabel was in there. I had to get her out.

I nodded frantically. "Do it."

Evelyn looked into my eyes, the hint of a smile at her lips. Then I was gone, pushed out of my body with such ease that I was sure she'd been waiting for this opportunity.

My body moved, joining Keir's vessel, and reached through the spirit barrier for the door handle.

As for me, I floated behind. Alive, bound to my body, but no longer part of the waking world.

The barrier opened immediately, allowing Keir's vessel and Evelyn to walk through, but resistance pressed me back when I tried to follow. I gritted my teeth, pain ripping through me. *Ow. I guess I'm too alive this time.*

The view within the house was as horrifying as before. The dead stood in a line in the hallway, skin etched with bloody symbols. Where had the enemy found them? Had they rounded up people off the streets? Whatever the case, I'd bet they hadn't come willingly.

"Evelyn, get Isabel out of harm's way," I called, floating right up against the barrier so I could see through to the room on the other side. "Then bring that barrier down."

"Really?" the Whisper's voice rang out. "Are you sure you want to risk that, Jacinda?"

Isabel moved into the light. She held a scalpel in her hand, her expression blank as she pressed it against her wrist. Evelyn would never reach her in time.

"Stop!" I shouted.

Cursing, I scanned the room for signs of Wanda. But aside from the dead, the only visible object in the room was the shimmering mirror at the back. It seemed to shine from within, white light flickering under the surface. Not unlike the pieces of enchanted stone…

Evelyn spotted the mirror, too, moving in that direction. The Whisper remained silent, but I tensed.

"Careful," I hissed, one eye on Isabel.

Keir's vessel moved in behind Evelyn, following her, but she already had her hands on the mirror.

The silvery surface shimmered under her touch—and her hand went *through* it.

I gasped aloud, an unbearable *tugging* sensation ripping at my spirit. Keir's vessel grabbed for Evelyn's hand, but they were already falling—disappearing into the mirror.

In the same instant, so did I.

Murky greyness filled my vision. Then it cleared,

revealing fog surrounding the top of a hillside. More rolling hills appeared silhouetted against the fog, too distant to reach.

Where in hell are we? The scenery looked like a countryside smothered in fog and silence. I floated above my body, my head spinning in confusion.

Keir swore quietly. "I don't think we're on Earth. I think we're... somewhere else." It was weird hearing Keir's voice coming from the dead man's mouth, but not as weird as watching Evelyn inside my body, crouching down in the grass.

"Evelyn, what are you doing?"

Footsteps crunched. The fog cleared a little beneath the vessel's feet, showing pieces of glittering white rock.

A large rock, broken into fragments.

"The stones," Keir said. "We came in here through the pieces of Moonbeam stone. I guess affecting shifters isn't their only power."

"What?" I turned on the spot, hovering above the hillside, but there was no sign of the mirror we'd come from. Another crunching noise drew my attention to the fragments of gleaming stone. They shimmered, reflecting the cloudy sky—and for a moment, an image of the room we'd left behind appeared in one of the largest fragments.

The stones and the mirror formed some kind of two-way portal to nowhere.

As it hit me, sensation rushed back so abruptly I sat down on the damp grass, back in my body. Evelyn had gone. The devious witch had abandoned me here.

"Jas?" Keir asked.

"Right here. Evelyn's gone walkabout again." I climbed

to my feet, scanning the rippling hillside. "Guess this is the Whisper's secret bolt hole. Seems empty."

Mostly fog and broken stones, by the look of things. This place might be a liminal space or the Ancient realm or even just the Scottish countryside—until we found a landmark, we wouldn't know.

I squinted into the fog, spotting something large and blocky further along the hilltop. "Aha. Civilisation."

I took the lead, Keir's vessel behind me, and approached the fog-smothered construction. A stone building came into view, weather-worn and overgrown with weeds.

"Bit run-down for a hideout," I commented. The eerie silence gave me the serious creeps. What could possibly have broken that shifter's stone? And why leave the pieces here?

Keir reached the small wooden door first and kicked it open. The space within was bigger than I'd expected—a huge cathedral-like space with a high ceiling supported by stone pillars.

Someone was tied to one of the towering pillars, a man with long dark hair and his eyes closed as though in a deep sleep.

Keir made a choked noise. His vessel swayed on the spot.

"Keir? What is it?"

"He—" He broke off, his gaze fixed on the man. "He's my brother. He's Aiden."

"*What?*" I stiffened at his side, staring into the cathedral. "How can—how can he be here?"

"I don't understand." Keir's vessel stepped into the hall, and the floor lit up as several symbols flared up along the edge. A barrier rose, semi-transparent and shimmering, stopping us from taking another step.

Then I spotted the second prisoner, tied to the opposite pillar. Wanda.

"What are you doing with her?" I shouted into the otherwise empty space. "What the hell are you playing at, Whisper?"

"Insurance." Her voice spoke from behind my shoulder. "The Mage Lord will come here. When the mages fall, I will gain what I desire."

The Mage Lord… she meant Vance. "He's not going to come," I told her. "He saw through your trick. You're working with Lord Sutherland, aren't you?"

"If the mage does not come, then the girl will die."

I threw myself against the barrier's edge, pain bruising my arms. Hemlock magic roared to the surface, lighting my hands in grey-green, and I hurled it at the barrier. The magic fizzled out on contact, sending sparks dancing across the floor. I couldn't leave Wanda behind—but I'd bet the barrier was the same as the other. Only the dead could pass it.

Keir's vessel slammed into the barrier. Maybe not. "Let me through," he snarled at the Whisper. "Or so help me—"

"You're nothing," she whispered. "Both of you."

Keir made a choked noise. His vessel collapsed, the light vanishing from his eyes.

"Keir!" I turned on the spot, and my pocket lit up with a white glow. The stone. I pulled it out, and the glow engulfed me. Reflections of the room full of zombies danced before my eyes. Maybe the individual pieces could act as portals, too.

My gaze snapped back to Wanda, my heart torn. *I can't leave her.*

The stone's glow brightened, and I screwed up my eyes, my grip slipping on the stone. I fell forward, and stumbled out of the mirror onto the damp floor of the abandoned house.

Chaos reigned. Zombies toppled into my path as though felled by an invisible weapon, their bodies falling to pieces as they stood—symbols and all. *What the hell is going on?*

The Whisper screamed in rage, her anger reverberating through the room. My head pounded. "Hey. Keir, where are you?"

"Jas, get over here!" Lloyd shouted.

I spotted him grinning at me from the other side of the shattered window. "What did you do?"

"Salt," he said triumphantly. "Turns out the barrier can't keep it out, and even specially enhanced zombies don't stand a chance against salt. Let's see what that piece of shit does with no army."

Another zombie fell across my path, his body dissolving. The zombies were falling to bits, even the most preserved ones. I'd spent so long thinking of ways to out-magic the enemy that it hadn't occurred to me that there might be a more mundane solution after all.

I turned back to Lloyd. "How'd you know that would work?"

"Morgan's guess," Lloyd said, nodding to the psychic standing just behind him. "We figured there must be a vulnerability somewhere. They're still undead, after all."

"Exactly," said Morgan, looking pleased with himself.

"They might be in stasis or whatever, but they're as dead as any old zombie."

"We figured we could be of use while you were off saving the day," added Lloyd.

"Not sure I've saved anything, to be honest," I said, my heart twisting. "Wanda's trapped behind a mirror in… in another realm, I think. The mirror's a sort of portal. Is Keir back in his body?"

"We have to get back there," Keir said, moving into view. "Jas—can you get out?"

"Ah." I took a step towards the window and the barrier pushed me back. "I can't get out. Evelyn's gone."

She'd left me stuck behind the barrier.

21

I swore and kicked out, but my foot bounced off the barrier. I was trapped in a room full of zombies and the Whisper.

"Really funny, Evelyn." I turned around, peering into the room. "Hey there, Whisper. Mind letting me out?"

Silence. Her screaming had stopped, too. Bits of dismembered zombies littered the floor, Isabel and Asher stood at the side, looking on blankly.

"Uh… Isabel?" I peered at her. Her gaze was out of focus, but she held a salt canister in her hands.

"I had a zombie give it to her," Lloyd explained. "I think she had just enough awareness left to use it."

"But she's still under the Whisper's control." I peered into Isabel's eyes and saw no flicker of recognition. "Evelyn, where are you?"

"Right here," she said, at my shoulder. "I thought you wanted to rescue your friend."

"You know perfectly well nobody alive can pass through the barrier," I told her. "Get me out of—"

A heavy object crashed into my skull. Eyes watering in pain, I staggered to face Isabel, who'd hit me over the head with the salt canister.

"What the hell?"

Isabel's gaze remained blank, but her hands glowed with bright, unfamiliar symbols. They warped, twisting, changing, and lashed out at me like a physical force. I flew back into the wall, pain rippling through my skin. *Ow.* So that's how it felt to have another coven leader's magic used against you.

"Isabel!" I gasped. "It's me, Jas."

Dark symbols glowed on her hands, lashing at me again. I dodged, cursing. I didn't want to hurt her. The Whisper was probably watching and laughing at us right now, though she'd gone awfully quiet.

"Heads up!" yelled Lloyd from behind the barrier. A spell sailed over my head, hitting Asher in the face as he crept up on me from behind. The knockout spell went off, and he fell unconscious.

"Cheers, Lloyd." I ducked another blow from the salt canister, my head throbbing with pain. *Sorry, Isabel.* Grabbing a knockout spell from my own wrist, I threw it in Isabel's face. She fell flat on her back, unconscious.

"Sorry," I said to her, my stomach turning over at the sight of those awful symbols on her hands.

"Can't you get those marks off, Jas?" Lloyd shouted from outside. "She must still have her own coven marks underneath them."

Yeah. She does. The Whisper must have shut them down.

I crouched down, taking Isabel's hand in mine. Her skin glowed with marks like tattoos, but which swirled and moved like a living force. Carefully, I held my palm over the symbols. Then, like with the zombie, I pushed my own magic into them.

Magic sizzled from my hand to hers, warping the symbols and turning them into bloody smudges. I swiftly moved to the next one, then a spark of magic answered. Isabel's eyes flew open, and light ignited under her skin in the form of silvery marks. They spread, her magic mingling with mine, until they reached the mark on her collarbone. The *control* mark, which forced her to serve the enemy.

Our combined magic swamped the mark, twisting it beyond recognition. As it faded out, a wordless scream of rage rang out, and I dropped her hand, recoiling.

"Whisper?" I asked into the silence. The scream had come from the *mark*.

Was that where the Whisper was hiding?

Isabel groaned. The silver marks flickered and went out, and she crawled towards Asher. "Help him," she whispered. "Help him, then get out, Jas—you have to stop her."

Isabel's eyes slid closed and she slumped to the floor again. She'd used all the power she had to break the Whisper's control.

I won't let it go to waste.

I moved to Asher next, using my Hemlock power to remove his symbols, too. When I reached the mark on his collarbone, a hiss of anger echoed from the mark.

The Whisper… was she in the symbols? The blood magic? Was that how she'd survived without a body or spirit?

I left Asher and Isabel unconscious, pacing back to the door. "I think I know what form the Whisper takes," I told the others. "She exists *inside* the blood magic symbols. I heard her scream when I destroyed them."

"You destroyed…" Lloyd trailed off. "Shit, Jas. There must be hundreds of zombies already out there. Can you destroy all of them?"

"She can't be in all of them at once," I said, though anything was possible where the Ancients were concerned. "Did the Whisper say anything to you when I was gone? Anything that might hint at her true form?"

"Nope," said Morgan.

"She's pretty weak," Mackie put in. "She has to use a proxy for everything. She's not like the Soul Collector—she can't even link mind to mind."

"She's still dangerous, though," I reminded her. "She can make witches do her bidding with a single symbol. And she can't be killed."

"She must have her spirit preserved somehow," Keir said. "Maybe—the original symbol used to summon her, if it was a ritual."

"It's not in here." Every symbol in this room was gone, burned out. "The enemy must have another base. I don't think she was behind that mirror either…"

"Summon another shifter and ask?" Lloyd suggested.

I recalled the shifter's words. "Someone summoned *her* to begin with," I said. "A witch. Probably a living one… Evelyn, now would be a fine time to tell me your plan." Other than start a war, that is.

I expected a reprimand or a sarcastic comment.

Not a dragon.

22

A tremendous roar came from outside. I jerked back, out of my body, and Evelyn stepped in, taking control. While I floated on the spot, reeling, my body jumped through the broken window and into the street.

"Hey!" I yelled at Evelyn. "Isabel's stuck back there, you selfish—"

A second roar drowned out my words, and a huge shape blotted out the sky, wings spread wide across the darkening clouds. A huge *scaled* body.

"Evelyn, what the unholy fuck did you do?"

The dragon was bright red, its huge body casting a shadow over the peaked roofs. A tongue of flame leapt from its mouth, setting the clouds ablaze, and I jumped back, smashing into the barrier. Ow. Evelyn had left and I was back in my body again.

Lloyd muttered a prayer under his breath. "If anyone needs me, I'll be playing dead."

"Likewise," Morgan said.

"It's not an Ancient," Evelyn said from beside me.

"Wow, I feel so much better." I clutched my chest, dizzy from the abrupt body-switching. "It's a *descendant* of the Ancients, then. You know, like the shifters *killing* people. Can you imagine that thing under the thrall of the Moonbeam? If it isn't already?"

"It isn't," said Evelyn. "And yes, it's a dragon shifter. Luckily, she came to help us."

"Lucky?" I shook my head at the huge majestic scaled shape in the sky. "That, Evelyn, is a monster. It's as likely to kill us as anyone else. Moonbeam or none."

The dragon released a jet of fire which brushed the tops of the nearby houses, and I threw up my hands. "Seriously!"

"It's coming this way!" Mackie yelped.

The dragon flew overhead, not so much as glancing down at us puny humans below. It must be seven feet long, easily, and those tent-like wings made it even more massive. But it was the flames that poured from its mouth into the street that made me certain that I looked upon my own death. I ducked my head, and Keir grabbed my arm. "It's not aiming for us. Look."

I lifted my gaze. The flames had soared right over our heads and crashed into the alley beside the empty house. Decaying zombies tumbled out of the alley, disintegrating, and the smell of burning flesh caught in the back of my throat.

"It's only burning the dead?" Lloyd said incredulously.

"They are intelligent beings, you know," Evelyn said. "Dragon shifters don't like the dead any more than we do."

"There's no such thing as dragon shifters," I said stupidly. "Come on, wouldn't we have had some kind of clue that they existed? Like villages being torched, people going missing…"

"Uh, Jas," said Lloyd. "The giant scary menace in the sky proves otherwise. Maybe it's just visiting."

"Where the bloody hell did it come from?" Morgan said.

"Evelyn strikes again," I answered.

What now? Evelyn had conveniently neglected to mention whether or not the Moonbeam could affect that shifter the same as the others. If it could, we'd all burn to a crisp.

The dragon continued to fly, breathing jets of fire at the city below. It was hard to trust Evelyn's word that such a huge and unpredictable creature might be on our side. It was almost as scary as the giant eye I'd seen in the forest.

"Evelyn summoned that thing… why?" Lloyd wanted to know.

"To save your necks," said Evelyn, loudly. "You're welcome."

"Who the fuck are you?" Morgan asked, staring at her ghostly form floating beside me.

Wait—now everyone could see her? "The person who's going to get us all killed," I said.

"Oh, come on," Evelyn said. "I had to do something."

"I'd rather you helped bring down this barrier." I waved a hand at the door. "Not summon a giant fire-breathing death machine."

"Or find the person who summoned the Whisper," Keir said. "Before they lure in the Mage Lord."

Crap. I'd forgotten, in the shock of the dragon's appearance, that Vance was the target. As much as it pained me to leave the others behind, the only way to end this was to find the person who'd summoned the Whisper.

The dragon roared, a thunderous noise that shook the peaked roofs and made everyone dive for cover. If nothing else, Evelyn had manufactured the perfect distraction. Pity it might kill all of us.

"So Wanda's in there?" Lloyd asked. "Behind the barrier?"

"She is," I said. "And obviously Isabel and Asher are there, too. If they wake up, they won't be able to get out, though…"

"And neither will my brother," Keir said quietly.

"What's he talking about?" Lloyd frowned.

"Keir's brother was taken by the Ancients years ago," I said. "We found him held captive in the same place as Wanda."

"Seriously?" Lloyd's eyes bugged out. "And Isabel's stuck in there, too?"

"I helped undo the marks controlling her and Asher," I said. "But she can't get past the barrier, obviously, even if I have Evelyn get back in there again. We need to find the person who made it."

"Someone's coming!" Mackie pointed down the ash-strewn street, where the dragon had dissolved the dead into nothingness.

Several figures approached. Unlike the dead, they walked perfectly steadily, though the glowing symbols on their exposed arms and collarbones spoke for themselves. A brief check of the spirit realm told me they were alive.

Damn. The fire had only hit the dead. Under the symbols, these witches were still alive. Maybe the dragon had a conscience after all, but the Whisper had upped her game. All of the approaching humans wore her symbol, and their expressions were blank, their will taken away.

"Damn." I took a step backwards, but they far outnumbered us.

As one, a dozen witches raised their hands. Magic poured out, serpentine and glowing, the same twisted symbols that Isabel had been forced to use against me.

I called my own magic, forming a shielding spell between them and us. The witches continued to advance, the marks on their skin glowing.

"Guys, they're alive!" Mackie said, her voice high. "We can't—kill them."

"Not without playing into her hands," I murmured. "There are too many. Necromancy doesn't work well on the living. Stand back—"

Two witches moved forwards, hands splayed, and my shield spell rippled. Shit, their power was strong enough to go neck and neck with my Hemlock magic.

"You will never find me," the Whisper said, her voice reverberating in the air. It seemed to come from everyone at once—every witch, every symbol.

My teeth chattered, my body shaking as the wall of magic pushed against me. If I let go, they'd take my friends to pieces.

"Guys, run!" I shouted. "Asher's shop's still open—I bet the place is packed with defensive spells." It was far from ideal, but there were no other safe places close by.

Panic brewed, my body trembling under the assault. I held my ground, drawing on all the Hemlock magic I could conjure. All my rage and fury—I poured it all into the rippling transparent shield.

"You won't harm them," I said through clenched teeth. *"You won't."*

My shield pushed back the witches, blocked the road with a shimmering barrier. The witches' hands pawed at it, but this time, it held steady. It wouldn't last forever, but it'd give us the chance to run. Nobody else would die today.

When I was sure the others were running, I backed away from the barrier, sprinting towards the market. It was far from the heroic thing to do, but the entire witch population of Edinburgh might be under the spell by now. We couldn't stop all of them, even if taking innocent lives was an option.

The five of us pelted down the alley into Asher's shop. The place looked like a tornado had hit it—shelves emptied, spell ingredients in piles, bloodstains on the floor. Isabel and Asher had put up a hell of a fight.

I threw a ward over the door, adding a heavy jolt of Hemlock power, and then backed into the shop, tripping over a half-open book. Beside it was a spell circle, recently deactivated, surrounded by chalked symbols.

"I think they were making a spell," Keir said. "When they were taken."

"Shit, you're right." A half-formed spell lay in the circle. I reached down, my hands still tingling with Hemlock power. "I think it's some sort of explosive."

Keir picked up the worn-looking book, showing me the open pages. Around the faded lines of printed text were drawings of a few symbols. "Are those the same symbols the dead were wearing?"

"No way." I read the text on the page. "No... it's an amplification symbol. They must have been planning to use it on the explosive to make it stronger. What would they need a huge blast for?"

"The barrier?" Keir frowned. "No… with that type of barrier, it requires the person who set it up to undo it."

"Or die," I said. "If we kill the person who made that barrier, would it be destroyed?"

"If it's like other spirit barriers, it would," said Mackie. "I did pay attention in training, believe it or not."

Morgan made a sceptical noise. "Not much help if we don't know where the fucker is hiding."

I read the page more closely. "We don't, but I don't think this spell is meant to be used against a person. It can destroy other spells. Including symbols."

Asher and Isabel had handed us the means of destroying the Whisper. But I had to complete the spell first.

"Come again?" said Lloyd. "Wouldn't you need to kill the witch behind this to bring an end to it? Destroying the symbols wouldn't do any good if the witch can just make more of them."

"True, but the Whisper is *inside* the symbols, somewhere," I said. "I bet this can destroy her, wherever her real form is hidden."

I returned to the spell circle, and one spark of Hemlock magic re-ignited both the circle and the chalk symbols surrounding it. Amplification runes. I *had* seen the symbol before, when Lloyd and I had found a poltergeist in a warehouse what felt like a lifetime ago. The symbols amplified magic, making any spell stronger than before.

"Can someone pass me some marigold leaves?" I asked.

Mackie ran to the nearest shelf to search, while I

reached for the book in Keir's hand. He didn't hand it to me. "Jas, have you read this?"

"Not all of it. Why?"

"Look at that." He pointed at some of the smudged handwriting in the page's corner.

I read the words. Then I reread them. "Oh, hell."

"What do you have to do?" Lloyd said.

"The spell's catalyst is blood. Blood magic. I have to draw the last symbol on myself."

"What?" Mackie surfaced from behind the desk with a handful of leaves. "What spell is that?"

"A spell that can destroy any other magic it comes into contact with. Isabel or Asher thought we'd need it. But… I'd have to tattoo myself."

"Is that what this is for?" Mackie picked up a lid-less pen which'd rolled under the desk. It was about as thick as a permanent marker, but its end glowed faintly.

I reached to take it from her. "This must be one of their tattooing implements. The Orion League's. Or the witches'."

"The what?" Mackie said.

"Before the invasion, there was a group of fanatics who forced the witches to use their magic against the rest of us." I put down the pen beside the spell circle. "The League used to tattoo ordinary humans, apparently, to turn them into supernaturals."

Lloyd swore. "What are you going to do? Mark yourself—like them?"

"If I want to use this spell, I might have no choice." I waved a hand over the simmering circle. "I take it the spell doesn't mention side effects?"

Keir's worried silence spoke for itself. I returned to the

circle, throwing in the ingredients Mackie had handed me. Never mind the laws on blood magic—if this went wrong, I might pull an Evelyn and utterly destroy everything. But Isabel wouldn't have started to make this spell if she'd thought it was too dangerous to use. I trusted her.

The spell circle shimmered brighter, the chalk symbols glowing, and I held my hand out to feed more power into the spell. "Evelyn, I don't suppose you've ever used one of those markers before?"

"Wait, now you're asking for her help?" said Lloyd.

"She's the only witch I know who isn't unconscious or under a spell." Which wasn't promising at all, but what choice did I have?

"No," said Evelyn. "I'd finish that spell before it burns out."

I continued to feed Hemlock power into the amplified circle. Flames leapt and shimmered, the ingredients merging, and becoming one.

"This can destroy the Whisper, right?" I asked.

Evelyn's grey-blue eyes met mine across the circle. "If you can find her."

And I'd need to amplify my own power to stand a chance against her. No less would bring down an Ancient.

"Jas, not that I don't trust you, but you're depending on the word of someone who set a dragon loose," Lloyd said.

"She's distracting the witches, actually," Evelyn said to him. "You're welcome."

"She?" Lloyd shook his head. "The dragon's a she?"

"They're coming!" Mackie yelled.

I grabbed the spell from the circle, and the ward on the door shattered. Keir slammed his foot into the door, knocking the first intruder off his feet. His vampire power lashed out, grabbing the nearest target, but the door flew wide with a blast of magic. The spell hit Morgan, knocking him into the desk. With a cry of fury, Lloyd threw himself at the attackers. His fist flew, and one of the witches reeled back, blood streaming from his nose. They were definitely still alive under the marks.

"Incapacitate them!" I ignored Evelyn's derisive snort, searching the spells on my wrist.

A trapping spell, boosted by my Hemlock power, slammed into the attacking witches. Rippling red lines filled the doorway, trapping two of them.

"Grab all the non-lethal spells you can!" I told the others. "Shields, knockout spells—whatever you can find."

Mackie moved to obey without a fuss, while Morgan staggered to his feet, rubbing the back of his head. Lloyd kicked down the witch he'd been fighting, but he rose to his feet immediately. Keir got there first, his vampire ability draining the man as he stood.

"Please tell me you're applying moderation." I pocketed the spell Isabel had left me and grabbed another shield.

"Can't make any promises," Keir said, tossing another witch over his shoulder into the wall. "He'll have one hell of a headache when he wakes up."

The man Keir had drained jerked to his feet. His eyes were out of focus, but he kept moving, the symbols on his hands glowing. "Uh… Keir. I don't think draining them works."

"Worth a try." His fist flew into the witch's solar plexus, sending him sprawling once again. I threw another trapping spell, catching three witches this time.

Their hands glowed, and the trapping spell strained, its lines fading.

I pushed back, pouring more power into the spell. The symbols glowed brighter, betraying the strain of trying to break the barrier.

"You're wasting your time," the Whisper's voice hissed. "You will all perish…"

"God, shut *up*." Mackie hurled a spell into the nearest witch's face, causing it to erupt in blisters.

I stifled a laugh, climbing over the fallen witches into the alley. The smell of burning caught in the back of my throat, making me cough. The dragon must have started a fire somewhere close, but all I could see was smoke.

"I can't sense the other witches," Keir said.

"Maybe the dragon scared them off." The path up out of the alley was clear, but without any clues as to where the person behind this was hiding, we'd end up running in circles. I reached into my pocket and slipped the new spell I'd made onto my wrist. "Evelyn, do *you* have any idea where the Whisper might be hiding? Is she possessing one of the witches?"

"No," Evelyn said. "She has no body or spirit… she exists only in the symbols."

"It's not possible to put your consciousness into a physical object," said Keir. "Let alone a symbol."

"The Ancients don't do rules," I reminded him. "So this symbol… it must be well-hidden. Not *on* one of the witches."

"It won't be a witch symbol," Evelyn said. "The Ancients had their own language, you know… close to ours in terms of its power, but not the same."

"Shit." The Whisper had implied something about

their own magic being lost, or stolen. But summoning a person required knowing their name. Maybe summoning an Ancient was the same. "It'll be at the ritual summoning site… which must be on a spirit line."

"Not necessarily," Evelyn said. "The spirit lines make it easier to summon beasts from between the worlds, but they're also volatile. Besides, the walls between the worlds are breaking down. I doubt it was hard for her to slip out."

Thanks to us. I pushed the thought away, recalling Ilsa's words when we were on the spirit line. "So this symbol… I guess it's like her talisman in a way."

"Talisman?" echoed Lloyd.

"Faerie thing," said Morgan. "Destroy a talisman and you take out the essence of a Sidhe's magic."

"The Ancients use them, too," I explained. Ivy and Ilsa both had talismans that contained the Ancients' magic. But theirs were static. The Whisper seemed to exist within everyone who bore her mark, as well as her origin point. "The symbol… it's got to be hidden somewhere that's well-protected, and that people won't just stumble across. I guess it's possible for it to be in a liminal space, but I'd have seen it when Ivy found those hellhounds."

Keir shook his head. "There must have been a sacrifice involved. A high surge of magic. It couldn't have happened on a spirit line."

"No…" I trailed off. "Never mind *where*—*who* knows symbols like that? It's not exactly the sort of knowledge you just stumble across."

A heartbeat passed. "It's someone with access to information nobody else has," Keir said, echoing my thoughts. "You already said the mages had been compromised…"

"By their own leader." Crap. "I can't think *why* he'd

summon an Ancient, but he *does* have a team of powerful witches on his side. I've never even met all of them. And he seemed confident he'd be able to protect himself even after he shut the witches out of his meeting..."

Because there was one already in the building.

"Shit, are you sure?" Lloyd said. "The mages summoned that—thing?"

"No, a witch did," I said. "It doesn't matter who—anyone can be controlled against their will, or coerced. Lord Sutherland has enough power that it doesn't matter."

"In that case..." Keir looked at me. "The witch must be hidden *inside* the mages' headquarters."

The air trembled. A blast of wind knocked us backward into the alley, and Vance appeared. His hands were wrapped in claws, and he stalked towards us with murder in his eyes.

23

I tensed, my heart sinking. The witches I'd trapped in Asher's shop would break free in seconds. Death by possessed witch or death by murderous shifter-mage? Not much of a choice there.

"Vance!" I said. "It's me. Jas."

His arms were covered in scales, his grey eyes had blanked out, and the aura of menace surrounding him made me take a step back despite my immunity. I sincerely hoped that as a part-shifter, he didn't have the same paralysing-with-terror power as the Ancients did.

He turned his back on me, stalking forwards, eyes fixed on the horizon.

"Er, Vance, where are you going? Where's Ivy?"

What had happened to Ivy's contingency spell? Wasn't it supposed to knock him out if he ended up under the control of one of those stones?

Speaking of stones... I reached into my pocket. The instant the stone's glow lit up, Vance turned around, his eyes narrowing.

"Hey, Vance," I said, holding the stone up. "I'm asking you to come to your senses."

I didn't quite dare try using magic, but his gaze was fixed on the fragment of stone in my hand. Then he shook his head, lifting a hand. A piece of stone was clenched in his own fist.

"What? You were holding it on purpose?" I blinked in confusion. "I thought you knew the enemy was trying to lure you in."

He gave me a glare, his eyes clearing. "Where is Wanda? You know where she is?"

Ah. "If I tell you, will you teleport us to the—"

"Hey, Vance!" Ivy ran up behind him. "Dammit, she's not here. This is way too risky."

"What *are* you doing?" I asked, lowering my own hand. "Why do you have a piece of that stone?"

"The only way to free the shifters is to move the stones far enough outside the city that they can't affect anyone," Ivy explained. "But he got it into his head that he can use it to track Wanda."

"You won't get to her," I said quickly. "She's behind a barrier that can only be passed by the dead. We're going to find the person who set it up, and we could use a teleporter."

Her eyes widened. "You know who did it?"

"One of the mages' witches," I said. "They summoned an Ancient called the Whisper—she's the one controlling all the witches, alive or dead, through those symbols."

Ivy swore. "And to think the bloody hellhounds were bad enough—where is this Ancient?"

"Inside one of the symbols," I said. "I'm guessing she's

still at the site of the ritual summoning. Is it even possible to use a symbol as a talisman?"

Ivy's mouth fell open. "The Ancients' language contains power. Every word. That's why the Sidhe stole it from them, I think—where is she?"

"I think she's inside the mages' headquarters," I said. "If anyone has access to the knowledge, they do—and they used a witch to summon her."

Ivy swore. "Sounds about right. Vance, we'll get Wanda back once Jas finds this witch. Can you kill her? The Whisper?"

I just nodded, hoping I was right. "What did you do to the hellhounds?"

"They fled from the dragon," she said. "You wouldn't happen to know anything about that?"

"Never mind the dragon. I have to deal with the witch first," I said. "Vance, can you transport us to the mages' place? As close as possible without getting us caught."

A white flash made me jump. Vance spoke through gritted teeth. "There's only so long I can resist. The stones are affecting every shifter within reach."

"I'll stop her first," I said. "Don't go after Wanda yet. The Whisper wants you to turn on us."

"I'll make sure he doesn't," Ivy said. "Jas—are you sure you can handle this?"

"Yes, she can." Keir stepped in behind me. "I'll go with her. Keep the others safe and we'll be back before you know it."

His faith bolstered me, but I shook my head. "Keir, if they catch you, you might lose your freedom."

"I'll risk it." He nodded to Vance. "I'm ready."

"Likewise."

In a rush of air, we landed in a deserted corridor. Vance disappeared a moment later, leaving Keir and me alone. The others wouldn't be happy at being left behind, but Ivy would help them. They'd stay safe. And I'd use my Hemlock magic to end this.

For Isabel, for Wanda, for everyone hurt by the Whisper. And by the Mage Lords.

I tapped into the spirit realm to scan for anyone present in the building. A few mages, stragglers from the meeting, maybe people hiding from the battle. But I didn't know every one of them by spirit sight. "It would help if you could just tell me where the witch is hidden, Evelyn."

"I don't know," she said. "I can't see everything from this view."

"You can see through the spirit realm, can't you?"

She gave me a look. "That's your area, not mine."

Shit, of course. I was a trained necromancer. Evelyn wasn't. She hadn't been present for most of my training, and besides, learning to extend your consciousness to find someone was a skill mostly developed intuitively.

"You can sense me, right? Same principle. Look around. Nobody can see you."

"I'm used to that, funnily enough."

"Ha."

What the hell, I'd had long enough to get used to her. And she'd be my only companion in jail, assuming she didn't leave my body to become a permanent ghost.

I slammed the lid on the thought and reached out my consciousness, searching every corner of the mages' headquarters. The Ancient, if she was here, would be trapped behind a barrier, but it wasn't possible to hide a spell so powerful without side effects. The place was too quiet. Maybe I'd guessed wrong.

"The whole building ought to be trembling," I said to Evelyn.

"Not if the spell is contained." She appeared at my side again. "You don't have much experience with rituals, do you?"

I didn't dignify that with a response. *The spell is contained...* like when I summoned a ghost into a circle of candles, its spiritual energy was contained within. The same principle applied when I used a chalk circle to create a spell. Without it, the raw energy escaped, causing damage to anything it touched.

To hold a god captive would require a hell of a powerful circle. A containment spell, at the very least. And the enemy didn't care what they sacrificed to do it. But *where* was it hidden? The mages' headquarters held no shortage of forbidden rooms and corridors.

Hang on. Their jail was underground, in the dungeons. Aside from a select few trusted individuals, nobody was allowed into the high security area. The place they locked up anyone who practised illegal magic and survived it.

I drove my consciousness down, below the earth. A faint glow caught my attention—barely a blip, but there was definitely something there. Magical. Alive.

"They did the ritual in the dungeon," I said to Keir, returning to my body. "I'm sure of it."

"Whereabouts is the way down?" he said, his face pale.

"Very good question."

Evelyn appeared beside us. "This way. It's warded."

"No shit." I ran after her floating form, Keir at my side. We moved through ornate corridors decorated with the portraits of Mage Lords past. I didn't stop to look at them, though stray thoughts chased through my head. How many of the mages worshipped as heroes had committed crimes as heinous as Lord Sutherland had? How far did this conspiracy stretch? I might be facing a lifetime imprisonment at the very least, but left to their own devices, the mages could do much worse than flood the city with zombies. They could kick-start another war with Faerie.

Finally, we came to a stairway leading down to a metal door covered in wards. My Hemlock magic lashed out, shattering the security as easily as cutting through paper. *They didn't even try.* They didn't need to. Soon, more than soon, they'd be able to do whatever they wanted without any outside interference.

I opened the door, checked Isabel's spell was ready on my wrist, and walked into the dark.

I'd been in the necromancers' dungeon a couple of times, and this place was built along similar lines. The guild rarely arrested anyone, because rogue necromancers tended to die before they could face trial. Here, too, most of the cells were empty. The smell of old wards, magic gone bad, filled the air, borne on an icy breeze.

Evelyn floated alongside me. "There are sealed chambers for magical criminals. This way."

I ran from one door to the next, following her lead. The cells became larger, the doors locked and barred, wards lapping at my Hemlock magic. *I know how to find which it is.*

I pressed my hands to the nearest door, pushing my Hemlock magic at the wards. No reaction. I moved to the next, my heart bouncing against my ribcage.

"Jas." Keir stopped outside one of the sealed doors further down the row. "My spirit sense can't go past this door. Someone's inside."

I moved to his side, reaching out. Even from here, my magic sparked at the feeling of *wrongness* on the other side. The antithesis of my magic.

Evelyn's hands lit up next to me, and she blasted the door with power. I did likewise. Wards sparked. The ceiling lights flickered on and off. My teeth chattered, and Keir swore quietly, taking a few steps backwards.

Break, damn you. Maybe Isabel's spell was intended to be used on the jail door and not the Ancient.

The door cracked open. Magic oozed out like slime, warping grey symbols snapping at my heels.

Evelyn and I pushed back with our combined strength, and the wards on the door snapped like a mousetrap. The door flew wide, revealing the room was covered in symbols, all over the walls and floor. They swam up and down, warping and twisting. *Witch spells.* The Whisper must be hidden somewhere underneath, protected by layers of magic.

Keir shifted behind me. "There *is* something alive in there."

A pair of eyes blinked at me from the wall, from behind the layers of symbols. I jerked backwards. "Crap. She's like the Hemlocks." The witch had been trapped here—ripped out of her body and trapped in her own magic. Now, that same magic fuelled the wards protecting the Whisper.

What kind of sick monster *was* the Mage Lord? He'd had her held captive beneath our feet the whole time, unable to escape.

The symbols on the walls warped and twisted, becoming tendril-like appendages. They crept out of the door, and grabbed my ankles, lashing me into the wall. Sparks exploded before my eyes. "Ow! I'm here to *free* you—"

Keir made a choked noise as more tendrils of magic tightened around his throat. I rose to my feet, and the sound of footsteps came from further down the corridor.

I met Keir's alarmed gaze. The witch wasn't contained by the cell. She'd kill anyone who got close. And if we ran, the mages would have me executed before I ever got above the ground.

"Let. Him. Go," I bit out, lashing at the witch with my own magic. Keir couldn't use his vampire ability on someone who was barely alive. "Let him go!"

Magic chewed into magic. Evelyn appeared again, her whole body aglow. The witch's gaze went to her—and Keir broke free, gasping for breath.

Threads of magic snapped, catching Evelyn instead of Keir. They swamped her, holding her in place. *Those spells can even trap a ghost.* Of course—they held the witch, after all, and if her body was still in that cell, I couldn't see it.

The footsteps grew louder.

Keir said, "I'll handle them."

I glanced over my shoulder in time to see him tackle one of the approaching mages. Then another thread of magic locked around my ankle, pulling me to the ground once again. I kicked it away, calling my Hemlock magic. *Evelyn.* She was trapped, her body suspended above the swirling mass of magic inside the cell. Despite the hunger with which the tendrils lashed at me, the magic inside the room felt stale, trapped.

Underneath was its barely beating heart—the Whisper.

"Let her go," I said to the witch. "You can't *want* to be trapped down here. We'll set you free."

"What she wanted ceased to matter long ago," purred the Whisper's voice from below the swirling magic. "You will not destroy me. You will be destroyed."

Evelyn screamed, throwing her head back, as the symbols rose to cover her transparent body. Unbearable agony tore through my own spirit, and I was yanked from my body, still glowing with magic.

The symbols were affecting our link, tearing us apart, inch by inch.

I gritted my teeth, forcing my way back into my body only to be torn free again. Magic swamped Evelyn, and through her, me. Threads of it, suffocating the life from both of us.

Then the threads recoiled as an explosion hit the symbols. Magic rose to swallow it in an instant, but the threads' grip broke on Evelyn for a brief second. I landed back in my body as Keir threw two explosive spells into the room. Spells I'd given him. They barely made a dent, but they'd won us time.

I plunged my hand into my pocket, grabbing the tattoo marker. No time for second-guessing. I'd use the spell or die trying.

"Did you mean to destroy me, Jacinda?" said the Whisper.

The marker in my hand exploded. Ink splattered the floor, luminescent and gleaming, and the Whisper let out a guttural laugh.

Shit.

More footsteps came from behind us. The mages must

have recovered. Swearing, Keir ran behind me to intercept them, but I couldn't take my eyes off the ink splattering the floor—my last chance.

Evelyn screamed, caught in the magical tendrils again. She couldn't use the ink. Only I could.

My fists clenched, and Hemlock power flooded my veins. Raw power vibrated in my hands, pushing the threads of magic away from Evelyn. She screamed something in my ear, but a roaring noise drowned out everything else.

More. More.

The ink *moved,* inching over my feet and up my legs, climbing to my hands, until my whole body was encased. It didn't feel like liquid, but more like standing under a waterfall of pure magic. The surface rippled with glyphs, like the walls in the Hemlocks' cave. Whoa. The tattoo markers, made by humans who hated witches, had trapped the magic in the ink. Now, it was free.

I eased Isabel's spell from my wrist and threw it into the cell, with the ink as the final catalyst.

The room exploded. Magic sizzled and burned, the walls warped, symbols merging together. The Whisper screamed, and so did the witch in the wall.

My back hit the floor with the force of the blast. My skin felt oddly loose. Ink swirled up and down my hands, my arms. I pushed to my knees, willing it to form runes. Amplifying ones.

And I pushed sweerything I had left into the shaking cell.

The magical tendrils recoiled, shrinking in on themselves, revealing a single symbol burning beneath. My vision swam, and I jerked my gaze away, continuing to feed destructive power into the room.

The ink dissipated, exploding outwards from my skin and mingling with the blast. The Whisper's high-pitched scream shattered windows, splintered doors, shook the spirit and physical realms all at once.

I squeezed my eyes shut against the blinding glare of light. When I opened them again, the symbol was gone. So was the witch whose eyes I'd seen staring at me from within the spell. She'd had no body left either. All that remained of her had been absorbed into the magic.

I stood, shakily. "Evelyn?"

For a heart-stopping moment, I feared she wouldn't reply—that the Whisper had severed our link forever. But I'd used her magic. *Our* magic.

And since when did I care if she lived or died?

She was unpredictable. Manipulative. Yet she'd almost destroyed herself to bring down the Whisper.

"Right here." Her voice spoke close to my shoulder, and I wheeled around, looking for Keir. He lay on the floor, thrown back by the blast, too.

"Shit." I ran to his side, staring down at his inert body. "Keir!"

His eyes opened. "Hey, Jas. I'm okay. Nine lives, remember?"

"That's my line." I heaved out a breath. "The mages—"

"I left them alive." He pushed to his feet, indicating several inert bodies. "I think."

I looked around. "Let's give them a new home. There's no shortage of cells in need of inmates."

Keir flashed me a smile. "Yes. There are."

We 'helped' the fallen mages into the nearest cell, and I

threw a ward over the door. With any luck, it'd be a while before someone came looking for them.

When I'd finished the ward, I checked my hands for tattoo marks. None remained. The ink had gone, burned out along with the Whisper.

We retraced our steps in silence, knowing there was no chance the mages wouldn't be waiting for us upstairs after the force of that blast. Someone would have felt it, and my luck was about to run out. I just hoped I could stall them in time for Keir to escape. He deserved to get his brother back, even if I never saw the light of day again.

When we reached the lobby, however, we found it deserted.

"What the...?" I approached the doors, baffled. "What happened?"

"Something big," Keir said. "Dragon sized, to be precise."

Through the window in the entrance hall, I saw it—huge, winged, bright red. The dragon had landed directly in front of the mages' headquarters. No wonder nobody was inside.

"This way," Evelyn said, beckoning us to follow. "Don't stand there gawking. I drew her here for a reason."

"The dragon's female?" Shaking his head, Keir backed away from the doors. I did likewise, following Evelyn's transparent form through the lobby to another exit. Unguarded. The wards had blown out, probably during my battle with the Whisper. Too bad I'd left no evidence behind. No proof that the mages were evil to the core.

"Almost there, Jas." Keir took my arm as we reached the exit, his firm grip communicating without words that he had no intention of watching the mages take me away.

Outside, the sky had gone back to its normal colour, but the sound of screaming came from about five directions at once."

"Tell me that dragon won't eat anyone," I said. "Well, she can feel free to take a bite out of Lord Sutherland. Evelyn?"

"Do you want to escape or do you want me to negotiate with a dragon?" Evelyn snapped. "Run for your life, idiot. Your friends are dealing with that spirit barrier."

"They got through the barrier?" I broke into a run, propelled by a fresh surge of energy, and Keir and I burst out of the guild's back gates into a deserted street. No shifter ghosts, no zombies or witches… "It's Isabel we have to thank for this. She saved everyone."

A rush of air heralded the arrival of Vance—and Ivy.

"Jas!" said Ivy. "You made it out. Did you kill her?"

"Both of them—the Ancient and the witch." I jerked my head over my shoulder. "No evidence, though—did you find Wanda?"

"Yes, but—" Ivy broke off as a rumbling growl came from behind the guild. "If anyone has a dragon translator, the mages might need one."

"I couldn't give less of a fuck if I tried," Keir said. "Did you find another man behind the mirror? My brother—"

"Was he the other prisoner?" Ivy asked. "Isabel and the other witch carried him out with your friends' help, since he was unconscious."

I sighed in relief. "Thanks. And the Moonbeam?"

"I buried all the pieces I could find," Vance said. "As for the mirror, the mages have it. Our mages, that is, not Lord Sutherland. As for the dragon… your friend might have to take care of it."

"Evelyn, what about the dragon?" I asked.

"What?" she said irritably. "If the mages tick off the dragon, that's their problem."

"It's our problem, too," I told her. "You don't piss off a giant fire-breathing lizard and expect it not to retaliate."

"I'll handle the dragon," Ivy said. "Wouldn't be the first time."

"Excuse me?" I said, but she just winked, pulled out her sword, and sprinted around the mages' headquarters.

Keir gave a laugh. "I think she'll handle it."

"You know, I think so, too," I said. "I guess she's dealt with the gods in person... will the dragon even be able to get home?"

"Of course," Evelyn said. "I can't say she won't expect repayment for helping, though."

"If she comes after us, you're dealing with her, not me." A favour owed to a dragon and a life sentence at the mages' hands. Not the victory I'd hoped for. But after I'd let Evelyn roam free, maybe it was the victory I deserved.

Vance cleared his throat. "Ivy can handle the dragon. Should I take you to your friends?"

"Please," I said, nodding to Keir.

In a blink, we all landed outside Asher's shop. The door still hung off its hinges, but the small shop was much more crowded than before, with Lloyd, Isabel, Morgan, Asher, Mackie and Keir's unconscious brother inside. Add Ivy, Keir, Vance and me on top of that and there was barely room to stand. But I brightened at the sight of Isabel on her feet, talking to Asher.

"Isabel." I made my way over to her. "Thank you so much. That spell—it saved us."

"Wish I'd had the chance to use it myself." She looked

down at her marked collarbones, grimacing. "I think I can get this off…"

"I know how," Asher said. "Trust me, it'll be fine."

I hope so. I cast my eyes around and saw Keir hurrying over to his brother.

"Is he okay?" I asked him.

"He won't wake up," Keir said.

"I tried a healing spell," Isabel said. "But he didn't respond. I think he's unconscious. He seems otherwise fine, Keir. Maybe he'll wake up in his own time now he's back."

Keir shook his head, just slightly, and I moved to his side. "What is it?" I murmured.

"His spirit," he said quietly. "It's gone."

My heart missed a beat. "Are… are you sure he doesn't need to feed on someone?"

He shook his head. "No. Trust me."

I tapped into the spirit realm, peered into the grey, but the confused jumble of everyone else's spirits made it difficult to tell.

Keir lifted his brother's body. "I'll take him back with me. See if I can help him…"

"Not alone," I said quickly, though I didn't want to leave the others either. Not so soon after the battle. Vance might have got me away, but the instant that dragon shifter left, the mages would come back…

The door flew off its remaining hinge, and three mages strode into the overcrowded shop.

"Jas Lyons," said one of them. "Come with us."

24

I was on trial again. Despite all the crimes committed, the only person facing justice today would be me.

I sat numbly in the cold metal seat of the interrogation chamber, faced with the row of mages. I'd seen this coming for weeks, and I'd even rehearsed what I'd say. But now, no words came. I'd been through too much—Keir's brother, the dragon, the battle with the Whisper, the witch, the mages' betrayal. My mind had utterly shut down.

Instead, Evelyn spoke. "I'm Evelyn Hemlock, and I think I'm the one you'd like to put on trial."

I sat back and let the council's shock wash over me. Two people exclaimed in alarm. Lady Anders, Lord Sutherland's blond second in command, rose from her seat. And Lord Sutherland's hateful face twisted in surprise. So he hadn't known about her. Or the Hemlocks. His only concern had been his own power. I wanted to ask him why he'd ordered his witch to summon the Whisper, what was in it for him, but Evelyn had total command, and Jas was in dire need of a nap.

"You're not Jas Lyons," Lord Sutherland said.

"Gods, you're even slower than you look," Evelyn said. "No, I am not Jas Lyons. The name's Evelyn. And if you lock Jas away, you lock me up, too. I'm not keen on being held in another prison, to tell you the truth."

She'd decided to part the curtains and reveal it all. Far be it from me to admit I was kind of enjoying the mages' shock. It might be the last bit of fun I had for a while.

"But you look like her," the Mage Lord protested. "You look like Jas."

"She's my host," Evelyn said. "We both belong to the Hemlock Coven, which predated even your almighty mage guild. And we will not be broken."

Even if I'd wanted to interrupt, I didn't have a chance. She was baring her hunger for power for the world to see. Nobody would be able to deny that our voices didn't sound the same and our mannerisms were different enough to be noticeable.

"The Hemlock Coven went extinct," one of the mages said.

"So did the Ancients, yet you summoned one in your own dungeon," Evelyn said.

"How dare you," said Lord Sutherland. "You attacked my son. You broke into my private quarters—"

"And found a witch in the middle of a ritualistic summoning, who you captured against her will." This time, I spoke, not Evelyn. "If I hadn't killed her, you'd all be dead. Was it worth it to you?"

Lord Sutherland shook his head. "She's a madwoman. She nearly killed my son in cold blood. She locked up three of my people."

"Frankly, I'd have preferred to kill them," Evelyn said blandly. "But I do as Jas asks, occasionally."

His face turned purple. Despite my satisfaction at watching him squirm, there was no visible proof he or his son were connected to the Whisper's revival.

After all, I was the one who'd woken her, when I'd used my Hemlock magic on the spirit lines.

Evelyn rose to her feet, and smiled, power welling in her hands. "This is for those of us you killed. We remember."

Evelyn. Don't—

The lights went out. Fog swarmed the room, and a wrenching scream came from outside.

Mackie? *Dammit, I told them not to interfere.*

Hands grabbed me, and the room vanished in a blur. I spun on the spot, disorientated, and another rush of cold air swallowed me up. I sucked in a breath and the world disappeared again.

The third time, it stopped. I staggered around and dropped to my knees, my head spinning. I'd teleported— once, twice, three times. Swallowing nausea, I looked up at Vance and Ivy.

"What did I say about not intervening?" I gasped out.

"Your friend Lloyd told us to get you out or he'd set an army of ghosts on us," Ivy said. "Three of the guild necromancers told me they'd unleash another zombie plague, while your vampire friend said he'd suck out my soul. You have very persistent friends, Jas."

"But—now they'll arrest you, too." Evelyn had disappeared mid-jump, probably dizzy from all the teleporting.

"No, they won't," Ivy said. "Your friends manufactured a diversion."

"Of course they did." I closed my eyes, opened them, looked around the room. Expensive-looking furniture filled most of the space, on a carpet patterned in hideous red and orange spirals. "This isn't the hotel room from last time."

"No," Vance said. "It's Lady Harper's country house."

"That's why it took three teleports to get here?" I shook off the dizziness and ran to the window. Fog covered the view outside, but I could make out the shape of a cliff jutting out over the sea. "They'll find me here. They know Lady Harper left me her property."

"The house is warded," Ivy said. "Heavily. It took us days to find the place, and only because Vance knows Lady Harper's style. The other mages don't. They won't find you."

"I'm still…" A fugitive. I could never go back to Edinburgh. "Lord Sutherland is still in power. I killed the witch he captured, but who knows what else he's plotting?"

"He won't get the shifters," Ivy said. "Vance and I already buried all those pieces of Moonbeam stone and took the mirror away. We'll bring him to justice."

"No, I will," said Evelyn. "I was about to kill him."

I groaned. "Evelyn has lost all meaning of subtlety. The whole supernatural world knows I'm a Hemlock witch now."

"Pretty sure it was inevitable," Ivy said. "Lady Harper probably saw it coming."

"Wait..." I looked around, seeing boxes piled up between the furniture. "Her boxes. You brought them here."

I ran to the nearest box, spotting the journal and the map. They hadn't disappeared after all.

"We moved everything we could," Vance said. "I'll come and speak to you later, but Ivy—we need to go back before the mages get suspicious."

"Aren't they already suspicious?" I said.

"Your friends made a pretty good diversion," Ivy said. "Not quite as good as the dragon, though. I wish I'd been able to convince her to stick around, but I don't think she liked my sword much."

"Wait," I said. "Are you sure Lord Sutherland won't haul my friends in for questioning?"

"He'll have to get through me first," Ivy said.

I pressed a hand to my forehead. Mere hours had passed since the battle. Too little time to take it all in. "All right, but I wouldn't put anything past him. Even a dragon couldn't stop him."

"The dragon was surprisingly placid," Vance put in. "Removing the leader of the mages is likely to require more of a delicate response."

"The hell it is," I said. "He tried to kill us."

"But he has powerful allies," Ivy said. "I don't like it either, but the forces protecting the mages go back nearly as far as the Hemlocks. Even that witch of his came from somewhere. I'd rather know if he has any other Ancients helping him before we make any sudden moves."

My skin crawled. "Yeah, well. Either he hunts me down or I do the same to him."

Nothing else would be acceptable.

"Finally," said Evelyn. "I'm glad you're taking your role seriously."

"Bollocks," I said. "You just wanted to declare yourself queen of the universe. You're not taking the Mage Lord's place, so forget it. And not all my friends have the mages' protection. What about Keir?"

"He's fine," Ivy said, apparently unperturbed by a ghost joining our conversation. "Isabel helped him move his brother… I'll tell him where you are. And we'll be back in a few hours."

"I—" I sank into an armchair, relieved beyond measure. I was free—relatively—and that was all I could ask for. "Thank you."

The idea of living in Lady Harper's property was kind of weird, but I'd got out of this alive and with both of my souls intact. Still better than being dead.

I hoped the house had decent heating. The Highlands got cold in winter.

———

Four hours later, Ivy and Vance returned.

"Things have calmed down a little," Vance said. "The mages' patrols are no longer searching the streets for you. They hired some necromancers to search the spirit realm and confirm you're not in the city any longer. They think you left for the forest."

"So even that isn't a secret."

"The mages know little, but they do know that the Hemlocks had their own private dimension," said Vance. "They'll never be able to find it, though."

"Not sure I want to go and live in there, either." I looked out the window at the foggy cliff edge. "I need to see my friends. Are they okay?"

"Sure," said Ivy. "Isabel and Asher claimed to remember nothing about the time they spent under the enemy's control. The mages didn't even bother bringing them in for questioning."

"Good," I said. "Keir, though… I have to speak to him in person. I don't know if he wants to stick around or not, but he attacked Neil Sutherland in self-defence and he drained three mages in the jail as well."

"Give me the address and I'll take you there, but I won't be able to give you long," Vance said. "It's the least I can do for what you did for Wanda."

When I gave him directions, he transported both of us to Keir's apartment.

Keir was at the door before I knocked.

"Jas!" His eyes widened. "You shouldn't be in the city. I thought you were safe."

"I'm okay—I'm staying at Lady Harper's safe house. Can I come in?"

"Ten minutes," Vance said from behind me, and Ivy gave him a poke in the arm. "Fifteen."

I ducked into the apartment. "I won't be here long. Not sure if I have an arrest warrant or a death sentence on my head, but it's safe to say I'm not welcome in Edinburgh anymore."

"I'm sorry." When we were inside the dimly lit hallway, Keir turned and embraced me. I rested my head on his shoulder, holding on tight.

"Can you tell Lloyd I'm okay if you see him?" I pulled

back. "I'll send a message, but I'm not sure there's a signal up on the cliffs, and I'm three teleports away. I can still reach you through the spirit realm, though."

"Then why risk coming in person?" He frowned.

"Isn't it obvious?" I sucked in a deep breath, my gaze going to the half-open door into his flat. "Is your brother really…?"

"He still won't wake up," he said, softly. "They took his soul."

Keir walked into the flat, the door closing behind us. The living room was dark, as though he'd never bothered to turn on the lights, and on the right, a door lay open. On the other side was Keir's brother's bedroom, the bed occupied by the man we'd rescued from the strange world on the other side of the mirror.

Aiden Langford looked like a taller and thinner version of Keir with a dark sweep of hair almost to his shoulders. He wore a T-shirt and faded jeans, and his face was lightly stubbled, his expression relaxed in sleep.

"His heart's still beating," Keir said quietly. "He has a pulse. But he's unresponsive, and his soul—it's gone."

"If he's alive, then so is his soul," I said firmly. "It's like… he's a powerful vampire, right? Maybe he can stay away from his body for longer than most people." There was no other explanation.

Keir dropped his head. "He's alive, all right, but he hasn't *aged.*"

A heartbeat passed. "What?"

"It's been eight years, Jas." His voice trembled. "I think the liminal space… I think it warped time. He's wearing the same clothes they kidnapped him in. You know they say time passes differently in Faerie? It looks like days or weeks have passed since he disappeared. Not years."

"How's that even possible?"

He shook his head, his face pale. "I don't understand, either."

"No…" I turned on my spirit sight. Keir was right… our two spirits were the only two present in the room. But if the soul disappeared, the body usually died. As far as I knew, nobody could restore a spirit that was lost. Not even a necromancer.

What had the Ancients done to him?

Keir's hands curled into fists. "It's been so long… and he won't even wake up."

I moved to his side, touched my hand to his. "We'll fix this."

He drew in a shuddering breath. His eyes were bright, shining. "It's fucking unfair. I spent years looking for him, and now—"

He buried his head in my shoulder, and I held onto him for a long moment, the same way he'd held me in the spirit realm in the Briar witches' empty house.

Keir sighed and released me, wiping his eyes with the back of his hand. "It wasn't supposed to be like this."

"I wasn't supposed to wind up a fugitive either." I heaved out a breath. "But just because I'm banned from the city doesn't mean I'm planning to stay away. I *will* help you fix this."

He gave a strained smile. "I'll hold you to that. And if there's any way to prove the mages are crooks, I'll be first on board. I notice none of them are *surprised* that there's a secret mirror that leads into another dimension. Not to mention the Moonbeam."

"I got the impression the mages own the mirror," I said. "Or they think they do. Vance said the mirror's safe and they got rid of the stones. Speaking of… did you see where the dragon disappeared to?"

"Flew away, I imagine," he said. "I'll have to do the same. The mages don't know where I live—aside from your friends—but if they take my brother, I'll kill them."

Oh, damn. A vampire who'd been imprisoned for years and apparently hadn't aged? They'd lock both him and his brother up for illegal magic, the way things were going. "Do you have a plan? Go into hiding?"

"They haven't come looking for me yet," he said. "Rumour says they temporarily dropped the registry idea —it's fairly obvious that the shifters and witches involved weren't in control of their own will. That much, they couldn't cover up. But that's not to say they won't revive their old plan later. I'm ready to run."

"If you want to come to Lady Harper's old house, you're more than welcome to," I said. "That house can host twenty people, easily."

"Yeah…" He looked down at his brother, biting his lip. "The mages… maybe *they* know how to bring him back."

"Maybe." They knew how to summon Ancients. Who knew what else they were hiding? "Lord Sutherland will come after me, for what I did to his son. He deserved it, but it drives me mad that the smug bastard is walking around free and I'm stuck in hiding. I still don't know what they hoped to gain from trapping that witch and forcing her to summon the Whisper."

"Yes, I did wonder," said Keir. "She wasn't the strongest Ancient. But…"

"Others might have got out," I said. "When I tore the spirit line… they broke free, and they can be summoned."

The Ancients were coming. No denial. No escape.

But I wasn't alone. Far from it.

Evelyn and I spoke at the same time. "Then we'll kill every last one of them."

ABOUT THE AUTHOR

Emma is the New York Times and USA Today Bestselling author of the Changeling Chronicles urban fantasy series.

Emma spent her childhood creating imaginary worlds to compensate for a disappointingly average reality, so it was probably inevitable that she ended up writing fantasy novels. When she's not immersed in her own fictional universes, Emma can be found with her head in a book or wandering around the world in search of adventure.

Find out more about Emma's books at www.emmaladams.com.